wolf girl

THERESA TOMLINSON

wolf girl

CORGI BOOKS

WOLF GIRL
A CORGI BOOK 978 0 552 55271 4 (from January 2007)
0 552 55271 2

First published in Great Britain by Corgi Books,
an imprint of Random House Children's Books

This edition published 2006

1 3 5 7 9 10 8 6 4 2

Set in 12/15.5pt Sabon by
Falcon Oast Graphic Art Ltd.

Corgi Books are published by Random House Children's Books,
61–63 Uxbridge Road, London W5 5SA,
a division of The Random House Group Ltd,
in Australia by Random House Australia (Pty) Ltd,
20 Alfred Street, Milsons Point, Sydney, NSW 2061, Australia,
in New Zealand by Random House New Zealand Ltd,
18 Poland Road, Glenfield, Auckland 10, New Zealand,
and in South Africa by Random House (Pty) Ltd,
Isle of Houghton, Corner of Boundary and Carse O'Gowrie Roads,
Houghton 2198, South Africa

THE RANDOM HOUSE GROUP Limited Reg. No. 954009
www.kidsatrandomhouse.co.uk

A CIP catalogue record for this book is available from the British Library.

Printed and bound in Great Britain by
Bookmarque Ltd, Croydon, Surrey

*In memory of
Delia Huddy;
editor and friend*

King Oswy's Northumbria

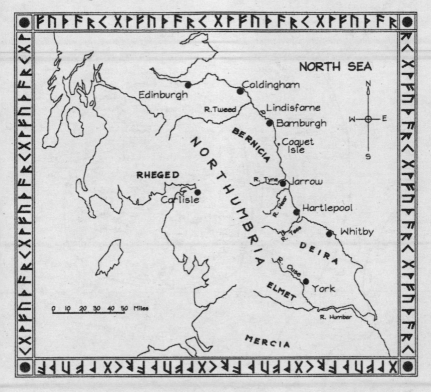

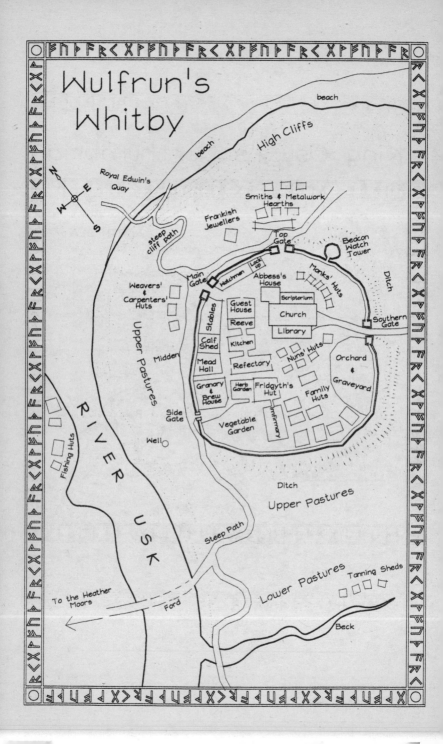

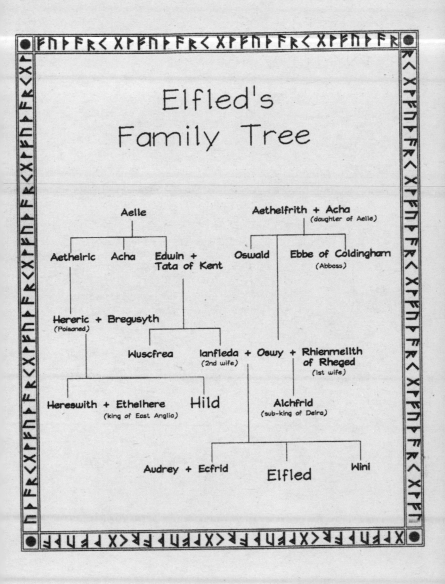

Elfled's Family Tree

prologue

The western horizon was flooded with bright orange light, intensifying to a deep blood-red as the sun began to sink behind the hills. A column of thunderous black clouds bridged the sky from east to west, marring the gorgeous colours of the evening. Six riders urged their horses down the steep hillside and onto the beach. They clattered across the shingle, their weapons and armour glinting red and gold in the dying light.

The first warrior turned to shout back at his companions. 'Too late,' he cried.

He pointed to a blazing beacon high on the clifftops to the east. The astounding news from the battlefield had flown ahead of them.

Both men and horses were lathered with sweat, for they'd ridden fast since noon. They reined in their steeds and stared at the choppy grey sea, growling out their anger. They could just see the small dark shape of a ship in the distance, its sail billowing out with the wind in its favour; then the image shrank, blurring into a dot.

'They've got away!'

'Bound for Kent, do you think?'

'Where else would they be bound for?'

The tallest man ground his teeth in frustration and drew his sword. He glared up and down the beach, which seemed to be empty but for a few small upturned fishing boats and a trail of deep indentations in the sand where horses had galloped eastwards. 'Not all have flown – some have taken their horses away towards Whitby.'

They all turned again to where the beacon could be seen in the distance, blazing away on the high cliff-top. 'Someone has given them aid and if Cadwallon or Penda find out who it is, they'll wish themselves at the bottom of the sea. They will not be pleased with us either,' said the tall man.

His companion shrugged. 'They have victory. Edwin's young cub is no threat to them, not yet! They've plenty of time.'

'Aye. No threat yet, but he will be!'

The beach was not as deserted as it seemed, for a young girl watched them through a tiny space, her cheek pressed into the bruising wet shingle beneath her father's upturned boat. The bottom of her skirt was soaked and she gritted her teeth against the freezing cold. She knew that she must not move or make a sound, for should the warriors

contents

notice the trail of wet shingle that led up from the water's edge to the boat, her life would be over.

Then, as she crouched in that painful position, there came a gentle sound that made her sigh with relief: a light pattering on the wooden hull that sheltered her. It was beginning to rain and the rain would wash away the trail, soaking the whole beach and all the upturned boats. This rain was blessed; it would hide her guilt. She closed her eyes and smiled. If she could just keep still a little longer, she would be safe.

Chapter 1

the keeper of secrets

Wulfrun looked out through the shutter of the webster's hut towards the wooden stockade that marked the inner monastic boundary. The new wooden church at Whitby rose high inside the stockade and ditch, its roof thickly thatched. Its pediment was carved with intricate patterns of fish and fowl, making it look like a powerful warlord's feasting hall, were it not for the simple wooden cross above the entrance. The ancient watchtower with its beacon, set just outside the stockade, towered high above everything. Seagulls swooped and mewed around it. That watchtower had been there on the high cliff-top long before the coming of the royal abbess, with her following of devoted monks and nuns.

The peace of the morning was broken by the sound of lowing cattle. 'Here they come,' Wulfrun murmured, as the cowherds led their eager charges out through the small side gate to graze in the steeply sloping meadows above the river Usk.

She smiled as she watched them go. For the moment she must stay here and work, combing raw wool until her arms and fingers ached. But later, when the sun was high in the sky and her mother Cwen had returned from the abbey, her job would be to take the geese out into the upper pasture. She'd be able to join her friend Cadmon, the cowherd, there.

She watched them as the last calves vanished round the curve of the stockade, then checked carefully that nobody else was coming down the path towards the webster's hut. While her mother was away, she might allow herself just one small treat before she returned to the dreary work of combing and spinning wool.

As she turned away from the doorway, Wulfrun's heart beat fast with guilty anticipation. She lifted the heavy lid of Cwen's marriage chest, thrusting aside the hanks of dyed wool to slide her hand down the side, searching for the special board. She had done this many times since last autumn, when she'd discovered the secret of this carefully crafted box.

There it was: she knew just where to press so that she could lift the loose board, making it fall forwards to reveal a dark hiding place. Her fingers closed about the heavy, clunky prize, and with shaking hands she lifted the necklace out of the shadows, smiling as she always did at the bright glint of the heavy gold beads shaped like shells from the beach and the richness of the many deep red stones that hung down from them, each in its own gold setting. She carefully lifted the treasure up into her hair like a crown, loving the weight of it against her brow; then stooped to pick up the small round of flat polished jet that they used as a looking glass.

Wulfrun moved warily to the window hole and opened the shutter just a little bit more, holding up the mirror so that she could admire herself. The sun struck deep into the stones and set them blazing with the ruddy shades hidden in their depths. Above her forehead hung a central pendant in the shape of a cross, supported from above by a beautifully crafted bird with wings spread in flight. Both cross and bird were fashioned from heavy, gleaming gold. On either side of the cross blood-red stones glowed with colour against her white skin, despite the darkness of the glass.

She stood there enjoying a moment of pure happiness, gazing at her reflection, but then a movement in the distance caught her eye and she heard her mother's voice. They were back much sooner than she'd expected. She snatched the jewels from her head and replaced them in their hidey-hole. Moving quickly, she spread the tangled raw wool back on top, then grabbed the hank that she was supposed to be combing.

Wulfrun had never spoken to Cwen about the hidden necklace that she'd found; some deep instinct told her that she must not. She felt sure that her mother could not know of the existence of the richly jewelled treasure that had been so carefully hidden away. The weight of the gleaming beads must surely mean that they were real gold. She thought that the blood-red stones were garnets, for she had seen just such jewels set into a gold reliquary box that was kept in the monastery church. The reliquary was said to contain a toe bone from the saintly King Oswald, who'd been killed in battle with the pagan King Penda. On special occasions people lined up to kiss the golden box and swore that it healed sickness. Only last Christmas the reeve's little daughter had been saved from a terrible fever by having the golden box brought to her bedside. Everyone spoke of it as a great treasure, and yet here were just the same gold and precious jewels on the necklace. Such a thing could not rightly belong to a simple weaver woman like Cwen. But who it really belonged to and how long it had been there was a mystery. At night Wulfrun dreamed of the jewels, and in her dreams she saw the shadowy, queenly shape of a mysterious woman who wore them.

Cwen the webster opened the strong wooden door of their hut. Gode, her younger daughter, jumped down the two steps that led onto the earthen floor. The walls of the hut were built from wattle hurdles, plastered with a daub of dried mud and dung. The floor was a sunken pit that had been dug out of the shale and ironstone layers on the cliff-top. It was a poor place compared to the fine new timber halls and guesthouses that the abbess was building above them on the windy cliff-tops, but Cwen was saving every bit of payment that she earned.

'That's another bag of grain.' Cwen was smiling broadly as she heaved the heavy sack up onto the wooden shelf that hung from one of the posts. She was so pleased with the sale she'd made that she didn't notice that Wulfrun looked a little flushed. 'There's more than we can eat so we can sell most of it.'

'We could buy another goose,' Wulfrun suggested.

But her mother gave her head a sharp shake and Wulfrun wished at once that she'd never spoken.

'They want another wall hanging,' Cwen went on cheerfully, ignoring the brief moment of tension. 'Twice the size of the last one, and I can use my own patterns. The guest-mistress begs me work as fast as I can and they'll buy every bit of weaving that I produce. They're hoping to get the new guestrooms furnished before the abbess returns.'

Everyone in Whitby knew that Abbess Hild had

gone off in a great fluster at the beginning of the Month of Weeds to see Oswy, High King of Northumbria, in his fortress at Bamburgh. It was rare for the abbess to display anger, but a message from Oswy's eldest son Alchfrid, Sub-king of Deira, had made the abbess's cheeks burn with rage. It seemed he wished all of Deira to adopt the Roman style of Christianity that he preferred.

Alchfrid was Oswy's son by his first wife, Rhienmellth of Rheged, and resented by many Deirans, who called him Alchfrid the Stranger. It was whispered that they would have preferred Oswy's younger son Ecfrid as their overlord, as he was grandson to the great King Edwin, through Oswy's second queen, Ianfleda.

Abbess Hild stuck resolutely to the simple ways of worship that she'd learned from Bishop Aidan and his Lindisfarne monks, but as Whitby was part of Alchfrid's sub-kingdom of Deira, it seemed the abbess might be forced to change against her will. She'd ordered the *Royal Edwin*, the twenty-oared galley that was always kept in readiness down in the harbour, and had gone by sea to beg support from Oswy, who had long been her friend. It was now the Month of Flies and there was still no sign of the royal boat returning.

'Every new guestroom is to have wall hangings on three sides,' Cwen told Wulfrun. 'What do you think of that?'

Wulfrun nodded and smiled. 'They'll need them, with the draughts they get up there.'

'They will!' her mother agreed.

Whitby folk looked on with amazement at the new buildings that were being raised high on the cliffs, exposed to every winter gale. Local people swore that when the wind came straight off the sea from the north, it was the bitterest known to man.

'You can't tell rich folk anything!' Cwen said, shaking her head. 'They'd have been warm and protected if they'd built snugly into the land folds down by the ford. I know it, you know it, the whole of Whitby knows it – but you can't tell them anything! Well, what do I care if it means they need more wall hangings and they're willing to pay me well?'

Four years ago the family had lived in Fisherstead, a little hamlet up the coast to the northwest. One terrible stormy night Wulfrun's father had been drowned while out in his fishing boat, and just a few days after the tragedy little Gode had been born. It had been a year of great bitterness mixed with this one small joy, for Cwen had lost many babies over the years. But to everyone's surprise Gode was born strong and healthy. This miracle had somehow forced Cwen to struggle through her sorrow, determined that they should all survive. Wulfrun had been ten years old at the time and she could remember only too well the hard winter that followed their loss. The family had lived very meagrely on their neighbours' charity, and when that had dried up, Cwen had done the thing they never spoke about, though Wulfrun knew she grieved over it every night. She had sold her son Sebbi to a passing thane to work as a slave at his villa near Catterick.

This was what made Wulfrun sure that Cwen could not know about the treasure hidden away beneath her wool and flax, for her mother saved every spare bit of her earnings so that one day they might manage to buy Sebbi back. Sometimes Wulfrun wondered guiltily if she should show Cwen the treasure, so that they could use it to reclaim her brother at once, but a deep sense of dread and uncertainty held her back.

The slave price for Sebbi had seen them through the winter, and then the following spring it seemed the fates had begun to weave a brighter thread into their lives. Cwen had packed her baby and her marriage chest onto a handcart and pushed it over the steep hills to Whitby, where she'd heard Abbess Hild was looking for women who were skilled at weaving. It had been a hard journey and ten-year-old Wulfrun had tramped sore-footed beside her mother, but when they arrived at the monastery and Abbess Hild discovered that Cwen was truly skilled, their fortunes changed at once for the better.

Cwen and her family were given temporary accommodation in the growing guesthouse and provided with a loom and wool. The sample work that Cwen produced had filled the abbess with delight.

'Why send over to the Frankish lands?' she had asked, staring intently at Cwen. 'Why bother with that, when there are women here like you, Cwen, who can do good strong work like this?'

Since that time they'd been given the small hut set just outside the stockade, along with the other weavers, dyers, washerwomen and hurdle makers. They'd been paid decently for the weaving they produced and were able to hold their heads high as respectable workers. Cwen kept six geese in the small wattle close outside the hut, and they sometimes sold their eggs to the monastery kitchens. They were allowed to graze the geese in the upper pasture, where the birds could scavenge for slops and waste from the granary and the abbey kitchens. They'd also bought a heavy iron cauldron for dying wool and flax, though just at the moment it bubbled with a thin barley broth for their meal. Despite their improved fortune Cwen still saved all she could.

Cwen set up her new wall hanging and Wulfrun combed wool, until Gode began complaining that she was hungry. They supped their broth, then sat back for a few moments of rest. Gode lay down by the hearth, her eyes heavy with sleep; Wulfrun and her mother nodded in the warmth, while the smoke curled up and escaped through a small hole in the heather-thatched roof. At last Cwen moved and yawned. 'Ah well . . . that wall hanging will not weave itself, I suppose.'

She struggled to her feet and lifted the wooden loom with its heavy dangling weights down from the wall, then went to unfasten the shutter on the southwest side of the hut, so that the afternoon sun came flooding inside to light her work. Wulfrun stretched and got up from the fire without being told, reaching down the goose-herding crook from its nail.

She squeezed past her mother. 'Come on, my old cacklers!' she called.

The upper pasture sloped gently downhill from the little side gate in the stockade, catching the afternoon sun. Wulfrun's stomach was full of broth and she still felt sleepy, but she knew she must not let her head droop and her eyes close until she'd set the hungry geese feeding.

Fat Sister Mildred, who worked as cook in the abbey kitchens, came out through the side gate and threw two buckets of slop onto the grass. 'There you are, my honeys,' she said, nodding kindly towards Wulfrun. She went back inside as the geese ran squawking towards the pile of vegetable peelings and boiled oats.

Wulfrun wasn't sure if it was she who was being

called 'honey' or the geese, but it didn't matter; it was a fine afternoon and she felt contented. The geese were feeding well; perhaps she could rest now and listen to the soothing buzz of Sister Fridgyth's bees, whose hives were kept in a corner of the upper pasture.

She loved this part of the day as the land was sheltered from the sea and the cold north wind. There was a fine view of the surrounding countryside and the many visitors who made the long journey to Whitby town, travelling down from the heather moors towards the ford that crossed the winding river Usk. A skein of lapwings fluttered and looped above the water. Wulfrun watched them lazily as Sister Fridgyth came out from the vegetable garden with charcoal smoking in a little pot; she blew smoke into one of the hives to make the bees drowsy, so that she could steal honey from them.

Wulfrun shaded her eyes, looking for Cadmon, who usually came and sat in comfortable silence beside her, while his cows cropped the grass and their calves suckled. She knew he must be somewhere below her, for she'd seen him setting out that morning. Then she spotted him in the distance and waved as he wound his way slowly up the steep zigzag path. Cadmon drove his beloved cows and calves before him with strange whimpers and grunts that his charges seemed to understand perfectly. He was older than most of the cowherds and some people called him 'simple', but Wulfrun had learned that it was only the humiliating stammer in his speech that made him seem slow-witted. Sometimes, when nobody else was near, he sang sweet songs to his beasts; at those times his words would flow like honey and Wulfrun loved to listen.

'Hurry!' she bellowed, as he came towards her. 'The sun will soon be gone!'

Chapter 2

elfled

When Cadmon arrived, he flopped down beside Wulfrun. For a few moments they enjoyed the peace and warmth together, while the cows tugged at the grass and the geese fed greedily. Then all at once the blissful quiet was disturbed by the sound of raised voices coming from inside the stockade. A girl, younger and smaller than Wulfrun and dressed in a layered, embroidered gown, burst through the side gate from the vegetable garden, her hair full of wild curls. She ran out into the pasture, screaming shrilly. 'No – I will not! I will not!'

Wulfrun sat up at once, angry that her peace should be disturbed. The noisy one ran towards them, heading straight for the patch of sun that they were enjoying.

Adfrith, one of the young men who spent most of his time painstakingly producing manuscripts in the scriptorium, ran after her. His monastic undyed tunic was splashed all down the front with the precious blue-black ink that the scribe monks spent many hours making. Wulfrun knew him, for he often came out to the pasture to beg long flight feathers from her geese to make his quill pens.

But today Adfrith had no thought of goose quills. 'Highness . . .' he pleaded breathlessly. 'Nobody can learn without hard work . . .'

Wulfrun saw that the young girl's hands were also stained with ink. Behind Adfrith, at a statelier pace, came a richly dressed young woman, a frown on her beautiful face. This was the Lady Irminburgh, well known to all in Whitby as a kinswoman of the abbess who aspired to be a nun. However, it was only the jewelled cross that hung from her neck that suggested she might be of a religious inclination.

'I warned the abbess,' Lady Irminburgh said. 'I told her you were far too young to teach anyone, Adfrith, let alone such a precious and highly sensitive one.'

'I don't care who teaches me.' The girl's nostrils flared and her blue eyes blazed. 'I won't make the shapes and join up the dots! Tell Mother Hild . . . tell her what you like! My hands won't do it! You can tell her to do it herself!'

The girl marched wildly around the pasture, flapping ink-stained fingers and sending the geese and cattle into a panic. 'I won't . . . I won't!' she shrieked.

Wulfrun scrambled to her feet, annoyed; even little Gode was better behaved than this girl, who must have seen at least ten summers. 'What do you think you're doing?' she demanded, hands on hips. 'Leave my geese in peace and stop that howling or I'll smack you!

Adfrith and Lady Irminburgh both stared open-mouthed and horrified as Wulfrun raised her hand. The girl in the braid-trimmed robe was so surprised at Wulfrun's anger that for a moment she stopped.

Then, before Wulfrun's hand could fall, Cadmon leaped up from the grass and hurled himself upon his friend. 'No – n-no!' he gasped. 'M-mustn't!' He dragged her away from the child.

Wulfrun was shocked, not so much by the girl's furious glare, or by Adfrith's look of dread, but by Cadmon's sudden attack. He usually obeyed her every wish, treating her with the devotion of a faithful dog, and she'd never known him act aggressively towards her.

'Ha!' the young girl cried with satisfaction, as though she'd enjoyed their performance. 'You had better not raise your hand to *me*!'

Wulfrun staggered back a little, taking more careful note now of the rich trimmings on the girl's gown and two intricately worked silver rings that adorned the small ink-stained fingers. The shouting had brought Sister Mildred out from her kitchen and Sister Fridgyth from the vegetable garden, both flushed with concern at what they saw.

Irminburgh recovered enough to call out sweetly, 'My darling, come here to me!'

The girl rubbed her belly and yawned, quickly bored now that the show seemed to be over. She wandered back to Irminburgh, who almost whimpered with relief. 'Darling Princess, please come back inside with poor tired Irminburgh.'

'Princess?' Wulfrun whispered. Had Adfrith also addressed her as Highness?

'Buttermilk!' the girl demanded. 'I want buttermilk sweetened with honey!'

'Yes, my darling! We'll go to the kitchen. Buttermilk you shall have. Come, Sister Mildred, get us buttermilk and honey!'

The girl seemed satisfied by the promise of a sweet drink and began to follow Irminburgh through the gate, but she paused to glance back at Wulfrun with a mixture of disdain and curiosity. 'What is sharp at the tip but makes us warm in bed?' she demanded.

Wulfrun stared open-mouthed, still restrained by Cadmon.

'It's a goose feather . . . Goose Girl. You should know that – with its sharp quill and soft down.'

Irminburgh took the young girl's hand and led her away, but she turned back once again, laughing. 'You should know that!'

Sister Mildred waddled after them, her cheeks still pink.

When they'd gone Adfrith wiped his forehead, leaving a dark smudge across his brow. 'Good heavens, Goose Girl!' he muttered. 'Are you mad or trying to get us all strung up?'

'I did nothing wrong!' Wulfrun insisted. She was still a little confused as to what had really happened.

Cadmon shook his head. 'No – n-no!' he stammered.

'Do you know who that was?' Sister Fridgyth demanded with sharp disapproval, hands on hips.

'No,' Wulfrun insisted, but that was not quite true. She had come to realize that the young girl must be a very important little personage indeed.

Adfrith raised his eyes to heaven and shuddered. 'You raised your hand to the Princess Elfled and you say you did nothing wrong? You raised your hand to the daughter of the great King Oswy. Had that blow fallen . . .' Words failed him.

Wulfrun frowned, trying to work out whether she should be ashamed of herself or not. 'That's no way for a princess to behave!'

'Huh!' Adfrith shook his head, still troubled at the thought of the catastrophe that had only narrowly been averted. 'Who are you to say how a princess should behave? Kings' daughters do what they want.'

A sense of chill began to creep over Wulfrun, even though the sun was as bright as before.

'Lady Irminburgh can't control her,' Adfrith acknowledged confidingly to Fridgyth. 'She's got little interest in her charge – ignores her most of the time and then fusses over her like a kitten. While the abbess is away, I am supposed to teach the princess to write her letters, but I don't know how! It's a different matter when the abbess is here; Elfled quietly obeys her slightest look of disapproval.'

'Hmm . . . most of us do,' Fridgyth acknowledged. She turned to go back to her garden and Adfrith followed her in through the side gate.

Wulfrun was angry with herself now. How could she have let her rage flare up so fast and in such a dangerous situation? She began to call her geese together, taking up her crook from where she'd dropped it. 'Go home,' she snapped at her charges, poking at them unusually savagely.

Cadmon ignored her as she left; he was concerned about his calves. His beasts were specially chosen for their pure white hides. He loved them as a father would, determined that they should not suffer during their short lives, for these selected calves would live only until the weather turned cold. At the start of Blood Month they would be slaughtered and their hides stripped by the tanners and used to make the precious vellum that Adfrith wrote upon. They cowered nervously together in the far corner of the pasture, rolling their eyes, while their mothers blundered about, bumping into each other and lowing loudly. Cadmon hated to see them in this state. Now that everyone had gone he crouched down on his haunches and began to sing under his breath:

'No *man will beat you,*
no ice will freeze you,
sleet will never chill you,
hail will never sting you . . .
so go to your mothers quietly
and hush, my little dear ones.'

At the gentle, rhythmical sound of his singing, both cows and calves turned their heads to listen. As his deep voice rose and fell, their confidence returned and the calves wandered back to their mothers to suckle, while the cows calmly returned to their grazing.

Wulfrun stumbled along the path after the geese, her head reeling. She knew well enough that the abbey was home to young Princess Elfled. Ten years ago King Oswy had vowed that he would give his baby daughter to the Christian God in payment for success in warfare. Against all odds, Oswy had won the great battle of the Winwaed, killing Penda, the pagan king of the Mercians, who'd been demanding tribute from the kingdom of Northumbria for many years and ravaging the country whenever he wanted more wealth. After his astonishing victory Oswy had been able to make himself High King over all the lands from the river Humber to the land of the Picts. He had kept his vow to the Christian God and sent the little princess, baby though she was, away from her mother and her home in the great fortress of Bamburgh where she'd been born. She'd been put into the care of Abbess Hild, who was her second cousin, though it seemed that like everyone else in Whitby the princess called the abbess Mother Hild. She would be brought up to be a nun, just like her respected guardian, and one day rule the lands around Whitby in Hild's place.

On rare occasions the king and his retinue came to stay at the fast-expanding monastery for a few days. On his last visit Wulfrun had caught brief glimpses of the royal child in the distance, carried on a litter or muffled in rich furs perched on her father's saddle. She had never seen her close up, let alone running amok in the upper pasture, with wild hair and ink on her fingers, so who could blame her for not knowing who the rude child was?

Cwen was waiting impatiently at the doorway to the hut. As soon as she saw Wulfrun approaching she threw her cloak over her shoulders. 'You must mind Gode and see the geese fastened up safely, for I need to go back to the guesthouse to consult with Lady Alta. I haven't the dyes she asked for and if we don't agree I can't set to work in the morning.'

Wulfrun nodded vacantly, her mind still on the princess and her tantrum. Obediently she locked up the geese in the small close that they'd built around their hut. Then she went inside, flopping down beside the warm hearth. Gode hurled herself cheerfully onto her sister's back, but was disappointed when she found herself thrust away.

'Play horsy! Play horsy!'

'No,' Wulfrun snapped. She was in no mood for playing horsy.

Gode knew better than to provoke her sister and wandered over to kick the swinging loom weights attached to the new wall hanging that her mother was just setting to work on. Cwen had already set up lengths of strong two-ply twisted wool to form the warps, with heavy stone weights to pull them straight. She'd woven a neat strip of soft undyed wool at the top to start the weft.

'Play wi' geese!' Gode announced sulkily, pulling aside the door hanging and going out into the small enclosure.

Wulfrun shrugged her shoulders and said nothing. The gate was fastened and both Gode and the geese should be safe enough within their own small fenced area. Wulfrun moved to the carved wooden chest, the cosseted young Elfled still on her mind. If she were a princess she'd behave with grace and dignity and not tear about like a screeching squirrel.

She went to glance through the shutter and saw that Gode had picked up the crook she'd left by the door. She was speaking with great authority to the geese, practising the art of goose herding; absorbed in her game.

Wulfrun let the shutter drop and opened the lid of the chest, searching for the loose board. She lifted the necklace out of its hiding place and undid the strong ring and hook, picking as she'd often done before at a small thread that seemed to be wound so tightly between two of the gold beads that she could never get it off. It did not mar the beauty of the necklace so she ignored it and fastened the jewels around her neck. The weight was quite heavy on her chest and shoulders as she moved to the window and lifted the wooden shutter again, the polished jet mirror ready in her hand. She smiled at her reflection, soothed by what she saw. The setting sun's rays bathed her skin in glowing pink warmth, while the jewels gleamed with a fiery radiance.

'Burning deep inside!' she murmured.

Her eyes feasted for a while on the thrilling sight of herself – the goose girl looking like a true princess – but when she directed her glance past the dark glass to check on Gode, what she saw made her drop the mirror.

Her little sister had somehow managed to reach the looped gate fastener and lift it over the upright stick that held it in place. Wulfrun just caught a glimpse of the geese before they vanished, waddling off towards the edge of the cliffs, followed by Gode. Wulfrun was after them in a flash, her heart thundering: those cliffs were known for their crumbling edges and the steep drop down to the rocks and wild sea. She rushed through the doorway but stopped in her tracks, for out of the main gate came Lady Irminburgh, past the guards. Sister Mildred followed, with Ulfstan, the abbey reeve, and her mother Cwen. They were heading straight for the webster's hut and Cwen looked distressed.

Wulfrun stood frozen to the spot, her thoughts in wild confusion.

'This is the one!' Sister Mildred pointed at her. 'The goose girl raised her hand as if to slap the princess!'

'Yes,' Irminburgh agreed. 'This is the one.'

Only then did Wulfrun remember that she was still wearing the necklace. Her hand flew to her neck, but it was too late: they were all staring at the precious heavy jewels. Her mind went numb and blank; even Gode toddling dangerously towards the cliffs was forgotten.

Cwen's face turned deathly white at the sight of her daughter decked out like a queen.

Wulfrun thought of running, but the reeve's hand shot out and snapped shut around her wrist with an iron grip.

Chapter 3

a deadly tangle

Sister Mildred was the first to recover her voice. 'A thief!' she cried. Her words were full of shocked disbelief. 'Not only did she threaten the princess, but she's a thief as well!'

Cwen opened her mouth as though to speak, but no sound came. Wulfrun stared helplessly back at her. A sudden rush of sickness surged from her stomach to her throat. What had she done? What would this mean? In just one careless moment she had turned their whole world upside down.

'She must come to the lock-up!' said Ulfstan. The reeve had a reputation for being fair-minded and efficient, which made his quiet words all the more chilling. He'd known the webster and her family since they came to Whitby and he and his wife had befriended them, but he could not deny the damning evidence of the jewels around Wulfrun's neck and his grip on her wrist did not give.

'No.' Cwen spoke at last, though her voice was faint. 'Please, Ulfstan, she's only a child.'

Neighbours peered from their huts as they sensed trouble.

'How old is the goose girl?' Lady Irminburgh was staring at the necklace as though she'd never seen its like before. 'She has the look of a woman about her – she must be more than eleven and so she must answer for her crime!'

The reeve nodded solemnly. 'That is right by King Oswy's law.'

The sounds of hammering in the carpenters' worksheds ceased, though the light had not yet gone, and a small whispering crowd gathered about them.

'She was fourteen last Easter Month, I swear,' a helpful neighbour supplied.

Wulfrun stood still, numb with fear and shock. It seemed to her that she was watching from a distance, as though it were somebody else accused. Then her mother spoke again and her astonishing words brought Wulfrun sharply back to the reality of the situation.

'No,' Cwen said calmly. 'Let my daughter go; the necklace is mine. My daughter is no thief and nor am I. These jewels were given to me as a gift, many years ago.'

There were gasps from all about them.

Ulfstan looked even more shocked at this, but he

let go of Wulfrun and took hold of the arm Cwen willingly offered him.

'No, Mother!' Wulfrun found her voice at last. 'Mother, no – it is my fault!' She screamed it out, reaching for her mother's hand. Sister Mildred roughly pushed the two of them apart, while Irminburgh reached forwards and dragged the necklace over Wulfrun's head.

She examined the jewels closely and seemed to catch her breath with surprise, but then she held the necklace high for all to see. 'How could any weaver woman have a right to own this? How could she?' She spoke the words as though with sorrow.

'She could not,' their neighbours responded with more shocked whispers. 'She could not!'

'It was payment!' Cwen insisted.

'Payment? For what?' Irminburgh asked.

Cwen was trembling violently now, but she still struggled to get her words out. 'A mother . . . with her two little children; it was payment for their lives! They could not wait for the tide.'

Irminburgh frowned in thought, but there were more gasps and murmurs and shaking of heads from the neighbours who stood around, arms folded, mouths gaping.

'She should be strung up for this!' they murmured. 'Hang her!'

'She could never pay compensation!'

'She must be sold as a slave!'

'But who may claim compensation?' a few puzzled bystanders asked.

'Stone her! This is a stoning offence.'

'There was a warrior and a monk.' Cwen turned frantically to Ulfstan. 'A tall dark monk – and a young woman, who pushed the boat out to sea, then rode away!' She was gabbling wildly now and desperate.

'A warrior, a monk,' Irminburgh sneered. 'Who will come next – the abbess herself?' Those around her sniggered as she thrust the beautiful jewels into Cwen's face and spoke low. 'Who was this mother? What was her name?'

Cwen could only shake her head.

'To the lock-up,' Ulfstan insisted. 'We shall see what the abbess says when she returns.'

'No, no!' Wulfrun screamed; her heart full of dread at the thought of losing her mother. She tried to grab at Cwen again, but Sister Mildred prevented her.

'But wait.' Irminburgh laid her hand on the reeve's arm, frowning in thought. 'I am closest in kin to the queen. While the abbess is away I should say what punishment shall be given.'

The reeve stopped, amazed at her, but he shook his head. 'Lady' – he spoke with courtesy, but firmly – 'the abbess left no such instructions.'

'Judgement is mine by right,' Irminburgh insisted. 'No instructions are needed.'

'Lady . . . if there is talk of hanging, or slavery, it is too serious a matter.' Ulfstan stood his ground. 'The abbess sits in judgement here at Whitby; she alone.'

Wulfrun watched them both, her mind a blur, her whole body trembling uncontrollably.

An angry frown marred Irminburgh's beautiful face, for she was not used to being denied. 'Then I shall take charge of these jewels,' she announced.

Ulfstan nodded at that and turned to call out the watchmen who acted as guards at the main gate.

'Take the webster to the lock-up,' he ordered, when a guard came running, pulling out the long knife they called a seax.

Cwen tugged at the girdle about her waist that was hung with all the tools of her trade. 'Let me give my child what she needs,' she begged.

Ulfstan let go of her for a moment and allowed her to loosen the belt and give it to Wulfrun. Cwen was trying to be calm, though her hands shook violently. 'Look after your sister, Wulfrun!' She forced the important words out. 'Look after your sister – keep her safe for me!'

'Mother!' Wulfrun howled. 'Mother . . . no!' She grabbed the girdle and clung to her mother too.

Ulfstan nodded to the men: they took hold of Cwen and began dragging her away, Wulfrun still clinging tight. Irminburgh and Sister Mildred slipped through the main gate ahead of them.

'Let go,' one of the guards growled.

But Wulfrun could not let go.

'Let go or you'll lose your fingers,' he warned, raising his seax against her.

Cwen gasped in horror and Wulfrun let go at last. Her mother vanished from sight and the gate was slammed in her face. Those gates were usually only shut late at night, but she could hear the heavy wooden bar being slid into place against her. When she turned round she found that all those who'd gathered to watch were staring coldly at her. These were her neighbours, her friends – or so she'd thought: the carpenters who'd helped them keep their hut repaired; the wattle weavers with whom Cwen had often exchanged warm rugs for woven hurdles.

Wulfrun's mind was full of blind panic. What could she do now? She tried to make her mind work – what had her mother said? *Look after your sister!* Gode had probably fallen over the cliff edge by now! She turned and ran that way, leaving her curious neighbours staring after her, strapping her mother's girdle about her waist as she went.

Though it was now growing dark, Wulfrun tore along the edges of the cliffs, calling wildly for Gode. Then she went down the steep path to the rocky beach below, still hopelessly calling her sister's name. She could see no sign of her or the geese. The tide was coming in and the sea was rough, crashing against the rocks below the high drop of the cliffs. Gulls wheeled overhead, screaming loudly, excited by the roaring waves. Even if Gode were trying to answer her, she'd never hear a young child's voice against this terrible noise. When at last she stumbled back to the hut, the fire had gone out and she couldn't find the iron striker or the flints. She hunkered down beside the ashes, her stomach churning. What had she done? She'd destroyed everything. Her chest was tight and her heart thundered; she'd never felt such despair. She was reminded of that terrible night when her father had been lost at sea and they'd sat together with their neighbours in a bitter agony of grief, cursing Woden and the fierce goddess Rheda, who brought death.

'But my neighbours will not help me now,' she muttered. 'And this cannot be blamed on any god or goddess . . . it is my fault – all my fault.'

She could get no peace crouching there beside the ashes – she felt as though she could never have peace again. She scrambled to her feet and went out into the dark.

All through the night she ran along the maze of cliff-top paths, crying out her sister's name. She went round the circling earthwork topped by the stockade that marked the monastic boundary.

When she hammered on the locked main gate the watchmen shouted at her to go away or she'd suffer the same fate as her mother.

Wulfrun swore under her breath.

Faces glanced out of doorways, annoyed with her for disturbing their sleep, but nobody comforted her; they just grumbled and cursed and went back to their beds. Her feet and hands grew numb with cold, but still she ran on and on, the tools on her mother's girdle battering her hips and thighs. The running and the bruising seemed to stop the pain of guilt a little, so she kept herself going, shouting until her throat was so sore that hardly any sound would come from it. Finally exhaustion slowly began to overtake her, promising some relief. She knew she'd have to stop eventually and drop down to the ground; perhaps when she dropped she could shut her eyes and never wake again. That might be best.

But at last, as the first faint streaks of morning light started to pattern the eastern horizon, she heard a faint reply to her cries. Could it be Gode? She shouted and listened again. The reply sounded like grunting, and after a moment or two of listening she began to understand. It was Cadmon calling her with the strange animal noises that he made for his cattle. She saw his dark shape struggling up the hillside towards her with his crook and she knew that she couldn't go on running any more. She bowed her head like a lost calf and went to him.

He put his rough hand on her cheek and stroked her wild hair, gentling her as though she were one of his beasts. 'C-come home, wild one,' he said. 'Gode's safe.'

She let him lead her by the hand back to the hut. The geese were all secured and quiet, and once inside she saw that Gode was there, fast asleep, with Sister Fridgyth sitting by their hearth, stoking the fire with scraps of wood.

Fridgyth looked up at her, unsmiling. 'Sit,' she ordered, pointing to the earth beside the hearthstone. As Wulfrun's knees crumpled beneath her, the herb woman pushed into her hands a warm beaker that smelled of hops, milk and honey. 'Drink!'

Wulfrun sipped the soothing pungent drink obediently, while the cowherd settled down quietly to guard the doorway.

'Sleep!' said Fridgyth, taking the beaker from her hands.

Wulfrun took off her mother's girdle, and clutching it to her chest, she let her eyelids close and slumped down onto the straw.

Sharp sunlight was shining in through the doorway when Wulfrun opened her eyes. She woke quickly and sat up, her heart beating fast, as though she'd had a bad dream. Something was terribly wrong and for a moment she wondered what it could be. Then she saw that Sister Fridgyth still sat by the hearthstone, feeding Gode oatcake and milk. Cwen's girdle with all its hangers and tools lay across her knees and the dreadful memory of what had happened last night came flooding back.

'Mother,' she whimpered.

Fridgyth gave her a warning glance. 'No good starting that wailing again,' she told her mercilessly. 'Not if you want to help your mother.'

'Mam!' Gode cried, picking up on her sister's distress.

'Where is Cadmon?' Wulfrun asked, trying to gather her thoughts into some kind of order.

'Gone to see to his calves.'

Wulfrun remembered Cwen's last instructions to her: to look after her sister. 'I . . . I lost Gode,' she said. 'I was to look after her, but I couldn't find her.'

'You should've come along towards Salt Scar,' Fridgyth answered her reprovingly. 'If you had, you'd have found your sister leading the geese across the rocks. A good thing I went up that way, gathering seaweed. I nearly didn't, the sea was so rough! The lass was soaked to the skin, so I took her back to my hut to get dry.'

Wulfrun shrugged with impatience. Fridgyth's

chastisement for letting her sister wander meant nothing compared to the horror of her mother being accused of theft and threatened with hanging. 'My mother,' she said again. 'Do you know . . . ?'

'I've heard it all from Mildred!' Fridgyth nodded.

'What shall I do?' Her voice cracked and faded so that she could only croak.

'Mam,' Gode whimpered. 'Where's my mam?'

Fridgyth stared into the fire for a moment and Wulfrun thought that she was too angry to speak to her, but then the herbwife began to fish inside the leather pouch that hung at her belt. She flung down onto the earthen floor two good-sized pieces of rough jet. 'Buy time!' she said. 'Make sure that Ulfstan takes no notice of what Irminburgh says. Try to buy your mother a bit of time! There's more rough jet where that came from. What else have you got to offer?'

Wulfrun looked desperately around the hut. 'Nothing,' she said, pressing her hands to her temples as though the pressure might make her think harder. 'We've nothing but hanks of wool and linen thread and mother's tools, but she will need them.'

That was not quite true, for Wulfrun knew that her mother had hidden away somewhere three silver sceattas that she was saving as the slave price for Sebbi. But she didn't know where Cwen kept them and she was also sure that her mother would never forgive her if she bought her time with the three precious coins; each one represented a whole year's work.

Suddenly Gode got up, smiling, as if they were playing a game, pointing at the sack of grain that Cwen had placed for safekeeping on the shelf. 'Mam sells grain,' she said.

Wulfrun saw that her little sister was thinking faster than she was. She got up and heaved the sack down. 'This was payment for her work,' she said. 'It came from the abbey. If I took it back to them, would it be enough?'

Fridgyth pursed her lips. 'I don't know. It might help.'

Then Wulfrun remembered the polished round of jet that was their mirror. She picked it up and tears sprang to her eyes again. What good was a mirror now that her treasure had been discovered and snatched away? What good was anything without her mother to care for them?

'Would they want this?'

'They might. They all seem to want these little jet crosses to dangle from their belts. I have no time for such things!' Sister Fridgyth was a strong, practical lay sister and the only things that dangled from her belt were a carrying pouch, work tools and a sharp pair of shears.

'What shall I do with them?'

'Take it all to the reeve and beg him keep your mother safe till Abbess Hild returns. Promise him more, if only he will wait. It's Hild who stands in judgement at Whitby in the king's name; no other has the right, whatever Irminburgh might say.'

Wulfrun frowned uncertainly. The abbess could be stern, all Whitby knew that. 'Might Irminburgh's judgement be kinder than the abbess's?'

'The abbess would be fair.' Fridgyth had no hesitation about that.

'If I take these things and beg for time, will Ulfstan release her?'

Fridgyth shrugged. 'Best not, I'd say.'

Wulfrun remembered the angry mutterings when the necklace was discovered. Fridgyth's answer told her that her mother might not even be safe from her neighbours were she to be released. She stared forlornly at the small collection of offerings, then began to pick them up.

'Wait.' Fridgyth suddenly looked hesitant and a little secretive. 'Before you go . . . there is one thing I can do.' She fished inside her pouch again and began to pull out a handful of little polished wooden twigs.

'The runes!' Wulfrun whispered, shocked. 'Oh, Fridgyth . . . how dare you? What if Abbess Hild knew?'

'Yes, but she does not,' came the answer.

Everyone knew that Fridgyth had been the local

wise woman before ever Hild came to Whitby. She'd made effective herb medicine for those who were sick, and Wulfrun had heard it rumoured that when people came to her with troubled minds, she would cast the runes for them. Once the Christians had arrived, she'd found new work that suited her well in the kitchen gardens and set up a small herb garden there with cuttings from her own plants. Hild had watched with approval, and when she saw how skilled the woman was, she'd asked her to take on the role of abbey herbwife. Like Cwen, the once pagan wise woman had become a respected member of the community high on the cliffs, but casting the runes was a pagan thing, forbidden by the Christians. Casting the runes meant calling on the help of the old gods; it must only be done in secret and in desperation.

Wulfrun shuddered, recognizing that this was a desperate situation and that Fridgyth was risking much for her by offering to do it.

Chapter 4

The Runes

Gode looked up at them, suddenly worried by the tense silence between her sister and the herbwife.

'Well?' Fridgyth asked. 'Shall I do it?'

Wulfrun nodded and went quietly to fasten the latch across the doorway, so that nobody could barge in and disturb them. Then she took her little sister into her arms and crouched down by the fire, stroking the child's hair to make her feel safe, though she herself felt far from safe. 'Do it,' she whispered.

Fridgyth took a small folded cloth of fine woven linen from her pouch and spread it carefully on the earthen floor. Then she gathered the little polished sticks together, each one marked with a powerful magical symbol. She closed her eyes for a moment and whispered into her cupped hands, 'Freyawife, Freyawife, pray tell us the strife.' Then with a fast movement she cast the runes down onto the linen cloth.

They sat in silence as she studied the way they had fallen, frowning a little, as though puzzled, at first, but at last came a small grunt of approval.

'Is it good, is it bad?' Wulfrun whispered.

Fridgyth snatched up the runes guiltily and returned them hurriedly to their pouch. 'There is hope,' she said cautiously. 'The runes say: "Help will come from where you least expect it."'

'What does that mean?'

The older woman shook her head. 'I don't know – the runes do not speak clearly; we have to be patient and trust them. Please remember this ancient saying, Wulfrun – it is very important: "When you consult the runes it is best to be silent."'

'I will be silent,' Wulfrun promised.

'Well . . . now I think you should go and beg the reeve to keep your mother safe till the abbess returns.' Fridgyth was back to being her usual practical self. 'Maybe the runes mean that Ulfstan will help: he is a just man.'

Wulfrun sighed and pushed Gode gently from her knee; she had hoped for something more. As she picked up the sack of grain she recalled her mother's satisfaction with the payment. It sickened her that it must be taken straight back to where it came from. She collected up the pieces of jet, looking anxiously at Fridgyth. 'Will you stay with my sister till I get back? I know I ask much.'

Fridgyth scrambled to her feet and held out her hand to Gode. 'I'll take her to the kitchen gardens. She can help me pull up weeds.'

Wulfrun stopped again, hesitating. Fridgyth had given help when all the other neighbours saving the cowherd had turned their back on them. 'I . . . I thank you for this,' she faltered. 'Only you and Cadmon . . .'

The herbwife nodded curtly at the awkward words, but she put out a gentle hand to stroke Gode's hair. 'I see it as the Christian thing to do. Oh, I may still cast the runes, but I do try hard to be a Christian. Abbess Hild says that Christians should show love to their neighbours and I think that a good and decent thing to do. Cwen is my neighbour, and though I've only known her since she turned up at Whitby with her handcart and her bairns, one thing I am sure about . . . she is no thief.'

'No,' Wulfrun agreed, relieved that at least one person believed that. 'It is all my fault,' she murmured.

Fridgyth bowed her head in agreement, but her words were full of sensible kindness. 'Do not waste time in guilt,' she said. 'Speak to the reeve with courtesy! Remember what the runes have said.'

Wulfrun marched determinedly up to the main gate, her heart beating painfully. Cadmon looked across from the upper pasture with sympathy, but she did not stop to talk to him. She went past the watchmen quickly, not daring to look at the small lock-up that was built against the palisade as a sturdy lean-to alongside their huts. She went straight to the front entrance of the guesthouse, dragging her bag of grain. The reeve's family quarters could only be reached through the great hall of the guesthouse; his wife Alta was guest-mistress there. Two lay sisters were sweeping used rushes from the floor, their long undyed woollen gowns hitched up and fastened behind them. They were Ethel and Bertha, a mother and daughter who'd once scraped a living gutting fish and shelling mussels down by the quayside. Wulfrun knew them well. They'd declared themselves Christians soon after the abbess had opened up her refectory and huts to those who wanted to take up the religious life.

'Where do you think you are going?' Bertha came over and blocked her way through. 'You are not allowed in there, Goose Girl.'

Her heart still beating wildly, Wulfrun made a quick curtsy to them, remembering Fridgyth's advice. 'Please, Sisters,' she said, trying to sound respectful, 'the reeve has locked my mother away and I must speak to him.'

'So it is true: it is Cwen the webster that they've locked up as a thief!'

'And is it you, Goose Girl, that was so foolish as

to wear a stolen necklace?' Bertha added with a snigger.

Wulfrun wanted to stamp and scream at them and deny any theft, but Fridgyth's words were still fresh in her memory. 'Please, Sisters, have pity on me. Let me speak to the reeve,' she said softly.

'What have you there?' Ethel, the old fish gutter, pointed with rough red fingers to the sack of grain.

Wulfrun hesitated. If these two took the grain and the jet she'd have nothing to offer the reeve, but without their help she might never get to see him. The grain she could not hide, but at least she could keep the precious jet in her tightly closed fist. 'This was payment to my mother for a large wall hanging that she worked on for a whole month,' she said. 'If you would help me to speak to the reeve, I would gladly give it to you.'

The lay sisters looked at each other, unimpressed. 'We've no need of extra grain,' Bertha said. 'The abbey feeds us well enough.'

Ethel sniffed. 'From what we've heard, your mother deserves to be taken out and stoned. We'd not want to interfere with a just punishment.'

'Theft is sin,' Bertha said sourly. 'That is what Abbess Hild tells us. Take yourself back to your geese, daughter of a thief, and be glad that you do not suffer alongside your mother.'

Wulfrun glared at them. How could they stand there, speaking so primly in their neatly stitched, soft woollen monastic habits. She wanted to slap their mouths and remind them that little more than a year ago they'd crouched by the quayside in rags, stinking of fish. She almost turned to run, but fear for her mother made her grit her teeth and try again; she hauled back the sack of grain and opened her closed fist to reveal the pieces of jet.

They smiled at each other then and picked up a piece. 'Just big enough for a cross,' Bertha said, holding a piece of jet against her hip as though testing how it would look if it were cut and polished to dangle from her girdle. 'What do you think, Mam?'

'This is heavier,' Ethel answered, carefully weighing another piece in the palm of her hand. 'And what is it that you still hide behind your back?'

Wulfrun was forced to reveal the polished jet mirror that she loved so much.

'Ah.' Bertha took it and held it up in front of her. 'Oh look – we'd be able to admire ourselves, Mam.'

Still trying to be patient and courteous and appeal to their better nature, Wulfrun tried again. 'The new Frankish polisher would cut these pieces for you and make them into fine, gleaming jewels,' she said.

'He would.' Ethel winked at her daughter. 'But he would need paying.'

'Aye – he'd need paying,' Bertha said, nudging her mother and sniggering. 'That Childeric would need paying all right. I might find a happy way of paying him!'

Childeric was the handsome son of the Frankish jeweller and Bertha was not the only young woman who admired him. She and her mother pocketed the jet and looked as though they'd return to their scrubbing, ignoring Wulfrun.

She watched them for a moment or two, feeling that she'd been tricked. 'You can have the grain too,' she said. 'You could use that to pay the jeweller.'

'That's more like it,' Bertha said, taking hold of the sack of grain.

'Now can I see the reeve?' Wulfrun begged.

'When he gets back.' Bertha returned to her scrubbing.

'Where from?'

'The tannery!'

'When will he be back?'

Ethel shrugged. 'When he's finished his business down there. Run along now.'

Wulfrun's hand clenched, making a tight fist. She had given them all she'd got and they hadn't helped her one bit. The tannery was far down the hillside near the beck, in a secluded fold of land, so that its stinking work was hidden away from the busy paths that led to the abbey. It would take her all morning to walk down there to the tanning pits and she didn't even know if she could trust them to be telling the truth about that. She wondered whether to try to grab back the sack of grain, but she knew that she'd have a fight on her hands and they were both strong women. At last she turned and ran out of the guesthouse, back through the gate.

She was furious with herself. What would she tell Sister Fridgyth when she asked what she'd done with the jet and the grain? The runes had lied. There was no help for her.

A gentle whistle made her turn to see that Cadmon was watching from the upper pasture. Wulfrun went to him, just as she had that morning. In a world that seemed to have turned itself upside down, the cowherd was almost the only one whose kindness she could take for granted.

'They've tricked me!' she cried as she strode towards him.

'Wh-who?' he asked, his brow furrowed with concern.

'Those two sluts who call themselves lay sisters, Ethel and Bertha. I could tell the abbess a thing or two about them,' she raged. 'I saw Bertha dancing with the lads last Yuletide, with mistletoe in her hair, and it wasn't only dancing she was doing either.'

'Wh-what?' Cadmon raised his eyebrows.

'They've stolen the jet and the grain that I was to offer Ulfstan.' She was shouting at him as though he were the guilty one. 'I was to buy my mother time. Fridgyth said I would get help if I were courteous. She lied like all of them!'

But Cadmon looked past her, ignoring the string of angry words. His finger flew to his lips in warning. Wulfrun understood at last that something was wrong and turned round. Her heart thundered as she saw that Princess Elfled had once again wandered out from the side gate. This time she must have crept down past the vegetable gardens and moved quietly into the upper pasture, for they hadn't heard her coming at all.

Elfled gave up any pretence of creeping up on them as Wulfrun turned to her. 'I thought it must be you,' she cried, her cheeks flushed and her eyes blazing blue. 'Was it you that kept me awake all night with your whining and your howling? How dare you disturb my sleep? Yesterday you complained that I was making a noise!'

Both Wulfrun and Cadmon glanced nervously behind her, fearing that Lady Irminburgh would also appear at any moment, but only Adfrith came through the side gate, looking as worried as when they'd last seen him.

'Oh, why can he not let me be?' Elfled cried, when she saw that he was following her.

'Please, Princess,' Adfrith begged. 'Please come

back. When the lady wakes from her rest she will want to see what you have done.'

'Huh! You do it!' she told him. 'Irminburgh will not know the difference! I want to speak to this girl who kept me awake last night. I could have her whipped; I have only to shout for the guards.'

It was too much; the battle to be courteous was lost. Wulfrun's chin went up and anger blazed from her. 'Then have me whipped!' she cried. 'What do I care if you have me whipped? You might as well have me hanged as well! Or if you decide to send my mother as a slave, then you should send me too, for I was the one who had the necklace.'

Chapter 5

from where you least expect it

Elfled opened her mouth to give a furious reply, but as Wulfrun's words sank in, she hesitated, closed it again and stared at them, puzzled. 'Hang you? Send you as a slave? What necklace is this?' she asked.

Wulfrun tried to answer, but her fury had left as suddenly as it came. Her mouth made to form words of explanation, but her lips went stiff and her chin trembled.

Elfled turned to the cowherd. 'Who is to be hanged?'

Cadmon could only stammer miserably, blushing scarlet.

'I don't think anyone is,' Adfrith explained. 'The goose girl's mother is accused of stealing a necklace of great value and Ulfstan has put her in the lock-up. I understand that my Lady

Irminburgh claimed the right to stand in judgement while the abbess is away, but Ulfstan has not agreed to that.'

Elfled shook her head, trying to make sense of it all. She looked back curiously at the miserable goose girl, seeing for the first time a world of uncertainty that she knew nothing about, but one important point had stood out in Adfrith's explanation. 'Irminburgh claims to stand in judgement?' she asked, frowning at the idea. 'Can she do that?'

Adfrith shrugged. 'Here in Whitby Abbess Hild sits in judgement as kinswoman to both the king and the queen; she is lady of all these lands. But it seems Irminburgh claims that she should have the right of judgement while the abbess is away as she is now the closest royal kin.'

'Huh!' Elfled's eyes grew round with outrage. 'Is she indeed? I thought Ulfstan was in charge while Mother Hild was away.'

Adfrith nodded thoughtfully, but still he seemed unsure. 'Yes, that has always been true in the past, but . . . the lady never claimed this right before.'

'Closest royal kin, is she?' Elfled pushed out her lower lip and turned to Wulfrun, beckoning imperiously. 'Come with me, Goose Girl. I shall show Irminburgh who is royal kin. Come now – do as I say!'

Wulfrun started in surprise and Adfrith looked troubled.

'Adfrith, this is more important than your scratchy work!' Elfled flung a delightful smile at him. 'Come, girl – we go to find the reeve.'

'But, Princess . . .' Adfrith begged.

Wulfrun looked to Cadmon for help, but he nodded encouragement, suddenly hopeful for her. Still unsure whether she did right or wrong, but feeling that things could not get any worse, Wulfrun set off obediently behind the young princess. Elfled strode back through the side gate, past Fridgyth and Gode, who stopped their weeding to stare after them, down the side of the stables and up the steps of the guesthouse. Adfrith followed them, looking more worried than ever.

Ethel and Bertha, who were still in the great hall, gaped at the sight of them. Elfled led the way to the reeve's chamber and knocked on the heavy oak door. As soon as the young monk who answered saw that it was the princess, he ushered them inside.

Wulfrun caught her breath. Ulfstan sat at a small table covered with counting boxes; he had been there all the time. He got up at once and bowed.

'Princess,' he murmured.

Elfled ignored his courteous gesture and demanded at once, 'Ulfstan, tell me, who is closest kin to the king and queen in Whitby?'

The reeve looked amazed, but he answered her at once. 'You are of course, dear Princess . . . you are their daughter.'

'Ha.' Elfled grinned with satisfaction. 'Then you must listen to me and not Irminburgh. Is that not right?'

Ulfstan opened his mouth as though to speak, but then he glanced at Wulfrun and Adfrith standing uncomfortably in the doorway and hesitated.

'Well' – Elfled folded her arms in a determined manner – 'I say that Irminburgh has no right to stand in judgement over the goose girl's mother. I am closest in kin to the king and queen, so I claim the right, not Irminburgh, and I say the woman should go free.'

Wulfrun's spirits soared with hope.

Ulfstan shook his head and sighed. 'Dear Princess . . . this is a matter of law . . . King Oswy's law. The king's appointed representative in Whitby is the abbess. Forgive me, Princess, but you are very young, too young to take on such a responsibility.'

Elfled fell quiet at the reeve's words. She bit her lips, suddenly looking very young and uncertain again; the great burst of confidence that had carried her was fading fast. They all stood in a tense silence for a few moments; then Wulfrun remembered something that Irminburgh had said the night before. She curtsied politely to the princess. 'May I ask the princess's age?' she said, unsure whether she should direct this question to the reeve or to the princess herself.

Elfled answered at once. 'I was eleven in the Month of Flowers – everyone knows that.'

Wulfrun's cheeks flushed with sudden hope. She curtsied again, this time to Ulfstan. 'Sir,' she said, 'when the Lady Irminburgh saw me accused me of theft last night, she said that I must answer for my crime as I was more than eleven years old.'

The reeve nodded thoughtfully. 'That would have been right by King Oswy's law – had you been the thief – but as Cwen admitted that the necklace was hers—'

'No, sir,' Wulfrun hastened on. 'What I meant was that if a young person must answer for their crime at the age of eleven, might not the Princess Elfled sit in judgement at that age too?'

'Yes, indeed.' Elfled understood at once. 'That is only right. I am eleven and that is the age of responsibility.'

Ulfstan scratched his head in thought and then rubbed his hands uncomfortably down his fine red linen tunic. 'Princess,' he said at last, 'I am unhappy about the Lady Irminburgh's claim to sit in judgement, but I am also unsure as to whether your claim should be upheld. This situation is beyond my knowledge. I must insist that the accusations that have been made against Cwen the webster will be heard and judged by no one but the abbess. Until then I shall keep the goose girl's mother safe in the lock-up. There will be no judgement, no slavery, and certainly no hanging unless Abbess Hild herself rules it.'

Wulfrun could see that this decision was fair and probably the safest course for Cwen. She shuddered with relief and suddenly burst into tears.

'What are you crying for now?' Elfled asked, turning to her with annoyance.

'I . . . I am crying with g-gratitude,' Wulfrun gulped. 'To know that my mother is to be kept safe is all I want.'

The reeve spoke kindly. 'Dry your tears, Cwen's daughter. I have always believed your mother to be a decent, honest woman and I myself will speak for her good character when the time comes, but the evidence of the necklace looks bad. Can you think of any reason why such jewels should rightfully be hers?'

Wulfrun racked her brains but could think of nothing to say that might help.

'Well,' the reeve continued calmly, 'you have a little time. We expect the abbess back before the bitter weather begins. If you can discover why those jewels were in Cwen's possession then you might help your mother's case a great deal.'

'Can I see her?' Wulfrun begged.

'No.' He was firm on that. 'But . . . I will see her myself and make sure she understands that we wait for Hild's judgement. I will tell her too that you and your sister are safe, but that is all I can do. There will be Lady Irminburgh to deal with and that will be difficult enough. Now . . . go back to your home, look after your sister and see if you can discover how that necklace came to be Cwen's – that is the best way for you to help your mother.'

Elfled folded her arms, frowning a little, unsure whether she'd achieved what she wanted or not. 'Well . . . so long as I am not to be overruled by Irminburgh,' she allowed.

Wulfrun curtsied to the reeve and turned to go, but then she stopped, realizing that despite all her early doubts the runes had spoken true. Help had come and it had come from a most unexpected source; she must not be ungrateful. She turned back and threw herself down at the feet of the young princess, snatching the small hand and kissing it with devotion. 'Dear Princess,' she said, 'I can never thank you enough.'

Elfled was taken aback for a moment, but then she suddenly smiled mischievously, seeing new possibilities. 'Oh yes you can,' she said quickly. 'I claim you as my slave in payment for helping your mother.'

Wulfrun looked up, shocked and surprised at her words.

'Oh, you can do as the reeve says,' Elfled allowed. 'You'd better see to your sister and your geese, but I want you to wait on me in the scriptorium schoolroom tomorrow morning.'

Wulfrun looked at the reeve for guidance.

He sighed and smiled reprovingly. 'Princess, you know what Mother Hild thinks of slavery.' Then he shrugged. 'But if it pleases you to have the goose girl spend a little time serving you, then I can't see the harm in that.'

'I will be there in the scriptorium, Princess,' Wulfrun promised. Then before any more could be demanded of her she got to her feet, curtsied again and ran back through the great hall, thumbing her nose at Bertha and Ethel, a huge smile on her face.

Fridgyth stood rake in hand by the steaming compost heap, Gode carrying a handful of weeds at her side.

'The abbess will sit in judgement and none other,' Wulfrun cried.

'Then you have bought your time.' The herbwife smiled at her excitement.

'The princess spoke up for me.' Wulfrun could not explain fast enough. 'So you see, help did come. I will never doubt the—'

Fridgyth frowned and pressed a finger to her lips.

'I know, I know,' Wulfrun remembered. 'It is best to be silent.'

'Then be silent,' the herbwife told her firmly. 'And remember that your mother is still to be judged.'

'The reeve told me to see if I can discover how my mother came to have the necklace. That might help to prove her innocent.'

Out in the sun of the upper pasture Wulfrun danced among the young calves, causing almost as much upset as the princess had. Cadmon simply followed her, smiling at her delight and making sure that she did no harm to his precious charges. Fridgyth and Gode followed her out of the vegetable garden and the little one joined her sister in her mad dance.

At last Wulfrun calmed down and went to thank Fridgyth for looking after Gode.

'There is much hard work ahead,' the herbwife warned. 'But I will help you all I can. Now, those geese of yours will need feeding and your sister too. I saw that there was little food left in Cwen's hut.'

'Very little,' Wulfrun acknowledged ruefully. 'And there is more work than you know, for the Princess Elfled has claimed me as her slave in payment for her help.'

Fridgyth's face showed instant disapproval. 'The abbess would not like that.'

'No. But the reeve has agreed that I should serve her. I am to wait on her in the scriptorium schoolroom tomorrow morning.'

'What can she want of you in the scriptorium?'
'To m-make the l-letters,' Cadmon suggested.
They both laughed at such an idea.
'Well . . . we shall see.' Fridgyth raised her eyebrows in wonder. 'Now let us see what we can do about food for you. Bring your sister and follow me!'

Chapter 6

Chose you can Crust

Fridgyth led them both back through the side gate, past the vegetable and herb gardens and into the great monastic refectory, where the monks and nuns were settling down to their noontide meal. Adfrith looked up from one of the long tables and smiled at them. He sat with the growing number of inky-fingered young men known as oblates, who were dedicated by their parents to God and were training to be monks at the monastery school.

'Sit here,' Fridgyth told them. They both scrambled over a bench and settled themselves at an empty table set close to the kitchen. Fridgyth went to speak to the servers, who were carrying out trays of food.

Bertha and Ethel turned round from the next table to stare and whisper. When Wulfrun looked about, it seemed that every face was turned in their direction with much muttering and expressions of outrage.

Gode's small hand crept up to cling to the crook of her arm. 'I want to go home,' she murmured. 'Go home to Mam.'

Wulfrun looked frantically round for Fridgyth and saw that she was talking to Sister Mildred, who stood hands on hips, looking in their direction. The cook pursed her lips, her expression grim.

Despite her fear of Mildred's anger Wulfrun's stomach churned with hunger. 'No, we must stay,' she told Gode. 'We're having our meal here . . . I think.'

At last Fridgyth came back to sit with them. 'Be patient,' she said. 'Mildred can only see guilt in the possession of such a necklace, but she will not have you starve.'

So they sat there patiently as they were bidden and at last Sister Mildred came over to them carrying a wooden tray. Still unsmiling, she set bowls of chunky vegetable soup and a hunk of brown barley bread in front of them. They were both so hungry that they snatched it up at once and began to eat, dipping into the wholesome soup.

'You can come here every day to eat,' Fridgyth told them. 'Mildred has agreed that it is only right. When you hear the summons bell you come along with the others and sit down at this table. It is for my garden helpers.'

'I'm your garden helper,' Gode insisted.

'Indeed you are, honey.'

'Thank you,' Wulfrun said. 'But . . . they all hate us being here.'

As Fridgyth's gaze swept around the room, many accusing eyes were quickly averted and heads went down. Nobody wished to offend the herbwife, for all were vulnerable to sickness, and who knew when they might need her skills?

'Ignore them,' she said.

Wulfrun tried hard to take this good advice, and as the meal continued, the resentful interest that they'd aroused seemed to wane. When her hunger was satisfied, she found herself staring round at the long tables and their occupants. There seemed to be a strict pecking order: the monks, with their hair long at the back and their heads shaved across the front from ear to ear, sat at a table at the far end of the hall; the nuns, in their simple undyed robes and plain linen coifs, sat at another. These austere religious men and women had dedicated their lives to chastity and slept in small solitary huts. They ate meagrely and in silence. The lay brothers and sisters, who lived as families, raising their children together, sat in the main body of the hall. They helped themselves from high piled stacks of bread and bowls of baked herrings, talking cheerfully and berating the children who sat at their sides.

When they'd finished their bread and soup and cleaned their bowls, Wulfrun wondered if they should creep away quietly, before the others left, but then an older nun with a slight limp came down to them from the far end of the hall carrying a tray of honey cakes. Every eye was turned in amazement as she placed one in Gode's empty bowl. The child's eyes grew wide with pleasure as her hands stretched out to grasp the sticky treat. Another cake was placed in front of Wulfrun. Such a delicacy was a rare delight for them. Wulfrun waited to see if Fridgyth would be given one and was puzzled to find that she was not.

'From the Princess Elfled,' the nun announced.

Heads turned quickly away and a new buzz of shocked gossip flew around Ethel and Bertha's table.

'Thank you, Sister Begu.' Fridgyth spoke for them, looking up at the nun with a smile.

Sister Begu gave a quick nod, then went back to the far end of the refectory. Wulfrun strained to see where the honey cakes were carried: at the very far end of the refectory a small table was raised on a dais. Elfled sat there with the reeve, his wife Alta and Lady Irminburgh. The princess looked in their direction and began climbing onto her chair, a wide grin on her face, her hand lifted as though to wave. Irminburgh and the guest-mistress were on their feet at once, admonishing her. She got down obediently enough, but continued to grin cheerfully in the direction of Wulfrun's table.

Fridgyth was impressed. 'Well, it seems you have friends in high places.'

Wulfrun began to eat her cake greedily, then suddenly stopped, overwhelmed with guilt. She broke a good-sized piece from the side of her cake to offer to Fridgyth.

The herbwife smiled and shook her head. 'Thank you, but today is Friday. Christians should fast on Friday: no meat, no cream, no honey or honey cakes. The abbess is both strict and sensible about it. These rules do not apply to children; those whose bodies are still growing should not fast.'

'But what about them?' Wulfrun indicated the next table, where the lay brothers seemed to be eating very well.

'It's different for those who labour for the monastery,' Fridgyth said. 'They need every bit of strength they can get.'

Wulfrun nodded. The table was full of muscular lay brothers who had recently arrived in the refectory, their clothes dark with charcoal dust from the bloom hearths, where they made iron, and sawdust from the carpenters' sheds. They were tucking into boiled eggs, baked herrings and a huge pile of barley bread, which they dipped into a honey pot.

'No meat for them on Friday,' Fridgyth said. 'But they get a good supply of fish and eggs.'

Wulfrun watched, fascinated. Though she had lived so close to the abbey, she had never understood that there were so many complicated rules for those who dwelt within the stockade. She recalled vaguely that she and Cwen had eaten here a few times when they first arrived at Whitby, but her memory of it was dim.

'Does Irminburgh fast on Friday?' she asked with sudden interest. She could not imagine the beautiful Lady Irminburgh denying herself.

The herbwife snorted with mirth, covering her mouth to mask the sound. She calmed herself quickly so that she could answer, though she did not quite banish the smile from her lips. 'Lady Irminburgh makes her own rules,' was all she'd say. 'Especially when the abbess is away.'

'But you labour in the gardens,' Wulfrun said. 'It seems wrong to me that you don't get honey, when you are the one who has to steal it from the bees. It is you who suffers the stings.'

Fridgyth smiled again. 'But the bees never sting me,' she said, her voice suddenly soft. 'They trust me. You are quick to see beneath the surface, Wulfrun. That is a good thing and should help you in your quest to prove your mother's innocence. It is important in life to know who you can trust.'

Wulfrun's thoughts flew back at once to her

mother and she began to get up from the table. 'I must take the geese out and try to get some weaving done. That wall hanging Mother started will bring us payment.'

'You are thinking well!' Fridgyth nodded approval, once again her usual practical self. 'Take Gode with you now, but I will have her help me in the gardens tomorrow morning, when you go to serve the princess. And while you are about your tasks, think carefully what your mother said about that necklace. Is there anyone who might have knowledge of it?'

Wulfrun shook her head; she could think of nothing that made any sense.

Fridgyth patted Gode on the head, as they all got up from the bench. 'Will you come and help Fridgyth again tomorrow?' she asked. 'I need a good helper like you.'

'Yes,' Gode answered cheerfully. 'I will pull weeds.'

As they left the refectory, Wulfrun noticed Bertha rather furtively handing over a bowl of honey cakes to the handsome Frankish jeweller's son, Childeric. It seems we are not the only ones getting special treats, she thought resentfully. Is he cutting a fine jet cross for her in return for honey cakes?

Wulfrun did not linger in the upper pasture with Cadmon, even though the sun was warm. As soon as the geese were fed she hurried them all back to the hut and opened the south-facing shutter, setting the heavy loom there on its hook. Now, what was she to do with Gode? She hardly dared take her eyes off her sister, remembering the neglect of her that seemed to have set off this whole terrible chain of events.

Then a picture came into her mind of her own early years, and she remembered how Cwen would get her to sit close by and comb wool with a dried teasel, rewarding her for a whole hank made smooth and ready for the spinning. Gode was young to be set to work, but she'd have to grow up fast, just as Wulfrun must.

'Come here, little sister,' she said, speaking kindly. 'You can comb the wool like Wulfrun does and be a big girl.'

'I'm a big girl,' Gode agreed.

But by the time Wulfrun had wound a hank of blue wool around the shuttle Gode had tired of combing and threw the teasel down. 'Play wi' geese now!' she said.

'No.' Wulfrun was adamant. 'No playing with the geese. Comb some more wool, then you shall get a reward.'

'No.' Gode shook her head firmly.

Wulfrun racked her brains. 'Honey cakes,' she said. 'More honey cakes.'

Gode suddenly smiled at that and picked up the

teasel. 'Honey cakes,' she said and returned to her work.

Wulfrun struggled with the weaving and managed to do a few more rows, but as the light faded she began to feel very tired and realized that the last row had somehow gone wrong – the warps were showing through. 'Freya's tears!' she whispered. 'I cannot get this right!'

Gode threw down her teasel again. 'Honey cakes now,' she demanded.

Wulfrun was grateful to hear the distant sound of the refectory bell summoning them to eat. She let the shuttle drop, took Gode by the hand and fastened the door behind them. 'We'll see if there are any more honey cakes,' she said.

She marched into the refectory, just as Fridgyth had instructed, and sat down. Bertha looked over from the next table and nudged her mother. 'They're here again,' she murmured.

Ethel looked up and spoke loudly. 'That table is for the gardeners.'

Wulfrun ignored them, sitting there as she'd been told, her cheeks burning. 'Where is Fridgyth?' she murmured.

'Honey cakes,' said Gode hopefully.

The lay workers on Bertha's table were served with a fine herb-scented fish stew and more barley bread, but still nothing came their way. The servers looked at each other, puzzled, and frowned at them as though they had no business being there. Wulfrun strained to see the raised high table at the far end of the refectory, but it was empty. Then at last Sister Mildred came out of the kitchen and saw them sitting there. She turned with sharp words to admonish the servers, and quickly two steaming bowls of stew and bread were put in front of them.

Wulfrun was so relieved that she didn't care that people stared any more; she just ate and so did Gode, but as soon as the fish stew was finished, the little girl began asking for honey cakes.

'I don't know whether there are honey cakes tonight,' Wulfrun admitted.

'You said honey cakes,' Gode accused.

'Honey cakes tomorrow,' Wulfrun tried.

'No,' Gode whined. 'Honey cakes now!'

'Be quiet!' Wulfrun hissed. She was aware of servers bringing out something else from the kitchen that smelled of apples, but at the same time all the faces were turned towards them with stark disapproval at the noise Gode was making.

'Now!' Gode demanded, slapping her small hand down hard on the wooden table.

It was too much. Wulfrun rose red-cheeked from the table, grabbed her sister by the arm and fled, dragging her behind, screaming and squawking like the geese.

'How could you shame me so?' she shouted once they were out of the refectory.

Cadmon emerged from the cowshed on his way to the evening meal.

'Wh-what is—?' he started, his brows furrowed with concern.

'Leave us alone!' Wulfrun cut across his slow, stammering speech.

She hurried Gode along, shaking her at every step and pushing her roughly in front of her. The geese set up a wild squawking as they burst in through the close. She flung her sister inside the hut, while she made sure the gate was securely fastened.

'I want Mam,' Gode wailed.

Wulfrun followed her sister inside. 'I want her too,' she bellowed. 'Do you think you are the only one?' She threw herself down on the straw and began to howl.

Gode went quiet at the shocking sound of her sister howling like the she-wolf she was named for. She sat very still and watched, eyes wide, cheeks white. At last Wulfrun saw how frightened her sister was and forced herself to calm down.

'Mam?' Gode murmured.

'Don't be fearful.' Wulfrun's voice was thick with crying and her nose was blocked. 'All's well . . . I'm better now. Let us be friends again.' She held out her arms and Gode went to her. They hugged each other tightly. 'Mam's gone away for a while,' Wulfrun whispered in her sister's ear, knowing she deserved a bit more explanation. 'But you are safe. I will look after you . . . and Fridgyth will help. Do you understand?'

Gode's mouth trembled, but she didn't cry. 'Yes,' she murmured.

Wulfrun built up the fire and they curled up together to sleep.

Chapter 7

a job shared

They were up early next morning and waiting at the main gate, which was opened as soon as the breakfast bell sounded, so that the silversmiths and jewellers could go inside to eat. Wulfrun was relieved to see that Fridgyth was there, sitting in her place on the garden workers' bench. They went to join her as the crowd of hungry lay workers and their children quietly took their places. The nuns' and monks' tables were empty and there were no bowls or food set out for them, though at the far end of the hall Elfled sat on her dais, accompanied only by Sister Begu, the reeve and the guest-mistress. She waved as though she'd been looking out for them, and neither Ulfstan nor his wife admonished her. They were soon served with steaming bowls of oatmeal, laced with cream and honey. Both girls ate quickly with appreciation; they could not remember ever tasting anything so delicious. Then Wulfrun suddenly stopped, overwhelmed with guilt.

'Will they feed my mother?' she whispered to Fridgyth.

'Certainly they will,' said Fridgyth. 'I was there in the kitchen when the reeve spoke to Mildred. She's to be offered the same food that the lay workers get.'

'But Sister Mildred hates us and believes my mother guilty of theft.'

Fridgyth shook her head. 'Mildred is more fair-minded than you think. She will obey Ulfstan's instructions, I can assure you of that.'

Wulfrun remembered that it was Sister Mildred who'd seen them fed last night. She tried to put the terrible picture of her mother starving and alone from her mind. 'When do the monks and nuns eat?' she asked, glancing across at the empty tables.

'Not until midday,' Fridgyth said with a smile.

'Only two meals a day?' Wulfrun was surprised. She'd thought of them as privileged.

Fridgyth nodded. 'The abbess orders me to eat breakfast before I set about my digging, and that is an order for which I am truly grateful.'

'I should think so,' Wulfrun agreed.

'And I must get to it.' Fridgyth stood up, holding her hand out to Gode, who went to her willingly enough.

Suddenly Wulfrun's stomach lurched at the thought that she must now go to the scriptorium at the princess's bidding. 'I must wash and comb my hair,' she fretted.

'Come to my hut,' Fridgyth suggested. 'I have all that you need there.'

She followed the herbwife round to the gardener's hut, which was placed conveniently at the junction of the herb garden and the kitchen garden and next to the small infirmary. It was bigger than most of the monastic huts, with two large lean-tos on either side. As soon as the woven door curtain was lifted a wonderful smell filled their nostrils. One lean-to was filled with onions, garlic, leeks, apples, pears and plums, all laid out carefully to dry in rows on shelves. The mouth-watering aroma of the fruits and vegetables mingled with the sharp scent of herbs that came from the other lean-to. Bunches of herbs dangled from the rafters there and clay pots and wooden spoons littered the shelves. Fridgyth's sleeping pallet took up little space in a cubicle in the middle and on every ledge stood growing seedlings, ready for the autumn planting. Rakes, spades and trowels were propped in every corner.

Both Gode and Wulfrun smiled at the pungent warmth that surrounded them as they stepped inside. 'I like Fridif's home,' Gode said.

'I can see why.' Wulfrun reached up to the end-less bunches of rosemary and thyme. 'Are so many medicines needed?'

'They are not all for medicines.' Fridgyth sighed. 'Sister Gudrun folds thyme into all the clean habits, once they're out of the drying house, and Lady Irminburgh pours rosewater into her wash. It takes a lot of petals to provide that.'

Fridgyth pointed to her bed and the small wooden cupboard that stood beside it. A pot of water had been placed there, with a comb and a clean cloth. 'Now, I prefer lavender water. I shall find a drop for you.'

'Thank you.' Wulfrun set about making herself as decent and tidy as she could. Her mother's girdle hangers bore heavy flax and wool combs, but nothing like Fridgyth's fine bone comb. She made her unruly tangle of hair smooth and brushed her worn linen smock free of feathers and dried dirt. There was nothing she could do about the old leather turnshoes that had once been her mother's. The soles flapped open at the front and needed stitching back in place.

Fridgyth put a drop of distilled lavender on the damp cloth and gently rubbed Wulfrun's neck and arms with the sweet, sharp scent. 'There,' she said. 'A touch of lavender brings calm and courage. Keep the comb; I have little need of it.'

Wulfrun gratefully added it to the collection of useful tools that swung from her mother's girdle. 'What can the princess want of me?' she asked, her stomach churning wildly now.

'If you go, you will find out,' was Fridgyth's practical reply. 'Just remember she is Woden's daughter.'

'What?' Wulfrun's mouth dropped open in surprise. 'But she is promised to the Christian God.'

'Yes' – Fridgyth smiled – 'that is true, but still the ravens fly around her shoulders. All the royal line of Northumbria claim descent from the old god Woden – don't forget it.'

'I won't,' she whispered.

Wulfrun walked round the refectory and past the library. The scriptorium was built above the oblates' dormitory onto the side of the great church. She hesitated at the top of the wooden stairs: she'd only been into the church, with its great carved beams, on a few very special occasions with Cwen, and she'd never set foot in the scriptorium before. She knew that some of the monks and nuns spent all their daylight hours carefully making copies of valuable books, but she had little idea of how they did it. She gingerly entered a small porch that led into a long, well-lit room that was set all around with benches. As soon as she stepped inside, many faces looked up at her from their work with an expression of astonished outrage. In the centre of the room were two tables occupied by nuns, but monks sat on the benches, their feet propped up on footstools, working away at squares of parchment that rested on a board across their knees. Some of them held a horn of ink in one hand, while they wrote with the other.

Wulfrun was so amazed at the skill with which they balanced the ink and their vellum parchment that she ignored their disapproving looks and stared back at them. At the far end of the long room a tall young man got up, carefully setting his work aside; she saw with relief that it was Adfrith.

He strode towards her, and as she opened her mouth to speak, he silenced her with a finger to his lips, then beckoned her to follow him. Heads turned as he led her through the room and into a small private study, with more chairs and benches around the walls and footstools set ready in front of them. A carved wooden cupboard with open doors revealed pots of ink and heavily weighted piles of parchment, some small tablets and a fine selection of goose quills.

'Are they from my geese?' she asked.

'Very likely,' Adfrith agreed.

He courteously pulled a chair forwards and indicated that she should sit. She felt a strange mixture of delight and fear, for nobody had ever held out a chair for her before. Indeed, she had never sat in a chair like this: simply made, but with a fine polished finish and a comfortable low, curving back.

'What am I to do?' she whispered.

Adfrith shrugged his shoulders and scratched his head, but there was no time to ask more, for they heard footsteps and a childlike voice in the big work-room. Elfled arrived, with Sister Begu hobbling beside her and a young nun carrying a cloak, a small jug and a silver-trimmed horn beaker.

Wulfrun rose from her seat and curtsied awkwardly, while Adfrith glanced nervously through the open doorway.

'If you're looking for Irminburgh, she's still in bed,' Elfled told him with a giggle.

Sister Begu looked heavenward, raising her eyebrows. 'Unfortunately that's true,' she said.

'I promised I should have some good work to show her and so I shall.'

'Let's hope so,' said Begu.

'Is there anything else, Princess?' the young nun asked, setting the jug and beaker down on a table and laying the cloak neatly over a chair back.

Elfled shook her head. 'This girl will serve me now.' She indicated Wulfrun with a wave of her hand.

The young woman glanced at Wulfrun with a touch of suspicion, but she and Sister Begu turned and left the room.

'Ha!' Elfled clapped her hands and smiled at them both. 'You are here and ready. Sit down – and Adfrith, pass the wax tablets. Do you know any riddles?'

'What are you doing, Princess?' Adfrith was full of suspicion.

'Today I have my slave. My slave will make the stupid letters for me and Irminburgh will be satisfied.'

'No!' Adfrith's hands flew up to his temples, horrified at the very idea. 'You cannot learn like that, Princess. You will not benefit in any way!'

'But I will have work to show Irminburgh and to show the abbess when she returns.' Elfled smiled broadly at him. 'Only you will know the difference and it is you who will be in trouble if they discover the trick.'

Wulfrun looked anxiously from one to the other, wishing to please the princess, but troubled at Adfrith's distress.

'I can't be a party to this.' Adfrith was adamant. 'And how can you expect the goose girl to make letters?'

Elfled turned to Wulfrun. 'Ignore him. Sit!' She pointed to a chair.

Wulfrun did as she was told.

'I know where to find all we need,' Elfled said, reaching into the cupboard. She picked out a small wax tablet set in a light wooden frame and a sharp pointed metal tool. 'You have to learn to use the wax tablet and the stylus first,' she went on knowledgably. Then she pointed to a neatly cut strip of vellum that was fixed to the wall and decorated with a pattern of shapes that had been laid out carefully in a neat row with small irregular gaps. 'These are the words . . . copy them carefully for me. Press onto the wax and make them neat, and while you work, I will ask you riddles.'

'No, Princess, no,' Adfrith begged. 'This simply will not do.'

'Just do it.' Elfled frowned, looking very determined.

'I owe the princess,' Wulfrun whispered uncomfortably, trying to explain to Adfrith why she felt she must do as she was asked. She bit her lips in anxiety, remembering how she and Fridgyth had laughed at the idea of the princess wanting the goose girl to write for her, but Cadmon had been right all the time. What else could she do but try?

Wulfrun picked up the stylus and began to scrape away carefully at the smooth wax coating. Her hand shook, but as she looked up at the pattern on the wall she realized with relief that she could do this. Her mother had often got her to copy weaving patterns onto scraps of tree bark, using a fine chipped twig and a bowl of dye. The pattern on the wall could be carefully copied with the little tool, just as a weaving pattern could.

As she scraped at the wax she quickly discovered the right amount of pressure to exert.

Elfled caught her breath with delight as Wulfrun worked through the top line. 'She can do it! She can do it!' she crowed. 'I have a slave who can write for me. Now . . listen to this riddle: *What is this . . . a miracle? Water becomes bone.*'

Adfrith gave a groan and put his head down on the table.

Wulfrun looked up and smiled; she had heard this riddle many times before. 'Ice,' she said. 'The answer is ice: frozen water becomes as hard as bone.'

'You *do* know riddles.' Elfled clapped her hands.

Adfrith raised his head from his hands and watched Wulfrun working away. 'Goose Girl?' he murmured.

Wulfrun turned to him and shrugged. 'It is easy – just like setting out a weaving pattern.'

'Dear Goose Girl,' he groaned, 'you have copied the words beautifully – I am astonished at your skill – but I am supposed to be teaching the princess how to do it. You would never have learned to do your weaving patterns so well if your mother had always done it for you!'

Wulfrun looked at him and paused in her work, beginning to understand his problem.

Elfled turned from one to the other, suddenly disquieted to see that Wulfrun was listening to what Adfrith said. 'Be quiet – you are both my slaves,' she said, determined to bring their attention back to herself. 'Get on with the writing, slaves, or I shall have you both whipped.'

Wulfrun's cheeks burned with the indignity of the reproof and she swallowed hard.

Adfrith's cheeks burned too, but he rose to his feet with quiet dignity. 'Princess . . . I am nobody's slave. I am a respected student at the monastery school and I hope to be accepted as a monk in time. If you will not accept me as your teacher I must confess my failure to the Lady Irminburgh. Perhaps she will set Brother Cenwulf in my place. He has more experience as a teacher than I.'

Wulfrun saw at once the hesitation in Elfled's eyes and knew that the strict elderly Brother Cenwulf would not be a welcome exchange.

'Princess . . .' Wulfrun's heart was beating fast, but she sensed the need for patience; she must not let a rush of anger bring chaos once more. This princess was descended from the fierce god Woden and she had already seen her lose her temper. 'Princess . . . there is another way. My mother always says that when two work side by side, the time passes twice as fast and the work goes twice as well. You could sit here beside me and together we might make the shapes.'

'Together?' Elfled looked at her suspiciously.

Adfrith opened his mouth as though to protest, but then quickly shut it again.

Elfled's cheeks flushed and she looked down at the floor with sudden childlike uncertainty. 'But . . . my hands will not do it,' she said.

Wulfrun got up from the table and walked round to where the princess stood. She knelt down before her, gently taking the small hands into hers. 'With the princess's permission?' she murmured. Elfled made no protest as Wulfrun studied her hands closely, turning them over to reveal that some of the nails were bitten. 'These are fine sturdy hands and the fingers are strong. You could do anything you wanted with these hands.'

'Do you think so?' Elfled's bullying tone had vanished.

'Yes, Princess, for certain. Will you try to work with me and Adfrith for just for a little while? Then if you prefer to work with Brother Cenwulf . . . we must all bow to your will.'

Elfled frowned, uncertain whether she was being tricked, but when Wulfrun got up she moved as though to follow her. Adfrith quickly gave the princess the chair he'd been sitting on and produced a small sheet of vellum. 'I think we may discard the wax tablets, Princess,' he said. 'Let us try vellum. I have already made small pinpricks for you to copy.'

He picked up two finely sharpened goose quills, split at the end to form a writing nib, and handed one to Elfled and another to Wulfrun. Then he set a small horn bottle of ink on the table.

'I want the goose girl's quill.' Elfled wasn't going to let them easily forget that they were her servants.

Wulfrun gave it to her at once and silently took the other quill from Adfrith. This time he handed her an offcut scrap of vellum.

'Now,' said Wulfrun as she took her place at the princess's side. 'Let us look up at the pattern we are to copy. First we need one straight swift stroke down with a tiny curl at the bottom. See how Adfrith has made pinpricks for you to follow.'

Elfled watched Wulfrun's bold stroke down and copied it carefully. 'You have no pinpricks,' she said, disturbed at the realization.

'That is because I'm used to copying weaving patterns. There,' Wulfrun said, looking at the princess's work with approval. 'You have done well – I knew those strong hands could do it. Now you need another stroke from the top to the side. I find it helps not to press too hard.'

Elfled's tongue peeped out from the side of her mouth as she completed the first letter and moved on to the next.

Adfrith drew up a chair and sat down beside them, closing his eyes for a moment of blessed relief.

Chapter 8

Tangled Threads

The morning wore on and Elfled continued to work steadily. Adfrith's spirits seemed to soar as he watched the princess produce a slightly shaky row of letters and words, but Wulfrun began to feel very weary. It was not the careful copying that tired her – she could do that easily – but the struggle to keep up a steady flow of firm and patient encouragement was exhausting. At last the distant dinging of the bell announcing the midday meal broke into the peace of the study, but before they had time to move, the door opened and Lady Irminburgh walked in.

The expression on her face quickly changed from serenity to amazement. 'What on earth is going on here?' she demanded.

Wulfrun got up from her chair and shrank into the corner, while Elfled and Adfrith both looked stunned; they hadn't prepared for this.

'What is the goose girl doing in here?'

Elfled was the first to recover; she was quickly on her feet and holding out her sheet of vellum with pride. 'I have learned a new way to do my words,' she said. 'The goose girl is my slave and I have decided to make her work . . . with me. When two work side by side, the time passes twice as fast.'

'What?' Irminburgh turned to Adfrith. 'What does this mean? You are responsible for the princess's learning.'

Adfrith struggled to his feet and bowed nervously, but then he pointed to the vellum sheet that Elfled waved with pride. 'The princess has made good progress this morning. She has worked hard and applied herself well.'

Irminburgh took the sheet, frowning at it. 'You have done this all by yourself, Princess?' she asked.

'Tell her,' Elfled ordered Adfrith.

'This is the princess's own work,' he agreed. 'The presence of the goose girl seems to have . . . helped the princess to concentrate.'

Irminburgh glanced across at Wulfrun, who looked as though she was ready to run. 'Poor girl,' she said sweetly. They all stood in silence while Irminburgh's eyes narrowed in thought for a moment. 'Well . . . we'll see,' she said at last. 'Now fetch your cloak and beaker and come for your dinner, darling.' She held out her hand to Elfled.

'Tomorrow morning . . . come here again,'

Elfled called back to Wulfrun as she was led away.

'Yes, Princess,' Wulfrun answered nervously. 'I'll be here.'

Adfrith sighed with relief. 'I thought we were all in deep trouble for a moment then – you never know with Irminburgh. But you have done very well today, Goose Girl.' He spoke with warm approval. 'Are you coming to eat now? I saw you in the refectory yesterday.'

'I left my sister with Fridgyth,' she said uncertainly.

'I'm sure Fridgyth will bring her to the refectory.'

She nodded and began to follow him out through the now empty scriptorium.

'What is your real name?' Adfrith asked as he opened the door for her. 'I cannot call you Goose Girl for ever.'

'Wulfrun,' she whispered, suddenly shy.

'It suits you.'

'Does it?' She frowned uncertainly; she'd often wished she'd been named for a swan or a flower.

'A she-wolf is a clever, determined creature. Fierce too,' he added.

She looked at him sharply, suspecting that he was making fun of her, but all she could see was warmth in his smile.

'You handled the princess very cleverly this morning. I have learned something from that.'

He walked beside her until they reached the refectory, then he gave a polite nod and went to join the other oblates.

Gode was already there, eating leek and barley soup with Fridgyth. The herb woman glanced up anxiously as Wulfrun came in, but was relieved to see the satisfied expression on her face.

'It's gone well?'

'Yes . . .' Wulfrun heaved a great sigh. 'But it was hard work. You will never guess . . . Cadmon was right; the princess *did* want me to act as her scribe.'

'Huh!' Fridgyth raised her eyes to heaven. 'Poor Adfrith!'

'Yes, he was fretting at first, but we found a way of making it work. I made the strokes and the princess copied me.'

Fridgyth put down her spoon and her eyebrows shot up in astonishment. 'You made the strokes . . . and the princess copied you?'

Wulfrun smiled broadly. 'It was easy.'

Fridgyth was speechless for once.

Wulfrun laughed at the herbwife's open-mouthed expression of amazement. 'I can copy a pattern perfectly. Mother has always praised me for it, so I copied the pattern that Adfrith's letters made.'

'Are you to go again?'

'Yes – tomorrow.'

* * *

After they had eaten Fridgyth went to mix her medicines, and Wulfrun took her sister and the geese out into the upper pasture. While Gode wandered happily among the geese and cattle, she flopped down in the sun with a sense of relief and related her experiences of the morning to Cadmon.

'It was just as you said. How did you guess that the princess would make me write for her?'

He shrugged. 'Lonely . . . little princess,' he said, shaking his head. 'She is looking for a friend, but d-doesn't know it.'

'Lonely?' Wulfrun stared at him, amazed. How could she be lonely with all the nuns and lay sisters fussing over her all the time and with fine young lads like Adfrith to teach her?

But Cadmon had more to say. 'She would like to run with the hares,' he insisted. 'But she must s-stay inside and make letters. No f-friends to run with her.'

Wulfrun sat there in the sun, quietly thinking about what he'd said. Perhaps Cadmon had sensed discontent in the princess, just as he sensed something troubling his calves. She tried hard to imagine what it would be like to live in comfort as Elfled did, but then she also began to see that the careless supervision of Irminburgh, the pious fussing of the nuns and the distant service of lay sisters might not hold much joy for one who was still a child. When did Elfled lie in the sun beside a trusted friend, enjoying perfect peace and harmony? She looked over at the cowherd with a grateful smile; she'd have liked to stay there in the sun with him for ever, but she remembered that her mother's loom hung from its nail in a fine old tangle and there'd be no payment given until it was finished.

'I can't sit here,' she muttered, struggling to her feet. 'However much I'd like to. Come, Gode, we must take the geese back now and start weaving.'

'Don't want to comb wool!' Gode was reluctant.

'You have to.'

Gode sighed, but followed her obediently. 'Fridif says I'm good at jobs.'

'Yes, you are very good,' Wulfrun said kindly. She must find as much patience for her sister as she had for the princess – that was only fair.

That afternoon Gode's small hands worked determinedly with the teasel and it was Wulfrun who sighed and growled as she tried to put her weaving right. At last, in despair, she stopped and threw down the shuttle. The light was beginning to fade but the wool was more tangled than ever.

Gode looked up at her sister. 'Mam coming home?' she whispered.

Wulfrun shook her head sadly. 'Not today.'

Gode accepted this without further show of distress and returned to her work. Wulfrun went back to her loom, close to tears, but as she stared at the tangled mess a memory came back to her so clearly that she almost thought she heard her mother there in the little hut saying: 'Go back to the beginning and start again – it's the only way, my honey.'

Wulfrun smiled and a tear trickled down her cheek. How many times had she heard her mother say those words? It was a dismal prospect, but it must be done. The monastery bell ringing to announce the evening meal interrupted her thoughts and made Gode's lips curve into a wide smile as she set her task aside. 'Hungry,' she murmured.

'Me too,' Wulfrun agreed, dashing away the tear.

That night, after they had eaten, Wulfrun set the loom up close to the hearth, as she'd seen Cwen do when a bit of work needed finishing fast. She steadily unpicked her tangled threads while Gode slept, working on until the last gleam had faded from the embers. When at last she settled, exhausted, to sleep, the wool had once again been wound into hanks and one neat row of undyed wool formed the weft again.

Wulfrun was already weary when she arrived at the scriptorium the following morning, but Adfrith seemed to be in good spirits and Elfled was already sitting at the table with a blank sheet of vellum in front of her.

'Here's my slave,' she announced cheerfully. 'Come and sit down here by me at once. Adfrith will let me write without the pinpricks today.'

Adfrith winced at the princess's tone and Wulfrun's tiredness made her prickly. 'I should like it if the princess would call me Wulfrun,' she said with formal courtesy, 'and not slave.'

Elfled frowned for a moment, but then she shrugged. 'Very well, *Wulf*run – come and sit here by me. Why are you named for a wolf?'

'Because my teeth are sharp and I fear nothing.' Wulfrun snapped back the reply that she'd often given to young lads who sneered at her name.

'Ha!' Elfled laughed and it was a merry, childlike sound that made even Adfrith smile. 'I shall call you Wolf Girl!'

Wulfrun shrugged; that name seemed better than 'slave'.

Adfrith cleared his throat to get their attention. 'Princess . . . today I have written some new words for you to copy.' He pointed to a fresh sheet of vellum that he had pinned onto the wall and decorated with a new pattern of marks.

'What are they?' Elfled demanded.

'*Elfled regia puella Northumbriae filia regis Oswy haec dicit*, which means: "Elfled, Princess of

Northumbria, daughter to King Oswy, says these words." '

'Aah!' Elfled sighed with satisfaction. 'I like these words. I will write them.'

Wulfrun looked sharply from Adfrith to the sheet of vellum, a marvellous understanding dawning on her. 'They are not just patterns,' she whispered. 'They are like runes, they have meaning.'

Adfrith smiled broadly, enjoying her moment of revelation. 'This is Latin, the language of the scholar. Each little piece of the pattern means something . . . this word means Elfled and this is the word that means king.'

Wulfrun's tiredness fled. 'You put these words in your great books?' She spoke with mounting excitement. 'This is how the abbess signs her orders and sends her messages.'

'I thought you would understand quickly. Now . . . let us begin.'

Wulfrun was so thrilled by this idea that she worked diligently at her copying while Elfled sat at her side, dutifully making the awkward shapes. As the morning wore on, Elfled became a little restless. Wulfrun worked on, ignoring her, but when the young princess raised her arms to stretch and yawn her embroidered sleeves fell back, revealing a beautiful bracelet. Wulfrun gasped in shock at the sight of it. Gold and garnets circled the slim wrist, with just one small gold cross supported by a bird with outspread wings.

'What is it?' Elfled asked, easily distracted. Wulfrun's exclamation was much more exciting than writing.

Adfrith looked up at them both with concern. He saw the colour draining from Wulfrun's cheeks as she stared at the dainty jewels. Elfled shook her hand in the air so that the jewels jangled in Wulfrun's face. 'Have you never seen jewels like these?'

It was too much: the goose girl clapped her hands over her mouth as though to prevent the words that threatened to come tumbling out. She had indeed seen jewels just like those.

'Tell me!' Elfled commanded. 'What is it?'

'I cannot . . . I daren't.'

Adfrith got up and approached her, gently putting a hand on her shoulder. 'What troubles you, Goose Girl – I mean Wulfrun? We were doing so well.'

'I must go,' she said, getting up from her seat.

'No!' Elfled thundered. But then suddenly her voice was soft and pleading. 'Do not run off, Wolf Girl,' she begged. 'Do not leave me to do my writing all alone.'

'I . . . I'm fearful,' Wulfrun told her. 'I'm fearful that what I've seen might bring more trouble.'

'Trouble to whom?' Adfrith asked.

'T-to me; to my mother.'

They both stared at her, puzzled.

'Tell me!' Elfled insisted. 'Tell me . . . and I swear that I will keep your secret.'

Wulfrun hesitated, but the shock of what she'd seen forced the words to come tumbling out. 'That fine bracelet,' she said; 'it . . . it is so like the necklace my mother was accused of stealing. The same gold and garnets, the same little golden bird with wings outstretched. It is the small twin of . . . that necklace.'

'The bird?' said Elfled, holding up her arm to examine the bracelet. She frowned as she touched the tiny shape. 'This is a sparrow in flight, just as it was on the battle standard of my grandfather King Edwin. Mother Hild told me that it was the flight of a sparrow that persuaded my grandfather to accept the Christian God, though . . . I do not really understand how.'

There was a terrible silence between them as they struggled to grasp what this might mean. Adfrith was quick to see why Wulfrun was so troubled. 'It is hard to understand how such a piece of jewellery could have lawfully belonged to Cwen,' he acknowledged.

'I knew I should not have told you,' Wulfrun whispered.

Elfled looked at them both uncertainly. 'Does this mean her mother is a thief after all?'

Wulfrun's backbone turned to ice.

Chapter 9

kin

Adfrith shook his head, trying hard to be fair. 'No . . . it does not mean that Cwen's a thief, but perhaps it's best if we keep this bit of information to ourselves, Princess – that is, if you wish Wulfrun to be allowed to continue as your helper.'

Wulfrun bit her lips and twisted her fingers together until they hurt. 'My mother . . .' she murmured.

Elfled sighed impatiently. 'Your mother – always your mother,' she said. 'I don't know why you bother about her so much. Mothers are of little use, I say.'

Wulfrun's jaw dropped with shock at the princess's reply, almost forgetting her own fear for the moment.

Adfrith intervened quickly. 'There is perhaps another way to look at this discovery.'

Elfled pulled a sullen face, but turned to hear what he'd got to say.

'Well,' said Adfrith, measuring his words with care, 'perhaps this tells us something important. If the necklace is truly of royal origin, then maybe we should ask ourselves how Cwen could rightfully own it. How could such a thing be possible?'

Wulfrun shrugged her shoulders; she had nothing sensible to suggest.

'If you have faith in your mother as you say you have, then . . .'

'Yes . . .' Wulfrun began to see the way that he was thinking. 'The answer to that question might help me to puzzle out the mystery.'

Elfled's eyes lit up at once. 'Like a riddle,' she said. 'We must try to find the answer . . . but this riddle is a hard one.'

'Yes, Princess.' Adfrith pursued the idea. 'Wulfrun, do you know how long your mother had those jewels in her possession?'

Wulfrun shook her head.

'As the princess says, they bear the symbol that was on her grandfather's battle standard, so they may be very old. Who would they have been made for?'

'Not for my mother,' Wulfrun admitted. 'That is for sure.'

'This was Queen Tata's bracelet – she was my grandmother, wife to the great King Edwin.' Elfled spoke with pride and held her arm up again. 'Mother Hild told me so.' Then she suddenly frowned: another thought had occurred to her. 'Who has got the necklace now?' she asked. 'If it belonged to my grandmother, then I should have it.'

'Lady Irminburgh took it.' Wulfrun shuddered at the memory of that terrible night.

There was silence then for a moment while they all thought hard. Wulfrun twisted her hands together in an agony of frustration.

'Let us ask ourselves another question,' Adfrith suggested. 'How could a royal necklace have rightly come to your family, Wulfrun? Was Cwen's mother ever a royal servant and given it as a reward for her loyalty?'

Wulfrun shook her head. 'My grandmother was a fisherwoman. Just a hard-worked fish gutter with scarred hands and a bent back. There is no help there.'

But Elfled's eyes gleamed with enjoyment. 'I will not speak of this riddle to anyone; we will puzzle it out in secret.'

Wulfrun glanced across at her with gratitude.

'Now,' said Adfrith, relieved that calm seemed to have returned, 'we must get back to your new Latin script, Princess, but . . . let us keep these questions in the back of our minds.'

Elfled folded her arms stubbornly. 'I would rather talk of riddles than make words,' she said.

Wulfrun saw that she must help Adfrith, who

was being so very kind, so she picked up her quill. 'These words are important, Princess; they spell out your name. When you are grown you will be able to write down your orders in Latin and sign your name as the abbess does and then everyone will obey you. Writing will give you power.'

'Power.' Elfled smiled at the word. 'I do want power.'

'Then pick up the quill, Princess.'

Elfled sighed and obediently picked up her quill; she set to work again, her small tongue peeping from the corner of her mouth. Wulfrun found it hard to settle back to the work, her mind now whirling with questions and ideas. When Irminburgh came to see them before the midday meal, she found the room quiet and studious, their heads bent over their script. The princess's fingers were pink with effort and only slightly smudged with ink.

Adfrith showed the work that Elfled had managed to produce.

'Hmm.' Irminburgh nodded. 'Darling, clever Princess – perhaps the goose girl may stay, as long as you are producing work like this.'

As Irminburgh led her away to the refectory, Elfled turned back and touched her finger to her lips in a brief secret signal. Wulfrun was about to follow them at a respectful distance, when Adfrith took a small rolled scrap of vellum from a leather bag that swung from his belt. 'This is something I prepared for you,' he said.

'For me?' She stared in surprise.

'Yes – have a look.'

Wulfrun felt that perhaps there had been enough surprises for one morning, but she opened the little roll of vellum and caught the smell of fish glue. Adfrith had inscribed it in his beautiful Latin script. The strip was made up of three small scraps, carefully glued together so that you could hardly see the joins. She saw at once that some of the words that he'd written were the same as the ones they'd been copying, but the first word was very different and the capital was decorated with a beautifully painted howling wolf's head, with a red lolling tongue and gleaming black eyes.

Wulfrun caught her breath as she guessed what it might mean, but hardly dared to hope.

Adfrith chuckled with pleasure at her astonished expression. 'Yes,' he said. 'That is your own name, Wulfrun, illuminated with the wolf's head and some more Latin words: *Wulfrun filia textoris Cwen haec dicit*. Try to work out the meaning.'

After spending the whole morning copying them, the Latin words and their meaning came easily to her. ' "Wulfrun, daughter of . . ." '

Then she suddenly smiled again as she saw that from the curling half-circle of the next capital swung a tiny shuttle suspended on a thread.

'Ha,' she whispered. 'That is my mother's name.'

Adfrith nodded, delighted by her quickness. ' "Wulfrun, daughter of Cwen the Webster, says these words." You see . . . you are already beginning to read Latin as well as write it.' He dropped his voice a little and his eyes were full of concern as he added: 'Now go for your meal and think carefully about what we discovered today. I would advise you again . . . speak to nobody of the similarity between your mother's necklace and the princess's bracelet.'

'I will not,' she said solemnly and they set off together towards the refectory.

Wulfrun clutched her small roll of vellum tightly in her hand as she ate, and when Fridgyth asked about her morning's work she found it difficult to answer. She wanted to tell her about Elfled's bracelet, but remembering Adfrith's concern she dared not speak of it even to her trusted friend. Instead she showed the lovely line of writing that Adfrith had given her. Both Fridgyth and Gode were impressed.

'A wolf for Wulfrun.' Gode held out a nervous finger to touch its sharply pointed teeth.

Fridgyth looked thoughtful and a little troubled. As they got up and walked away she touched Wulfrun's arm gently. 'Adfrith . . . he is promised to the Church, you know – an oblate. He must become a monk. They say he is born to it and the

most promising scribe in the school – that's why he
was chosen to tutor the princess. They will soon be
shaving the front of his head and putting him into
monk's robes.'

Wulfrun looked at her, surprised. She knew that
most of the young men brought up in the abbey
school were destined for the Church. Why should
Fridgyth be making such a point of it with Adfrith?
Then suddenly she understood and smiled. 'You
think that I am falling in love with him. No, no –
it is just that he has been so very kind to me.
Nobody has ever taken such trouble for me . . .'
Then she added with sadness, 'Nobody except my
mother and . . . and of course you.'

Fridgyth shrugged and smiled. 'Take no notice
of me; I'm a silly old woman.'

That afternoon Wulfrun tried to snatch a few
moments of rest in the meadow beside Cadmon,
but she could not settle and her eyelids refused to
droop.

'You . . . you're disturbing my b-beasts,'
Cadmon told her.

'Me? How?' she demanded.

'Th-this,' he said and did a fine imitation of her
twitching shoulders and heavy sighs.

Wulfrun could not help but smile. 'I'm troubled
about my mother.' She tried to explain her distress.
Then suddenly she had an idea: it was simple and
foolish but it might make both her and Cwen feel

a little better. She got to her feet and began to pick a bunch of long-stemmed meadow blooms that flourished all around: buttercups, daisies, clover and vetch. She sat down again beside Cadmon and carefully began to weave their stems together into the pattern that Cwen called Kin. It would be a message that they'd both understand; a message without any words that would remind Cwen that her daughter loved her and thought of her.

Cadmon watched. He began to hum, and then words came into his head and he sang them softly as Wulfrun wove her pattern.

'Buttercups; small gleams of gold, bring us
warmth and sun.
Daisies, the eyes of truth, see through the
darkest night.
Clover brings a touch of nectar, sweet reward
for those who work.
Vetch clings tightly, binds together those
whom fate has torn apart.'

Wulfrun's fingers grew still and she turned to look at him; the cowherd had tears in his eyes. 'I will take these flowers and beg the guards to give them to my mother,' she said. 'I wish that I could take her your song.'

Cadmon smiled ruefully. 'N-no,' he said, blushing a little.

'You were thinking of your own mother too?'

Cadmon nodded and bowed his head. He would never speak of his kin and Wulfrun could only guess that he must now be alone in the world. She stretched out to press his arm warmly, then struggled to her feet, her heart full of determination. She carried her delicate woven spray in through the main gate, marching bravely up to the guards who sat by the lock-up, engrossed in a game of Merrills. They had set out their game with white and black pebbles from the beach and marked out the lines in the dirt. Wulfrun stood quietly waiting, afraid to disturb them, but then one of the men looked up at her and nudged his companion.

'The wicked webster's brat wishes to play,' he sneered.

Wulfrun swallowed hard and spoke up. 'I wish to give these flowers to my mother,' she said.

They laughed and made foul comments, as she knew they would, but at last one of them took pity and went to the lock-up. Wulfrun followed eagerly, thinking it well worth suffering the humiliation if it meant she'd see her mother, but she stared with dismay, for the man unbarred the door and it swung open to reveal an empty hut.

'Where is she?' she demanded.

The man shrugged and shook his head. 'The reeve took her – that is all I know.'

Wulfrun was shocked and confused. What did

this mean? She stumbled on towards the guest-house, wondering if she dare confront Ulfstan, but instead of him she met his wife Alta heading down the steps towards Fridgyth's herb garden with a basket in her hands.

'Lady.' Wulfrun bobbed a respectful curtsy to her. 'My mother is not in the lock-up and I am fearful that something terrible has been done to her. The reeve promised—'

'The reeve keeps his promises.' Alta cut through her worried words. 'I cannot tell you where your mother is, child. But you can trust my husband to do his best for her. She is safe – I promise you that.'

Alta walked on ahead, dismissing her. Wulfrun followed behind, despairing, not daring to ask more. As she wandered past the monastery kitchen that thrummed with hard work and loud voices, another thought came to her mind and all her fiery determination came flooding back. Sister Mildred was her enemy, but she was in charge of all the food prepared for those who ate within the walls of the stockade; she must know where her mother was kept.

'Shoo, Goose Girl!' Sister Mildred flapped her floury hands as soon as she caught sight of Wulfrun sidling into the great kitchen with its row of clay ovens and smoking chimneys. 'I can't put up with beggars in here. You must wait until the evening meal, then you can eat your fill and more than you deserve, I'm sure.'

Wulfrun's cheeks flamed scarlet, but she stood her ground as Sister Mildred pounded dough vigorously on a trestle table. 'I ask for nothing, Sister, but to put this posy with the food my mother will be given. I know the food she gets must be made in here.'

Sister Mildred looked at her, amazed. She paused in her work and scratched her head, leaving a trail of flour on the tie-back of her linen veil. Ethel looked up, red-faced and flustered from stirring the huge cauldron that hung from a three-legged stand and bubbled with pottage. Wulfrun waited for a nasty comment from her and looked about for Bertha.

'If you're looking for my lass, you'll not find her here,' said Ethel, her face glum. 'She's serving my Lady Irminburgh – can't be bothered with her mother these days.' Surprisingly, the old fish gutter seemed to wish to confide, but Wulfrun could feel little sympathy.

Everywhere there was smoke and steam and good smells. Wulfrun held up her small posy for Mildred to inspect. 'You can see that I have sent nothing that will aid her to escape.' She laid the woven flowers carefully down on the end of the trestle, away from the flour and dough. 'It is nothing but a few meadow blooms to tell her that I . . . still . . .'

The words she wished to speak choked in her throat, but Mildred reached towards the posy with her floury fingers, then drew back delicately. She gave a curt nod and turned to a plain wooden tray set aside from the other boards and platters. 'Lay them on that tray,' she said. 'Your mother will get your flowers and she'll know who sent them.'

That evening Wulfrun sat up late again, carefully picking through the warp threads with her shuttle and correcting the work at once if she made a mistake. As she worked, many thoughts chased around her head. Perhaps it wasn't only woollen warp and weft that could get tangled, for it seemed as though the very threads of their lives had twisted too. Trying to struggle on without un- ravelling first might only make things worse and worse, but at least with Fridgyth's help and the reeve's fair judgement the tangling threads of their lives seemed to be held in place for a while.

She sighed. This situation could not go on for ever, and as soon as the abbess returned a judge- ment must be made. 'Go back to the beginning,' she suddenly told herself, speaking out loud. 'Go back to the beginning and unravel the threads.'

'Mama . . .' Gode murmured in her sleep.

'Hush,' Wulfrun whispered gently.

She racked her brains again. Where was the beginning? The necklace could have been there in her mother's chest long before Wulfrun had so foolishly brought it to light. How had it got there? Wulfrun put down the shuttle and went over to the chest. She quietly lifted the lid and let her hand slip down the side into the empty hiding place. She checked the other side . . . no hidey-hole there, though the wood was just as thick. Suddenly she realized that the chest had been so cunningly put together that it must have been made especially to hide the treasure. Adfrith asking about her grand-mother came to mind. Who would have made the chest? They had brought it with them to Whitby on the handcart, pushing it over the cliffs from Fisherstead.

Next morning, while they carefully penned their letters, Wulfrun shared her thoughts with Elfled and Adfrith. 'If only I could go back to Fisherstead I could ask my mother's closest friend Emma. Her husband gave us money when we left in return for our old hut and we sold him almost all that we owned, but not the chest.'

Elfled was at once full of bright curiosity. 'I have never been to Fisherstead,' she said. 'We could take horses from the stables and ride out to find your old home. Let us go now . . . at once.'

Adfrith frowned and shook his head at so wild a plan. 'Princess . . . you would have half of Deira looking for you.'

'Well' – Elfled folded her arms across her chest –

'I am weary of sitting in this stuffy chamber, wearing my fingers to the bone with scratchy quills.'

'Work well today,' Adfrith promised, 'and I will try to find a proper way for us to go to Fisherstead.'

Chapter 10

magpie

They said no more about riding out and worked on obediently. When Irminburgh came to fetch Elfled, she was clearly relieved to see the work that was being produced with so little effort on her part.

Adfrith cleared his throat and started tentatively. 'As the princess is working so well now, I thought that perhaps we should move her education on a little.'

'What do you mean by that?' Irminburgh frowned.

'I think the princess should get to see a little more of the kingdom of Deira.'

'Oh . . .' Irminburgh was puzzled. 'Would you call that education?'

'Oh yes indeed. The princess should learn about the lands that the abbess rules.'

Irminburgh began to look bored and Adfrith went on quickly. 'I suggest that just one day in seven the princess might ride out and visit some of the places that lie close by. I offer myself as tutor and escort. I would inform the princess of the history, fauna, botany and geography of the lands that we see. I'm sure the abbess would approve – after all, one day she must—'

'Yes, yes,' Irminburgh cut in, shrugging her shoulders.

The two girls waited in silence, not daring to speak in case they said the wrong thing.

'I couldn't let the princess ride out without a woman to wait on her,' Irminburgh said, suppressing a yawn. 'I'm far too busy to go riding over the cliffs and moors to study the land, and Begu is not up to riding at all.'

Elfled opened her mouth in eagerness to speak, but at a warning glance from Adfrith she said nothing.

'I understand.' Adfrith bowed his head respectfully. 'You bear such a burden of care and duty, lady, but . . . perhaps the goose girl could escort the princess. She is proving to be both obedient and discreet, despite—'

'Oh . . . very well.' Irminburgh flapped her hand carelessly in Wulfrun's direction. 'I suppose she may take one of the rougher mares. Come along now for your meal, dear Princess.'

Elfled went willingly, flashing them both a smile of wild joy.

But as soon as the swish of their skirts and the high-pitched chatter of Elfled had faded, Wulfrun turned to Adfrith, her eyes wide with fear. 'But . . . I have never been on a horse . . . I cannot ride.'

Adfrith smiled kindly at her. 'Anyone who can learn to read and write as fast as you, Wolf Girl, can certainly learn to ride.'

That night, as Wulfrun sat weaving, she went over the day in her mind. It seemed strange that since the terrible imprisonment of her mother, her own life had become so exciting. That thought was quickly followed by a great wave of guilt that there should be enjoyment while her mother was imprisoned and surely worried sick. The guilt was quickly quashed by a flood of fear as she remembered that she must get up on a horse and learn to ride, but still her spirits rose again as she remembered Adfrith's encouraging words. How many weavers' daughters could ride anything other than a mule?

She rose early next morning, leaving a sleepy Gode with a yawning Fridgyth. Adfrith had told her to meet him by the monastery stables straight after the morning service he called Prime.

She skirted the vegetable garden and headed for the stables, but before she could go inside, the cloaked and hooded figure of a man turned the corner and almost bumped into her. It was

Childeric, his fair hair almost covered by the hood. He stopped for a moment, shocked to see her there. He opened his mouth as if to speak, but then closed it again and pushed past her roughly.

'Watch out,' she grumbled, staring after him.

What was he doing inside the monastic boundary so early? He seemed to be in something of a hurry and was heading for the side gate. She watched until he vanished, then remembered that she had much more important things to think about and went into the stables. She was glad to see that Cadmon too was there, though he muttered that he could not stay for long as his calves were waiting.

He led the way into the great barn-like building, where the horses were kept in stalls separated by woven wattle dividers. The stable lads were just waking in the little booths where they slept side by side with their charges. They began to drag away the soiled mats that were set beneath the horses' rumps, replacing them with fresh ones. Wulfrun wrinkled her nose, but smiled as she saw the lads scraping the manure into a handcart. That cart was familiar to her, for she'd often seen it tipped into the corner of Fridgyth's herb garden, ready to feed the soil.

Adfrith was waiting inside; he held out a pair of rough linen men's breeches. 'You will not be able to ride properly if you are worrying about modesty,' he told her, quite matter of factly.

She took them a little uncertainly but could see the sense in what he said. He turned his back discreetly as she stooped to pull them on. She fastened them tightly round her waist and tried lifting up her legs, smiling at the sense of freedom they gave. 'Why don't all women wear these?' she murmured.

Adfrith turned round, a wry smile on his face. 'Are you ready now, young sir?'

Wulfrun looked nervously at some of the great horses that stamped in their stalls. 'Yes, I'm ready, but . . . it doesn't need to be a big one, does it?'

'Let Cadmon choose,' Adfrith said. 'There's nobody better at sensing the nature of a beast than Cadmon.'

'This one looks sweet natured,' Wulfrun suggested as she passed a smaller silver-grey mare that stood in her stall next to a larger gelding with identical markings.

'Ah, that's Sea Mist.' Adfrith shook his head, though his lips twisted in amusement. 'Sea Mist and her brother Sea Coal are twins, but Sea Mist is usually ridden by the princess. Even if that were not the case you'd find her skittish; she's not for a beginner.'

'Yet they let the princess ride her?' Wulfrun was shocked.

Adfrith chuckled. 'You haven't seen how valiantly the princess rides!'

'I see.' She swallowed hard, though somehow his words did not surprise her. 'Well . . . I hope that she will not expect me to keep up with her.'

Adfrith raised his eyebrows in amusement. 'Abbess Hild insists that all goods are held in common at Whitby, but I think Elfled would challenge anyone who claimed to share her favourite mare. The princess is an exception to many rules.'

Wulfrun had learned that quickly enough. 'Elfled and Irminburgh,' she said. 'Why is Irminburgh so much obeyed when she behaves so—?'

Adfrith looked at her sharply and shook his head. 'Beware how you speak of her,' he advised. 'Irminburgh is distantly related to Elfled's half-brother, King Alchfrid of Deira, through his mother, Oswy's first queen.'

Wulfrun had heard of this queen, who'd died quite young and been swiftly replaced by Elfled's mother. 'She was the one who brought Oswy the lands of Rheged?'

'Yes,' Adfrith agreed. 'Irminburgh also claims her mother was linked by blood to King Edwin and that she is a distant cousin to the queen. Irminburgh's sister has married Prince Centwine, son of the King of Wessex, and she's likely to become queen when the old king dies. Irminburgh could cause a lot of trouble if she put her mind to it. There are many who say she should have married Alchfrid the Stranger – then he'd have had a better right to rule Deira.'

'But doesn't Abbess Hild have a claim to the throne of Deira?' Wulfrun was sure she'd heard her mother suggest such a thing.

Adfrith smiled and nodded. 'None could have had a better claim than Mother Hild. When her older sister Hereswith married King Ethelhere of East Anglia, many wondered if he would use his wife to make a claim on Deira, but like her sister, Hereswith only wanted peace. If Hild but clicked her fingers all Deira would rise in her support – but she will never do it. Peace is all that matters to her. Oswy puts great trust in the abbess. I do not think the same can be said for Irminburgh; she never lets anyone forget her royal blood.'

'Why do they not banish her?' Wulfrun asked.

Adfrith frowned and shook his head. 'That would be the quickest way to see her return with a warrior husband at her side and an army at her back. No, they play a different game: they hope to keep her sweet and encourage her to become a nun as Hild has done, but even that is a dangerous game. An abbess can have as much power as a princess and she will have no husband to answer to.'

'I understand it better now.' Wulfrun nodded. 'I will be very careful with Lady Irminburgh.'

She hesitated to ask what next came to mind, remembering Fridgyth's concern, but curiosity got the better of her. 'Adfrith . . . I know you are an oblate, promised to the Church by your parents,' she said. 'But do you really want to be a monk?'

He smiled at her and looked thoughtful. 'The abbey gives me the training and the opportunity to do what I love best. I don't have to worry about food, clothes or shelter; I just paint and draw and write and I am happy . . . most of the time.'

Wulfrun smiled shyly then. 'I loved the fierce wolf you made for me,' she said.

Adfrith looked as though he might say more, but Cadmon backed out from one of the horses' stalls, holding the leading rope and patting the rump of a sturdy black and white dappled mare. 'Th-this one,' he said. 'Magpie.'

Wulfrun flinched at the size of the beast.

Cadmon walked the mare towards them. 'Magpie is a c-clever bird.' He sang out the words. 'This bird will not fly, but she will carry you steady and strong, as a wide flat-bottomed boat rides the waves.'

Wulfrun could not help but smile at his words; she took the leading rope from him, still nervous. 'If you say she is right for me, then I will trust her.'

'Stroke her nose, then she will catch the sweet scent of Wulfrun and know that she can trust you too,' he advised.

She put out a hesitant hand, but quickly found the hairs on Magpie's smooth nose warm and pleasant to the touch. The mare snorted a little, but accepted the caress.

Cadmon cupped his hands to help her mount. 'Put your foot here,' he said.

Wulfrun could not have done it for anyone else. It was a terrifying feeling to be thrust up so high into the air and expected to scramble across the horse's back; she was glad of the breeches. At last her stomach stopped skittering about, so that she could manage to sit upright and cling to the strong tufts at the base of Magpie's mane. Cadmon left them to find his calves, though Wulfrun felt like calling him back to stay at her side and help her.

Adfrith took the leading rein. 'Just sit tight,' he said. 'You will soon get used to the way she rolls.'

He began to walk the mare at a steady pace out of the stables, past the abbess's house and the rows of tiny monastic huts towards the southern gate. 'You are quite safe,' he said. 'Grip her sides tightly with your legs.'

Wulfrun gasped: she had never been so high above the ground before, but she did not want to look a fool in front of Adfrith. He led her along the cliff-top path, past the beacon, then suddenly with a lurch of her stomach she saw that he had unfastened the leading rein, though Magpie still walked on steadily at his side.

'What are you doing?' Wulfrun asked in a shaky voice.

Adfrith turned calmly to her. 'I am doing nothing,' he said. 'You are riding Magpie all by yourself.'

Elfled was already waiting for them in the scriptorium when they got back, with vellum and quills all ready. 'Can she ride yet?' she demanded.

Adfrith frowned at her abrupt question. Elfled bit her lips for a moment, then turned to Wulfrun and asked politely, 'How are you getting on with your riding, Wolf Girl?'

'Well,' Wulfrun replied.

'Can you gallop?'

Wulfrun's eyes widened with alarm. 'I trotted a little,' she said defensively.

'By Friday you must learn to gallop,' Elfled said. 'Well . . . are we not doing our writing?'

'Yes . . . Princess.' Wulfrun and Adfrith both rushed to join her.

'I have been doing my own bit of investigation into the mystery of your mother's necklace,' Elfled told them with a satisfied smile, as they settled to their work.

'Have you?' Wulfrun's heart began beating fast, though she made herself continue copying the work that Adfrith had set them.

'I went into Irminburgh's chamber,' Elfled went

on. 'I wanted to find the necklace. She has no right to keep it there – it should be mine.'

'Oh, Princess.' Adfrith could not help but reprove such behaviour.

But Wulfrun had no such scruples. 'Did you find it?' she asked.

'I did.' Elfled smiled, pleased with herself. 'She had hidden it away in a rosewood box that contained other jewellery.'

'Did you take it?' Adfrith asked, full of anxiety.

'No.' Elfled scowled at him. 'I am not stupid, Adfrith. I compared it to my bracelet and I saw that they were exactly the same, but of course the necklace is bigger. I'm sure the same jeweller must have made them both.'

Wulfrun frowned. Suddenly she remembered something puzzling, but it meant forcing herself to go back to that dreadful moment when she'd been accused as a thief. 'Why did Irminburgh not recognize King Edwin's symbol in the design? She spoke of it as valuable, but . . . she did not point out the little sparrow that makes it so very special.'

Elfled's eyes narrowed with suspicion and resentment. 'Yes . . . why didn't she say at once? She must have recognized it – she has seen my bracelet many times and admired it. When I saw the necklace there in her room I wanted to take it from her and wave it in her face and claim it there and then – but I didn't.'

'Princess, that showed great wisdom.' Adfrith swallowed with relief.

Elfled smiled confidently. 'I thought so too, but why didn't Ulfstan see the sparrow on it and give it to me?'

Wulfrun shook her head, trying hard to recall what had happened. 'Irminburgh took it before he or Sister Mildred could look closely,' she said, remembering how the lady's white fingers had snaked out so fast and lifted the gold and garnets over her head.

'She wants it for herself,' Elfled insisted. 'That's why she did not tell Ulfstan how like my bracelet it is.'

They all frowned in thought as they continued with their work.

Chapter 11

the maker of the chest

Every morning for a week Wulfrun went early to the stables to ride Magpie. At first Adfrith patiently strode or ran at her side, but once she could walk and trot with confidence he used the leading rein again to make Magpie canter and eventually gallop round in a circle. On Thursday he brought out of the stable a huge black gelding named Midnight.

'I'm not climbing up onto him.' Wulfrun backed away.

Adfrith laughed out loud. 'No, I shall ride Midnight,' he said. 'No leading rein today – I'll ride at your side.'

'If you say so.' Wulfrun gritted her teeth and leaped up onto Magpie's back unaided.

That morning her confidence grew fast. Magpie obeyed her slightest dig with her knees or spoken command. Beside Midnight, she felt safe and close to the ground on the sturdy mare. Cadmon had been right: Magpie would carry her like a steady broad-bottomed boat; all she needed was a bit of gentle steering.

On Friday morning Elfled met them at the stables, attended by Irminburgh, who kept yawning and shivering in the early morning chill. Wulfrun saw that Adfrith had stuck a sheathed seax into his belt and fastened a shield and short spear to Midnight's saddle.

Elfled led Sea Mist from her stall; the little mare was eager for exercise, tossing her head and blowing her nostrils wide.

'Never let the princess out of your sight,' Irminburgh warned Adfrith. 'Stick to all the well-used tracks. The abbess would never forgive us if—'

'I will take the greatest care,' Adfrith promised.

They rode out through the main gate, saluted by the watchmen, who stared after them curiously. Wulfrun lifted her chin as she went past, trusting Magpie to carry her onwards. 'They will not look down on the goose girl now,' she murmured. Then she remembered that her mother was still a prisoner and the purpose of this ride was to find proof of her innocence.

Harvest Month had now begun and the moors were a sea of purple heather; the honeyed scent carried in the breeze. The ride across moors as the sun climbed high in the sky would have been sheer pleasure, if it hadn't been for Elfled continually urging Sea Mist to a gallop, so that Adfrith had to dutifully race ahead, begging her to be careful.

As they began to descend the steep slope to the small fishing village that sheltered beneath high cliffs, each tree and rock they passed brought memories of early childhood to Wulfrun, making her sad.

'What are you thinking about, Wolf Girl?' Elfled demanded, seeing her wistful looks. 'Have you seen a ghost?'

'Almost a ghost,' she admitted, and with the emotion strong in her she spoke without thinking. 'I used to come up here with my brother Sebbi to gather bilberries.'

'Your brother?' Elfled was amazed. 'I never knew you had a brother! Why does he not come to help your family when you need him?'

Wulfrun bit her lips in shame, wishing she'd been more cautious. 'He . . . had to go away,' she said. 'He knows nothing of our troubles.'

Elfled was not quite satisfied with this reply. 'You should send someone to fetch him,' she insisted. 'That's what I would do. Brothers can be fun – I would send for my brother Ecfrid, if I were in trouble. Even though he's now married that old woman Princess Audrey and seems to obey her every whim, I would still expect him to come to his sister's aid if I needed him.'

Wulfrun racked her brains for an answer, but as they reached the bottom of the steep path Elfled was distracted by the sight of the poor dwellings, crowded close together in the small spaces beneath the cliffs. Smoke drifted from the chimneys and rose in twists and twirls, and a great cloud of fishy steam hung over the staithe. 'What are they doing down here to cause such a stink?' she asked.

'They're boiling freshly caught crabs, just as they do on Whitby staithe,' Wulfrun told her.

'Why have I never been down to Whitby staithe?' Elfled turned to Adfrith.

He shrugged his shoulders. 'Perhaps we could go there next Friday,' he suggested.

Elfled stared about her with interest: she'd never seen such ragged folk, all hard at work mending nets, scraping out shellfish, baiting lines and cleaning fish. A few rough nags with panniers were being loaded up with fish and crabs at the bottom of the bank.

Wulfrun climbed down from Magpie's back and led her mare towards the tiny hut that had once been her home. Their arrival was causing a stir in Fisherstead, and a great many faces stared out wide-eyed from the ramshackle sheds. The gnarled old women who were boiling the crabs turned to them with a challenging look at first, but as they took in Elfled's expensive riding dress and the armed young man at her side, they began to bow and curtsy with respect.

Wulfrun was unsure whether anyone would recognize her, but as she approached the doorway of her old home a plump woman came towards her and dropped the two loaves she was carrying. 'Blessed Freya . . . is it Wulfrun?'

'It is.' Wulfrun stood there awkwardly, holding Magpie's reins. 'It's good to see you, Emma.'

'Dear girl.' Emma left the loaves on the ground and hugged her tightly. Then, as she stood back, she glanced nervously over Wulfrun's shoulder at her strange escort. 'But what is this?' she whispered. 'You have done well, child.'

'No.' Wulfrun was quick to deny it, stooping to pick up the loaves. 'No, I have done ill – my mother is accused of theft and I need your help. Can we speak in private?'

Emma curtsied anxiously towards both Elfled and Adfrith, took back the loaves and drew Wulfrun inside the hut, her face full of concern.

Wulfrun quickly explained what had happened, and when she mentioned the garnet necklace, Emma's hands flew to her mouth in horror. 'Did you know my mother possessed such a thing?' she asked.

'No.' Emma shook her head vigorously to refute any knowledge. 'But . . . I knew that Cwen kept a secret. She would not tell, for she did not wish to burden me with the knowledge. But . . . yes, I did know that there was something that she dare not speak of.'

Wulfrun sighed. 'I had hoped you might know how she got it – you see, she kept the necklace in her chest and that chest was the only thing that we took with us when we left Fisherstead.'

All at once Emma looked at her with a new alertness. 'Her marriage chest,' she said.

'Yes – yes,' Wulfrun agreed quickly. 'Did you know that she kept something valuable hidden in it?'

'No. But I do know who made that chest for Cwen and I remember that she visited the carpenter so often while he was making it that his wife complained.'

Suddenly Wulfrun herself knew too. 'Leofrid the woodsman,' she murmured. 'I should have thought of it.' Cwen had often walked over the cliffs to see Leofrid, and her father had been annoyed about it, saying that there was a decent carpenter in Fisherstead. 'Mother always liked Leofrid – she said he was to be trusted.'

Emma nodded vigorously. 'She said the same to me and I never understood what she meant exactly, but now you tell me about this hidden necklace . . .'

'Does he still live where he used to?'

'Yes . . . but I hear he is become a hermit since

his wife died. He sees nobody and gives short shrift to any who offer him work.'

Wulfrun remembered the man as hearty and full of humour, always ready with a riddle for the children. It seemed that much had changed since they'd left Fisherstead. 'Still . . . I must find him,' she insisted. She hadn't come all this way to shrink at the first sign of trouble. She turned to leave, clasping Emma's hands in gratitude. 'Will you keep this to yourself?' she begged.

Emma nodded and kissed her.

Wulfrun went back outside and found Elfled picking at a steaming crab claw, surrounded by fisher folk. Adfrith stood at her shoulder, alert to any possible threat. The villagers watched quietly, huge smiles on their faces, a little awed by the importance of their visitor.

'Ha! I like to eat like this.' Elfled laughed and blew on her fingers.

'Wait! Wait! Princess.' One of the women came rushing from her hut with a fine woven square of linen in her hands. She wrapped the hot crab claw in it and handed it carefully back to the princess. 'Now you can eat and not burn yourself.'

Wulfrun hesitated to break up this happy gathering, but she was impatient to act on the information that she'd received. Elfled looked up and saw her there. 'Have you discovered anything?' she asked.

'Yes, Princess.' Wulfrun nodded, but then fell silent.

'Then we must go.' Elfled quickly understood that they shouldn't speak of it in front of an audience.

The villagers insisted on escorting them up the steep hill, net-mending and line-baiting set aside, full of curiosity about this delightful young princess. It was not until the three riders had set off once more across the heather moors on horseback, leaving the villagers behind, that Wulfrun felt she could explain to her companions. They rode close together, keeping the horses at a slow walking pace. '. . . And so you see,' she finished, 'I must try to find this carpenter and ask if he can tell me more – it isn't far from here that he lives.'

Elfled's eyes were wide with interest. 'Then lead us there at once,' she said.

Wulfrun glanced at Adfrith, unsure whether her luck could hold out, but he nodded. 'The princess is seeing the lands that Abbess Hild rules and meeting the inhabitants. Lead on, Wolf Girl – we will follow.'

Wulfrun moved ahead and led them down the track that she remembered well from early childhood, but as they moved further away from the well-trodden route she slowed Magpie up a little, feeling disconcerted. The track was becoming hard to follow, as it was overgrown with bilberries and prickly gorse. 'This used to be a wide clear path.' She turned to Adfrith. 'Now these great fronds of bracken stand in our way. People travelled up and down it with their carts, carrying away the chests and boxes that Leofrid made. Emma told me that he keeps himself to himself since his wife died, but . . .' Her voice trailed off in uncertainty.

'Are you sure it's the right path?' Adfrith asked.

'I thought I was sure.'

'It is a while since you walked this way.' Adfrith's courteous uncertainty made her begin to doubt herself.

'It looks so very different,' she acknowledged.

They struggled on for a while in tense silence, but the undergrowth became so thick that it was difficult for the horses to pick their way through. A tangled copse loomed before them and it seemed there was no way through it.

'But . . . I do remember a copse,' Wulfrun said. 'Leofrid's hut was in a clearing in a copse. If only I could find the path that once cut through to it.'

Adfrith had come to a halt and was looking worried. 'I think perhaps we should turn back,' he said. 'We must make the princess's safety our first concern.'

Sea Mist blundered into an obstacle hidden beneath thick grass and reared a little, but her mistress quickly quietened the mare. 'I'm not turning back.' Elfled spoke with determination.

'This is a broken gate, hidden beneath brambles.'

'Ah.' Wulfrun was confident again. 'The gate led to the clearing . . . it is just that now it is all so different.' But then she looked ahead and glimpsed through the trees some rotting thatch that was almost hidden. 'This is it,' she said. 'I see his place, though it is in such a sorry state.'

Elfled urged Sea Mist forwards, not at all put off by the neglect and mess. 'The man lives like a hermit in the woods,' she murmured, fascinated.

They dismounted and fought their way forward on foot, pushing branches aside. No smoke curled from the many holes in the thatch, but Leofrid was there, hard at work, it seemed, in a crumbling lean-to. As they got closer, they saw that the knife he worked with was small and the object he carved was hidden in his big hands. Wulfrun strode through the bracken towards him, making a great crackling beneath her feet. When the man looked up at the sounds, she was shocked to see his dishevelled appearance, dirty face, hair and beard grown long and unkempt. Leofrid had once been a fine-looking man whom all the women admired.

But Wulfrun was not the only one who was shocked. Leofrid turned pale at the sight of her. 'Cwen?' he murmured.

'No' – Wulfrun quickly understood – 'it is me, Wulfrun; Cwen's daughter.'

Leofrid dropped his work into the bilberries that

grew all around. 'Of course . . . couldn't be Cwen.' He shook his head. 'Cwen is as old as I am . . .'

'This is the Princess Elfled and her tutor Adfrith.' Wulfrun felt it only right that Leofrid should understand the importance of his visitors.

Leofrid struggled to his feet and bowed, brushing down his dirty work tunic with trembling hands. There was shame in his eyes that both he and his hut should be discovered in such a state of neglect. Wulfrun wished that she'd been able to prepare him a little, but then the urgency of her mother's plight wiped all such thoughts away.

'Leofrid . . . I need your help. My mother is accused of the theft of a valuable necklace and held prisoner at Whitby to await judgement. Can you remember the oak marriage chest that you made for her? It contained a secret hiding place where this treasure lay hidden.'

They could see at once that Leofrid remembered well, but he hesitated to give them an answer. 'I would not say aught to harm Cwen.'

'No . . . no,' Adfrith intervened. 'We are her friends and we wish to prove her innocence. Anything you can tell us might be of help.'

'Do you remember . . . you slid your hand down inside the chest?' Wulfrun asked, hoping to revive his memory. 'And then . . .'

'Yes, yes,' Leofrid said at last. 'You pressed the third board down.'

'Ah.' Wulfrun sighed with relief, but the carpenter still looked troubled.

'If we could be sure that Cwen held the necklace in her possession before she came to Whitby,' Adfrith said, 'that would make things a little clearer . . . it would help us.'

'That is certain.' Leofrid nodded quickly. 'But . . . I never knew that her treasure was a necklace. I made the hiding place for Cwen and she swore that it was safer for me not to know. She showed me the size' – he made a small shape with his hands – 'and I made the space.'

Wulfrun sighed with frustration: just as she'd begun to hope that she'd find a clear answer, it seemed she was almost back at the beginning again.

Chapter 12

mathematics

While Wulfrun and Adfrith had been questioning Leofrid, Elfled's sharp eyes were straying to the undergrowth and now she swooped down on the spot where Leofrid had been working.

'Oh.' She gasped with pleasure as she lifted from among the bilberries a tiny carved horse. It was made so beautifully that you could see the eyes, the fine mane, with each hair seeming to ripple with life, and even the delicate curve of the nostrils. 'This is what you were carving.'

'Yes, Princess.' Leofrid bowed his head respectfully, though his cheeks flushed as though he were embarrassed at what she'd discovered.

'And here is another.' Elfled bent down to pick up another perfectly carved creature, this time a ram with curling horns.

Wulfrun wanted to ask more about her mother's chest, but she could not help but be distracted: now they had started to look they saw that tiny carved animals were lined up on every surface in Leofrid's workshop. They made a strange contrast with the dust and dirt that covered the heavier tools and stacked-up seasoned wood. Elfled went from one to another, crying out with delight. 'Look, here is a deer and here another deer; there are cows and calves and cockerels and hens.'

'Leofrid?' Wulfrun spoke gently, puzzled by this strange but enchanting work. 'Are you selling these? Who are these beautiful creatures for?'

Leofrid shook his head and his eyes filled up with tears. 'Foolish,' he mumbled. 'What a fool I am. I make them for the little one – the little one that can never come.'

Wulfrun frowned at his strange words, but then she remembered what Emma had said and began to understand. 'I heard that your wife had died, Leofrid.'

'Yes.'

'Was she . . . with child?'

'Yes . . . at last. We had longed for children, but the years passed and none came. My Martha became very bitter; she was jealous of other women who seemed to have children so easily, like your Cwen. Cwen and I were always friends but Martha never had a good word to say for her. Then last April, though it was so very late, Martha began to grow round in the belly and it seemed we'd have our wish. But when the baby tried to come, Martha died in the struggle to give birth and the child went with her.'

Wulfrun remembered how all the children had been afraid of Leofrid's wife's sharp tongue. 'Poor Martha,' she murmured, pitying her now.

Elfled went to pick up a beautiful carved wooden boat built like a house. 'I know,' she said, stroking it gently. 'Mother Hild told me the story – how Noah built an ark.'

Leofrid shrugged. 'A young man called Cuthbert came walking over the heather moors from Whitby and he stopped at Fisherstead for a night.'

'I know Brother Cuthbert,' Elfled said with a smile.

'He walked carrying only an oak staff and the clothes he stood up in.'

'Yes,' Elfled agreed. 'He is quite mad, but I love him dearly and he tells such good stories.'

Leofrid nodded. 'He told us the story of Noah, then he set off again across the moors saying that he was on his way to Melrose. Dear Princess – take these creatures and the boat back with you to Whitby Abbey.'

Elfled gasped and smiled with delight at the prospect of claiming such beautifully carved treasures, but Wulfrun frowned, uncomfortable about the gift. It did not seem right to her that they should simply ride away with the beautiful result of months of work that had clearly meant so much to Leofrid.

'I would treasure them,' Elfled said graciously.

They stood there quietly for a moment and then Adfrith found a solution. 'You have put your heart and soul into the making of these creatures, Leofrid. If you really would like the princess to have them, bring them to the abbey at Whitby. Mother Hild has need of good craftsmen and likes to use local workers. I would take you to see the reeve and he would pay you for them. When he saw the quality of your carving, I'm sure he would offer you more work.'

Wulfrun nodded encouragement then; this seemed a much fairer way to take the gift. But there was more to it than that: maybe this clever suggestion might draw Leofrid away from the sadness of his memories and bring him back to living and working again.

'Will you come and bring them?' Elfled was anxious that she'd lose her gift, but she managed to retain her dignity in accepting the correctness of Adfrith's suggestion. 'May I just take this little horse?' she begged.

'Yes,' Adfrith agreed. Then he turned to Leofrid. 'Will you think about it?' he asked.

'Yes.' Leofrid smiled.

Wulfrun stooped to pick up a pair of calves, their eyes wide and alive, ears so sensitively made you thought at any moment they'd twitch. 'I should so like to show these to my friend Cadmon,' she said. 'He rears the vellum calves with such loving care.'

'Take them both for him.'

Adfrith insisted that they must go if they were to be back before Irminburgh started to worry about them, and Leofrid walked a little way with them. When they turned to say goodbye he hesitated again, as though a new thought had occurred to him. 'That marriage chest was not the first box I made for Cwen,' he said at last.

'Was it not?' Wulfrun turned to him with interest.

'No. I made her a small box with a secret catch that only we two knew how to open. I made it when we were naught but children.'

'So very long ago?' Wulfrun was amazed.

'How old would Cwen have been?' Adfrith was quickly aware that this might be significant.

'She was about as old as the princess is now,' Leofrid said, bowing respectfully to Elfled.

'Thank you,' Wulfrun said. 'That might be very important.'

As they rode back over the heather moors, Elfled raced wildly ahead and Adfrith struggled once more to keep her in check. Wulfrun followed more steadily on Magpie and almost lost her grip on the reins as she tried to count on her fingers.

'If mother was eleven . . .' she murmured.

Adfrith was anxious that they were late and Irminburgh might be angry, but when they rode in through the main gate there was no sign of her. Sister Begu was waiting in the stables to escort the princess to the abbess's house. 'My Lady Irminburgh is busy,' she informed Adfrith with a humorous glance and raised eyebrows.

Wulfrun was still trying to count as Adfrith helped her down from Magpie's back. 'What is this?' he asked as he saw her twisted fingers.

'I cannot work it out,' she said in frustration. 'How many years have passed since my mother was the same age as Elfled is now?'

Adfrith nodded seriously, understanding the importance of this question. 'How old is Cwen now?'

Wulfrun frowned; she had to admit that she wasn't quite sure. 'She is more than thirty, for I remember her saying that she was widowed soon after she'd turned thirty and that was the year that Gode was born.'

'And Gode is four or five?'

'She is five.'

'Then let us say that Cwen must be about thirty-six. So . . . we all know that the Princess Elfled is eleven years old. That means that Cwen would probably have been eleven in the year six hundred and thirty-three. Ah . . . that is very interesting.'

'How can you know that?' Wulfrun was astonished.

Adfrith shrugged. 'Simple mathematics – but do you know what this means?'

Wulfrun stared at him with resentful respect. 'That you are even cleverer than I realized,' she said.

Adfrith threw back his head and laughed. 'It is not the method of finding the date that is important – it is the date itself.'

'Do not laugh like a howling dog.' Wulfrun was annoyed with him now. 'I can see all your teeth. Tell me quickly why this date is so important. I can hear the supper bell ringing and we must go.'

Adfrith sobered up, but his face was still animated. 'The year six hundred and thirty-three was the year of terror. King Edwin was killed in battle against Penda of Mercia and Cadwallon of Gwynedd. Both Celt and Saxon fought together at Hatfield Chase to break the power of Edwin of Northumbria.'

'My mother told me of this terrible year.' Wulfrun frowned, her thoughts flying around in confusion.

All laughter had fled as Adfrith ignored the supper bell to explain, his expression grim. 'Penda and Cadwallon ravaged Northumbria, burning crops and dwellings, killing any who resisted. They were determined to make Northumbria subject to them.'

'Yes . . . it must have been terrible. But how does this help us work out the puzzle? My mother was still a child: how could she have come to own a precious necklace by fair and honest means?'

Adfrith shook his head. 'That I do not know, but Queen Tata and her daughter Ianfleda, who is now our queen, had to flee the land. At such a time of chaos the jewels could easily have been lost or . . . or . . .'

'Or stolen.' Wulfrun regarded him with a stony look.

'That is not what I was thinking,' Adfrith said, but then he grabbed her arm. 'We must run,' he said. 'The supper bell has gone silent and we'll both miss our meal.'

In the refectory Fridgyth questioned her closely about her day of riding and Wulfrun told her cheerfully of her visits to Emma and Leofrid. Gode was enchanted by the two tiny calves. Wulfrun gave her one carved beast to keep, feeling sure that just one of them would delight Cadmon as much as two.

'You are trying to find out more about that necklace,' Fridgyth said, her eyes sharp and alert.

'Yes,' Wulfrun agreed cautiously. 'I think I have discovered when it was that my mother somehow got that necklace.'

'Well, I have been noticing some secretive

comings and goings while you were away.'
Fridgyth dropped her voice a little. 'Our so-called
Sister Bertha went sneaking out through the
gardens and met the jeweller's son by the side
gate.'

'Huh!' Wulfrun was not surprised. 'She has long
been trying to catch his eye and I surprised him
sneaking across the courtyard a few mornings
ago.'

Fridgyth pulled a knowing face. 'They were
there together for an age, whispering and glancing
around, looking guilty.'

'Perhaps she tries to persuade him to become a
lay brother.' Wulfrun giggled.

Fridgyth laughed. 'More like to take a wife.'

Wulfrun worked all Saturday at the wall hanging,
thinking hard and carefully as she picked her
shuttle through the threads. Might Elfled know
something about the year her grandfather was
killed and her mother forced to flee? She feared it
would upset the princess to be forced to think of
that terrible time and discarded the idea of asking
her about it.

On Sunday she took Gode and the geese with
her to the upper pasture, where they found
Cadmon and his calves. He was delighted with the
gift she'd brought and touched it gently all over.
'This man Leofrid – he knows the beasts well,' he

said. 'H-here is the muscle that runs along the flank. He makes the calves as fine as Freya makes them.'

'I knew you would like it,' Wulfrun said.

After the noonday meal they helped Fridgyth with her weeding, which was an interminable task. Gode was becoming skilled at it and Wulfrun found herself being instructed by her small sister. 'Do not yank the weeds out hard,' she told her. 'Fridif says that if you pull them gently they come out willingly all in one piece.'

'Yes, Gode.' Wulfrun pulled a wry face. She seemed to be discovering that many things in life worked better if given a bit of care and gentleness.

As she worked hard with her trowel, trying to follow Gode's instructions, she heard the rustle of silken skirts and glanced up to see that Irminburgh was hurrying round the outer garden path towards the side gate. She looked across and saw Wulfrun's curious stare. She stopped for a moment, startled, but then smiled in a surprisingly friendly manner.

'Goose Girl,' she said, 'I wanted to see you. Come with me.'

'Me?' Wulfrun was immediately nervous despite the sweet smile.

'Yes. Come with me. Now that you are working as the princess's servant I think you should have a decent gown.'

Wulfrun glanced back to where Fridgyth was energetically pulling up parsnips; Gode was safe for the moment. She rubbed her soil-stained hands self-consciously on her worn tunic and followed Irminburgh round to the abbess's house. Elfled was sitting in the abbess's parlour with Sister Begu, struggling to stitch fine linen. She looked up in surprise when she saw Wulfrun there.

'Come, darling Princess,' Irminburgh called. 'Let us find a gown to dress your Wolf Girl in. You cannot have a servant who looks like a beggar.'

Elfled willingly set aside her work, while Begu pulled an exasperated face.

'I do not really care how my Wolf Girl looks,' Elfled said, but she got to her feet, glad of any distraction from her needlework.

'But *I* care, Princess. Come with me.'

Irminburgh led them into her chamber, where they found Bertha, carefully brushing a finely felted gown. Wulfrun stared about her in awe. The walls were draped with colourful hangings and six carved wooden chests stood in a row. They proved to be full of clothes. Irminburgh threw open one after another, pulling from them gowns, tunics, cloaks and mantles. 'Your Wolf Girl is tall, but not as tall as me, so they may need a little altering. You may have these,' she said to Wulfrun, lifting out a pair of gleaming leather ankle boots with latchet fasteners. 'See if they fit – they are far too clumsy for me.'

Bertha looked on with disapproval, though it seemed that she too had benefited from Irminburgh's generosity, having discarded her plain religious habit for a braid-trimmed over-gown. Wulfrun swallowed hard and kicked off her old turnshoes; they'd never done much to protect her feet. She took the new boots with trembling hands and slipped them on. They felt warmer and softer on the inside than anything that had ever touched her feet before. 'Thank you so much. You are very kind,' she whispered. 'They fit me beautifully.'

'Here is a good warm felted cloak,' Irminburgh said. 'Now . . . you may search these chests. Choose two over-gowns and two under-gowns and then you will begin to look something like a royal servant.'

Sister Begu had followed them and stood in the doorway. 'Ah, Sister.' Irminburgh smiled again. 'Would you be so very kind as to shorten two gowns for Elfled's Wolf Girl?'

'I thought her name was Wulfrun,' Sister Begu answered a little sourly.

'Bertha will help you.' Irminburgh nodded to her servant. 'Remove any fancy braid or embroidery; that would not be suitable.'

Bertha looked up sullenly, while Elfled dived

into the chest and pulled out a madder-dyed linen under gown with embroidered cuffs. She held it up against Wulfrun. 'This would do.'

'It is too good,' Wulfrun protested.

Elfled shook her head. 'These are her old clothes – things she never wears.'

Wulfrun looked round to see if Irminburgh was offended, but the lady had vanished, leaving them to rummage freely among her finery.

'Where has Lady Irminburgh gone?' Wulfrun asked, a little disconcerted by her disappearance.

'Where indeed,' Begu said.

Chapter 13

daughter of the brigante tribe

Wulfrun could not suppress a bubble of excitement at the wonderful gifts she'd been offered. Even the oldest gowns were finer than anything she or her mother had ever owned. She chose a green linen over-gown with wide sleeves to go with the rose madder under-gown, and another warm over-gown of softest felted wool, dyed dark blue with woad.

'That should keep me warm when the cold weather comes,' she said with pleasure.

'They are not very fancy.' Elfled pulled a disappointed face.

'Wulfrun has chosen sensibly,' Sister Begu insisted, glancing meaningfully up at Bertha. 'She will attract envy if she parades like a peacock.'

Wulfrun suddenly saw herself entering the refectory dressed like a lady, with her sister beside her in ragged hand-me-downs.

'What is wrong now?' Elfled demanded, seeing the sudden stricken look.

'I would rather take something for my sister,' Wulfrun whispered. 'I do not really need four gowns.'

'Take what you want,' Elfled said.

Wulfrun hesitated, very much aware of Bertha, working away behind them and listening to all that was said. 'But . . . the lady only said four gowns,' she insisted. She could not afford to give anyone the chance to accuse her of taking more than she should.

'I have the solution.' Sister Begu smiled. 'By the time I have shortened all four gowns, there will be plenty of cloth left for me to make a nice warm tunic that will fit Gode. Leave it to me.'

Wulfrun was overcome with gratitude, so that tears sprang to her eyes.

'Why are you crying now?' Elfled asked, astounded. 'You are supposed to be my fierce Wolf Girl. You are not supposed to cry.'

As they left the chamber, Wulfrun turned to Bertha. 'I thank you for your help in altering these things,' she said.

Bertha shrugged. 'I've little choice in the matter.'

'But still I thank you,' Wulfrun repeated, her heart warm with gratitude even towards Bertha, after she'd been given this wonderful gift.

As they walked away from Irminburgh's

chamber Bertha stared after them, frowning in thought. Had Wulfrun really thanked her so politely? Guiltily she put her hand down to touch the finely carved jet cross that hung at her waist.

Later Wulfrun told Fridgyth all that had happened. 'Irminburgh has been so kind,' she said.

Fridgyth was unimpressed. 'She has many gowns – it is not so very generous of her, and while you were busy in her chamber my Lady Irminburgh herself went creeping back along the hedges to meet young Childeric by the side gate. I think that, after all, the lad may have a more exalted admirer than Bertha. Lady Irminburgh speaks the Frankish tongue and few in Whitby do.'

Wulfrun's mouth dropped open with shock at the idea. 'Irminburgh and Childeric . . . surely not?'

'That is what I saw with my own eyes.' Fridgyth raised her eyebrows in disapproval. 'Though I made sure they did not see me looking at them. It would not happen if Hild were here.'

'Do you think Irminburgh wanted me out of the way?' Wulfrun murmured, thinking aloud. She could not help but feel some sympathy. What young woman would not prefer the attentions of a handsome flaxen-haired lad to the restricted life of a nun? 'Did she fear I'd spread rumours about her? I would not speak ill of the lady; she has been kind to me!'

'Fair enough,' Fridgyth agreed.

When they went to the refectory for their Sunday supper, Sister Begu came down to their table, bringing the newly altered clothing all tied up in a parcel for them.

'You have worked so fast.' Wulfrun was impressed. She saw with gratitude that Begu had unpicked the embroidered panels as she'd been ordered, but had added instead a simple trim of braid, patterned with ivy leaves.

'I made the princess help us,' Begu chuckled. 'She preferred it to her embroidery.'

Gode wished to try her new gown on at once, but Wulfrun insisted that they wait until they were back in their hut.

Sister Begu nodded at Fridgyth. 'This one has brains,' she said.

'What did she mean?' Wulfrun asked as the nun hobbled away.

Fridgyth smiled. 'She saw that you had better sense than to start trying on gifts from Lady Irminburgh while all of Whitby watches you.'

As the days passed they fell into a hard-working pattern. Wulfrun studied beside Elfled in the scriptorium in the mornings, then tended her geese and helped Fridgyth in the afternoons. Each evening she struggled to weave, but often fell asleep over her shuttle. She enjoyed wearing her new clothes and even more the lovely Friday rides on Magpie's back. They visited the fishing villages close by and rode inland across the heather moors towards the city of York. Adfrith promised them that he'd try to arrange a longer visit for Elfled so that she could go to York and stay for a few days, visiting her half-brother in the great hall that he'd built there.

'Alchfrid is so pious and gloomy.' Elfled spoke with little enthusiasm, as they sat in the school-room planning their next week's outing. 'Now if it were my other brother Ecfrid, that would be a different matter. He is full of fun, even though his dreary wife wants to be a nun.'

Wulfrun stared at Elfled, quite shocked.

'Princess!' Adfrith admonished.

'But it is true – you know it, Adfrith. Irminburgh talks about it all the time.'

Wulfrun turned to Adfrith to see if this strange information could possibly be true.

Adfrith sighed. 'Prince Ecfrid is married to Princess Audrey,' he explained. 'She is a very holy lady, the widow of King Tondberht of Gyrwas.'

'She is twelve years older than my brother,' said Elfled, her eyes wide with disgust. 'And though she is his wife she refuses to go to bed with poor Ecfrid. Can you imagine that?'

'You cannot know such a thing.' Wulfrun shook her head in doubt.

'It is one of the more interesting things that Irminburgh talks about.' Elfled spoke with relish. 'My brother is the handsomest man I know and the funniest. All women love him, except for his wife.'

Again Wulfrun looked at Adfrith for confirmation, but he simply shrugged and tapped the line of script they were supposed to be copying. Wulfrun returned to her work, more puzzled than ever by the strange ways of royal folk.

One evening at supper time Adfrith approached the garden workers' table with Leofrid at his side. The carpenter had come to the abbey as they'd hoped he would. Ulfstan had found him space in the craftsmen's quarters and work inside the expanding guesthouse.

'I have brought these for the princess,' he said, holding the carved Noah's Ark in his arms.

Wulfrun glimpsed tiny carved animals filling a bag slung across his shoulder. 'She will be delighted,' she told him.

'But I do not like to approach her.' Leofrid spoke shyly. 'Will you give them to her when the moment is right?'

Wulfrun thanked him and promised that she would, but as soon as he put the lovely work down on the trestle top, Gode pulled the roof off the boat. She discovered more tiny carved sheep, pigs, deer and horses inside it, and began pulling them out, exclaiming with delight, before anyone could stop her. Soon heads were turning and a small friendly crowd gathered about them, admiring Leofrid's work and begging him to make animals for their own children.

Wulfrun and Adfrith smiled at each other. It was very satisfying to see Leofrid standing among the lay brothers and sisters, his tunic clean, his hair and beard trimmed, nodding eagerly at their many requests.

Weeks passed and still there was no sign of the *Royal Edwin* returning with the abbess. Wulfrun would almost have been happy if anxiety about her mother's fate had not nagged at her so much. The weather turned cool and it grew blustery, with high tides and rough seas. One Monday morning Adfrith announced that he would introduce a little simple mathematics into his teaching as the princess was getting on so well as a scribe.

Elfled looked at him impatiently. 'I'll learn anything you like, Monkman,' she told him. 'But first you must let me tell you of a discovery that I have made.'

'What is it?' Wulfrun was alert at once.

Adfrith gave up for the time being, knowing that he had little chance of being listened to.

Elfled's eyes were bright with intrigue. 'There are two necklaces,' she said.

Wulfrun stared at her, but Adfrith understood only too well what this must mean. 'Princess . . . you've been poking about among the Lady Irminburgh's belongings again. I cannot approve of that.'

Elfled dismissed his concern. 'She pokes about in everyone else's business. There are now two necklaces hidden in her jewellery box, when before there was only one, and the most interesting thing is that they are almost exactly alike, except for one tiny thing. At first I thought I must be seeing visions like old Begu, but when I touched them I knew that they were both solid and real.'

'What is this tiny difference?' Wulfrun was avid to hear.

'The second necklace has no sparrow. It is set with garnets and made of the same heavy gold, but a little pouncing cat supports the cross instead of a bird. The difference is almost unnoticeable and the cat is delightful; it is so beautifully made.'

'And yet,' Adfrith acknowledged, 'the difference is huge, for without the sparrow the jewels do not represent King Edwin's family, for it was the brief flight of the sparrow that persuaded the great king to turn to the Christian God. A necklace with a cat on could belong to any rich woman.'

'How could a sparrow make King Edwin into a

Christian?' Wulfrun asked. She could not believe that such a small, fragile thing could bring about such a huge change.

'But it did happen so,' Adfrith insisted. 'One of the king's companions began comparing our short life on earth to the flight of a sparrow through a feasting hall: it flies in at the eaves and quickly out again through a smoke hole. King Edwin suddenly realized how soon this life is over and how much more important the afterlife might be. He decided to become a Christian like his wife, hoping that this would secure him a place in the Christian heaven, and he set up the image of a sparrow on his battle standard.'

'Since then sparrows are our family symbol.' Elfled raised her small chin with pride.

But as they spoke, Wulfrun suddenly remembered Irminburgh's secretive meetings with Childeric. Perhaps, after all, it was not his handsome face that made Irminburgh wish to meet him in secret. 'Is the second necklace newly made?' She turned sharply to Elfled. 'Childeric has been working very hard of late: there's been no more creeping round the vegetable garden and he is never out of his workshop. Has he made this other necklace for Irminburgh?'

The girl shook her head. 'No. It looks old; the edges of the gold are darkened a little with age.'

Wulfrun sighed. 'Well if both the necklaces are old, that cannot be.'

Adfrith intervened. 'I think you still may be right,' he said. 'I've heard that the Frankish jewellers have the skill to make new jewellery look old. So clever are their secret processes that nobody can tell the difference, but I cannot think why Irminburgh would wish to do such a thing.'

'She can never have enough jewels,' Elfled said. 'She keeps most of them hidden from Mother Hild.'

'Please do not visit the lady's rooms again, Princess,' Adfrith begged. 'Now . . . as I was saying – simple mathematics . . .'

Neither Elfled nor Wulfrun found Adfrith's mathematics simple. One day, as they struggled to add and subtract, a wooden abacus set between them, Wulfrun at last plucked up the courage to ask Elfled something that had long been on her mind.

'When we came back from Fisherstead, Adfrith used mathematics to help me,' she said. 'He worked out that my mother had her first secret box made by Leofrid soon after the time they called the year of terror. I think she must have had the necklace since that time.'

Elfled stopped work, giving her full attention.

'I wondered . . .' Wulfrun continued, hesitating

a little. 'I wondered if the abbess told you much about that year. If I knew what happened to Queen Tata and Queen Ianfleda at that time, it might help me to see how my mother could possibly have a royal necklace that should really have belonged to them.'

Elfled stroked her chin with the soft end of the goose quill. At least she did not seem upset by this line of questioning. 'Mother Hild did tell me something,' she said, frowning a little as she tried to remember. 'She told me that I should study the history of Northumbria, but I found it very dull.'

'Far from dull, Princess.' Adfrith tried to interest her. 'It was a terrible year for Deira. The pagans ran amok and slaughtered beasts and people, burning crops and taking slaves.'

'Yes . . .' Elfled admitted. 'And Mother Hild did tell me something about my other mother, but . . . I cannot remember what – I wasn't listening.' She suddenly began counting aloud on the abacus as though her life depended on it.

Wulfrun could see that Elfled was upset now and seemed not even to want to speak her real mother's name. 'Never mind,' she said soothingly and returned to work.

Nothing more was said that morning, but while Wulfrun was eating her noonday meal alongside Fridgyth and Gode, Begu came hobbling along to their table. 'May I join you?' she asked.

'You are most welcome,' said Fridgyth.

Gode watched wide-eyed as the nun settled herself beside them. 'You made my gown,' she said, fingering with pleasure the two-coloured smock and the neatly braided cuffs that the nun had stitched for her.

'So I did, and you are most welcome, honey.' Begu beamed at the little one.

Heads turned towards them with curiosity, but strange visitors to Fridgyth's table brought little surprise these days, and the need for good food after a hard morning's work soon drew their neighbours' eyes back to their bowls.

'I cannot keep up with our princess,' said Begu. 'But you seem to be a good influence on her, Wulfrun. She is calmer than she was, a little more contented with her lot.'

'I'm glad of that, Sister,' Wulfrun said.

'Now' – Sister Begu leaned forward and spoke in a confiding tone – 'I understand that you are interested in the history of Elfled's family and especially the year of terror.'

'Yes, Sister.' Wulfrun looked up eagerly.

'Well . . . I think I can give you a bit of advice about that.' Begu gave a knowing nod. 'My husband was killed that terrible year, and when at last King Oswald came and brought us peace, I went to be a nun. With this bad leg of mine I doubted I'd ever find another husband and I kept dreaming of a church, high above the sea. I thought those dreams meant that I should go to the abbey at Hartlepool – though now I wonder if it was Whitby Abbey that called me. I thought at least I'd be safe and quiet as a nun.'

Fridgyth nodded. 'Many widows felt the same.'

Begu nodded with wry humour. 'I was safe and quiet at Hartlepool – until Bishop Aidan sent Hild to take charge of us.' She chuckled again. 'Hild quickly put paid to our easy life.'

Wulfrun gaped a little in surprise.

Begu laughed at her reaction. 'Don't get the wrong idea, honey. Hild was like a breath of fresh air, we loved her. She filled our lives with hard work: suddenly we were spinning, weaving and dying wool, keeping cows and pigs, digging gardens, and on top of that we were all supposed to learn to read and write. Hild brought us to life again.'

Wulfrun smiled with understanding. She too had discovered the excitement of learning new things.

Begu continued, 'When Hild said she was up and off to Whitby to start a new monastery from scratch, I was one of the first to vow that I'd go with her. We came from Hartlepool by boat, and even the journey was terrifying, for we were tossed in a storm off Boulby Head. I can't forget the sight of the great cliffs of Whitby and the watchtower reaching high above as we approached. "Where are we going to build the new abbey?" we asked. "Up there on those cliffs," Hild told us. We looked at each other and whispered that she was mad, but it didn't surprise us. Nothing she said or did surprised us by then.'

'I remember you coming,' Fridgyth joined in, smiling at the memory. 'Whitby was a smaller place then, but we all went crowding down to the harbour to see her arrive, expecting a princess. We'd all heard of Princess Hild, daughter of Hereric . . . she could have claimed to rule Deira.' Fridgyth lowered her voice and murmured, 'And through her mother too!'

'Through her mother?' Wulfrun was surprised. 'Who was her mother?'

Begu and Fridgyth exchanged a glance of understanding.

'Bregusyth.' Fridgyth whispered the name. 'A daughter of the warrior Brigante tribe, whose family ruled in Deira long before the Saxons came and even before the Romans. They served the wild goddess Brig and were as fierce as she – Bregusyth is little spoken of, but the older ones do not forget. Hild has warrior blood: her very name means Battlemaid.'

Begu put a finger to her lips. 'Hush . . . hush,' she warned, glancing at Gode, who was listening wide-eyed.

Fridgyth nodded and returned to her memories.

'When Hild arrived in Whitby we expected a princess decorated with jewels; what we saw was a tiny woman in plain homespun, standing in the curving prow of the great royal galley. She carried a lovely little girl in her arms; she held the child up and made the little one wave at us. 'She's just a mother,' we whispered. Since then she's been "Mother" Hild to us all. I think we needed a mother more than a princess.'

'And that child was Elfled.' Wulfrun sighed at the happy picture it brought to mind, but then she sat up, alert again and fearful that she'd never get the answers she needed for Cwen. 'But . . . that was a long time after the year of terror, was it not? King Oswy had beaten Penda in battle by then.'

Fridgyth saw her anxiety and got up from the table, taking Gode with her. 'Enough of my memories,' she said. 'I'll leave you two to talk in peace.'

Chapter 14

warning

Once they were left alone, Begu cast her mind back and struggled to remember the year of King Edwin's defeat. 'When I think of that year, all that comes to mind is fear and madness, but . . . now this is what I wanted to tell you: there was one who came to Whitby with us in that boat, who could tell you a great deal more than me.'

'And who is that?' At last Wulfrun seemed to be getting somewhere.

'She is called Nelda, but you will know her by a different name and she lives not far away from here. She was nurse to Hild and followed her fosterling wherever she went. When she had lived three score years and ten Nelda took herself off to Uskdale to try the life of a hermit.'

Wulfrun's eyes grew wide with understanding. 'The hermit of Uskdale Forest,' she whispered. 'I've heard that she is very old – and fierce.'

'She was Hild's nurse, appointed by Bregusyth,

but she is fierce only in her devotion to her nursling. You'd be surprised how many folk go tramping through the forest to find her when they need some good advice. And one who still goes tramping there is her own foster child.'

'Mother Hild?'

Sister Begu smiled. 'Hild did not get her reputation for wisdom from nowhere. Some say it comes from the Christian God, and of course as a good nun I must agree with that, but I would say that a little of it comes from Nelda in her forest lair.'

Wulfrun was fearful at the thought of going through the woods alone to find the hermit, but then she suddenly realized that she would not have to do that. 'Adfrith will take us there,' she said. 'I'm sure he will think it good for the princess to visit the hermit.'

'Speak to her with respect,' Begu warned. 'She was there with Hild in the year of terror and they both served Queen Tata and the child Ianfleda, who is now our queen.'

'I thank you for telling me this,' Wulfrun said with feeling. 'Did the princess disclose to you the reason for my search?' she asked hesitantly.

Begu reached out and pressed her hand. 'I only know that it has something to do with your mother. You may trust me to say nothing of this, child. The abbess should be home before the

winter frosts and I swear she will see justice done
by your Cwen.'

'Thank you,' Wulfrun said again, wanting for a
moment to cling tightly to Begu's warm hand.

'Remember this old saying,' Begu told her. ' "It
is wise to know how to ask." Keep on asking, Wolf
Girl. Ask with courtesy – but keep on asking.'

It wasn't difficult to persuade Adfrith that next
Friday morning's ride should take them in the
direction of Uskdale Forest, but Wulfrun was
worried that Elfled might be upset by the visit. She
would need to ask the hermit questions about
Ianfleda, and the princess was clearly angry and
upset that she'd been given away as a baby.
Wulfrun could only guess how that might feel: she
herself knew that her mother loved her, despite the
terrible mistake she'd made which had brought
them so much grief.

'The princess never willingly speaks of her
mother,' she confided to Adfrith the following
morning, as Elfled and Irminburgh swished away
from the scriptorium, leaving the scent of roses in
their wake.

Adfrith looked thoughtful and solemn. 'Being
given away to God is not an easy state,' he agreed.

Wulfrun looked up at him with concern, remembering that he too had been given to the monastery
as an oblate when he was very young.

'How old were you?' she asked tentatively.

'I was seven,' he answered her comfortably enough.

'So young . . . did you not miss your mother?'

'Dreadfully. But I loved having a full belly and I loved the skill of scribe that I began my training in.'

'A full belly? Were your parents not rich?' Wulfrun had always assumed that, with his dignity, cleverness and clear speech, he was the son of a nobleman.

Adfrith shook his head. 'No – Mother and Father could not feed us all and so one of us must be sent away. Because I was the quiet one who spent my time scratching pictures in the dust, they thought it best that I should go to the abbey. I have no regrets.'

'Better than to be sent as a slave,' she murmured, thinking bitterly of Sebbi.

'Much better.' Adfrith bowed his head in agreement. 'Mother Hild will take on any youngster, rather than let them be enslaved. Somewhere within the monastery she'll find space for them.'

Wulfrun left the scriptorium, her cheeks burning with shame at his words. If only they had understood that, maybe they could have kept Sebbi with them. Was it too late to get him back? But no good could come from letting her mind race ahead like that – she must get her mother back first. Oh, why had Gwen not sold that precious necklace rather than her eldest child?

'Uskdale? No, no – you cannot take the princess to see that old witch.' Irminburgh looked alarmed when Adfrith announced their intended destination at the end of their lessons on Thursday.

'But Nelda is the abbess's respected foster mother,' he insisted with polite formality. 'The life of a hermit is something the princess should have knowledge of and understand.'

Irminburgh glanced at Wulfrun, who was standing quietly behind Adfrith in her fine boots and gown, struggling to hide her anxiety. 'And I suppose you will take the Wolf Girl too?'

'Of course,' said Adfrith. 'You yourself insisted that the princess have a woman to wait on her.' He began to expand a little on the educational value of such a visit, while Irminburgh frowned, but then she suddenly interrupted him, flapping her hand in dismissal. 'Oh, very well then – if you insist on going to that wild place, you must go. I have much to do and must hurry now. Come, Princess.'

Later, as Wulfrun left the scriptorium, she saw Bertha emerge from the abbess's house and cross the courtyard carrying what looked like her old religious habit, neatly folded. For a moment she thought Bertha might stop and speak, but then she seemed to think better of it and hurried away through the main gate.

The following morning Wulfrun strode into Magpie's stall, wearing breeches beneath her gown, excited at the thought of the day ahead. She acknowledged the mare's snorting greeting with a friendly stroke on the nose and was just about to back her out of her stall, when she saw that somebody had been there before her and chalked a sign on the wooden cross beam above the mare's head.

Wulfrun caught her breath at the sight of it. It was the only rune she could recognize: two straight sticks down, linked by a diagonal.

ᚺ

'Hail!' She breathed the word.

Adfrith walked Midnight past and stopped to look in on her. He saw that she was staring up at the chalked rune, her face white. 'A warning,' she whispered. 'I know the meaning – it is a warning of trouble to come.'

'Pagan superstition.' Adfrith shook his head. 'Rub it out at once before Brother Cenwulf sees it, and take no notice of it.'

With a trembling hand Wulfrun obeyed. 'Nonsense,' she told herself as she rubbed the chalky mark away, then she backed Magpie out of her stall.

Elfled was waiting outside the stables, with Begu fussing a little about her and no sign of Irminburgh. A low sun shone warm on the backs of their heads as they went down towards the river. Magpie got into a rolling canter and Wulfrun's spirits rose. As they approached the first ford over the Usk, two riders on big geldings splashed through from the direction of the heather moors, barely slowing down for the shallow water.

'Visitors in something of a hurry,' Adfrith commented. They'd had to hold back, to avoid getting a good soaking.

Elfled did not care about this discourtesy; her mind was on the day ahead. 'Will the hermit know me?' she wondered. 'She saw me often when I was a little girl.'

They went more sedately through the water and set off along the western bank of the river. As they rode, Wulfrun tried to acknowledge her debt to Elfled. 'It was kind of you to send Begu to talk to me,' she said.

Elfled shrugged. 'Old mad Begu – it's more a matter of stopping her talking. At least it meant that I was free of her visions and her babble for a while.'

'But you would not prefer the company of Irminburgh, I think.' Wulfrun raised an questioning eyebrow.

'Certainly not,' Elfled agreed. 'I'd rather be with you.'

'Would you?' Wulfrun was touched.

'Yes, Wolf Girl – you are my slave and must do all I say.'

Wulfrun sighed at that and rode on in silence: being Elfled's slave required a lot of patience. Gode would have suffered heavily for a reply like that. Adfrith caught her eye and raised his eyebrows in silent communication.

They forded the river again close to where the Usk curved round by the corn mill, then set off up the steep track that took them inland, leaving the marshy flood plain behind. As the horses plodded steadily uphill, the grass became dry and speckled with gorse and heather. But before the thickness of the heather moors surrounded them they turned south towards the large stretch of woodland that was Uskdale Forest.

'Speak to me, Wolf Girl,' Elfled commanded, weary of her companion's silence.

'I will speak as long as you answer me with courtesy,' Wulfrun replied.

'Are you angry at me for calling you Wolf Girl?' Elfled asked.

Wulfrun shook her head. 'No – I am angry that you called me slave.'

'Huh . . . even though—' But then Elfled thought better of the answer that sprang to her lips and bit back her thoughtless words.

As they rode into the forest beneath the dark canopy of ancient trees, Elfled and Wulfrun slowed up a little and rode companionably closer, forgetting their disagreement. They allowed Adfrith to lead the way into the murky depth of green, where the sun struggled to penetrate.

'Have you been here before?' Wulfrun asked Elfled.

'No, never, but I remember the old one from when I was very small. She had whiskers growing on her chin and silver hair.'

'Were you afraid of her?'

Elfled looked thoughtful. 'No, I was never afraid.'

They went into the woods along a narrow winding path that fell away to the right of them above a fast rushing stream. As they went further along the path, the rocks above them became steeper and steeper; the drop below deeper and deeper, until they found themselves moving cautiously, halfway up the side of a dramatic ravine.

'Keep away from the edge,' Adfrith warned. Wulfrun saw the tension in his face. He reined in Midnight and seemed to be listening.

'What is it?' Elfled was quick to pick up on his concern.

'I thought I heard another horse.'

They all stopped then and listened: they could

hear nothing but the distant rushing of the water below them.

Soon the woodland became so overgrown that for safety they had to dismount and lead their horses. The sounds made by the water grew louder. Adfrith seemed to hesitate and then stopped, making Wulfrun's heart thud with uncertainty. 'What is it?' she asked. 'Have you lost the way?'

'No,' he said, 'I'm quite sure that this is right, but it occurs to me that it wouldn't have hurt to have a few guards to escort us. You'd think Irminburgh would have insisted on it – perhaps I should have made the suggestion.'

Wulfrun wanted to remind him of the warning rune that he'd dismissed, but thought better of it. It was all too late to take any heed of it now.

'Never mind,' Adfrith said, walking on again. 'I'm sure we are almost there.'

As they moved on, the sounds of water became so loud that it was difficult to hear one another speak.

'There!' Elfled bellowed, pointing ahead. Her sharp eyes had picked out the dark mouth of a cave perched high in the rocky side of the ravine above a waterfall.

Wulfrun reached out and shook Adfrith by the shoulder. He saw where Elfled was pointing and nodded, looking relieved.

Elfled's eyes were wide with curiosity. Wulfrun

wondered how the old woman could live in a place like this. Adfrith led them down to the bridge that crossed the water. They could see a narrow path cut into the rock leading up to the cave.

They left the horses carefully tied to sturdy trees and crossed the bridge above the wild rushing expanse of tumbling water. The upward path had been hacked out of the rock face and Wulfrun thought she'd be afraid to climb it, but changed her mind when she saw how carefully it had been made. It had been cut into the hillside like a winding trough, so that the outer side was still in place and formed a protective wall, well above ankle height. It gave confidence to those who struggled up it, even though the incline was steep.

Elfled became too confident and began peering over the edge, though Wulfrun firmly pulled her back.

Adfrith went in front, signalling for Wulfrun to bring up the rear, so that Elfled was safe in the middle between them. They struggled up the path and were almost there, when suddenly two rooks launched themselves screeching from the sheer rock face above them, flapping and shrieking. In their wake it seemed they'd set a small rockfall skittering down from high above their heads.

'Beware!' Adfrith shouted frantically back to them.

Wulfrun did not hesitate to throw herself on top

of Elfled, bringing her down to the ground with a thud. They fell with such force that Wulfrun saw nothing but a great black flash, and it seemed to her that the sound of the waterfall faded and vanished for a moment. She opened her eyes to find Adfrith bending over them both with concern.

Elfled wriggled out from beneath her, looking angry, but her expression changed as she turned to look at Wulfrun. 'Bleeding,' she yelled, cupping her hands to her mouth.

Adfrith pointed urgently ahead to the safety of the cave.

Elfled scrambled to her feet and ran the short distance. Adfrith stooped to pick something up; then took Wulfrun by the arm to help her.

'Right inside,' he bellowed as Elfled hesitated at the dark opening.

They went into the darkness.

'I cannot see a thing,' Elfled complained, her voice full of uncertainty. 'Is the old one here or not?'

It took a few moments for their eyes to grow used to the gloom, but inside the cave the waterfall's roar was muted and they found they could hear again. Wulfrun saw then that Adfrith's face was white and worried. 'Just a bit of blood – no harm is done,' she said, wiping the sore spot with the back of her hand.

'A deal of harm could have been done,' Adfrith

insisted. He stared down at the small piece of rock that he'd picked up.

Wulfrun saw that it was egg-shaped, just big enough to fit into a man's fist. 'Is that what fell on me?' She reached out and took it from him, gasping with surprise at the weight of it. 'Ironstone,' she said. Then she looked at Adfrith with understanding. 'This is the heavy rock that the smiths call dogger – something is wrong.'

Elfled looked at them both as though they were stupid. 'But it's only a rock.'

Wulfrun shook her head. 'If it had fallen from the rock face it would have a sharp flat side where it had freshly broken away. This is completely round and smooth . . . you find this dogger on the beach. How could it come to be flying down from the rocks above us?'

'How indeed?'

They turned round, startled, for the voice that spoke was deep and breathy; it did not come from any of them. An old woman was looking in at them from the open mouth of the cave. They were all a little shocked, unaware that they'd been followed. Elfled was the first to recover. 'Old One,' she whispered. 'Do you know me? Do you remember me?'

'Of course I remember you, child, and I would know you anywhere – you are the very image of the young Ianfleda.'

'Am I?' Elfled murmured.

Wulfrun moved forwards, still rubbing her head, curiosity getting the better of fear. Elfled's confident words told her that this must be Nelda, the hermit of Uskdale.

Chapter 15

the hermit of uskdale

For a moment they stared at Nelda in silence, but then Adfrith remembered his manners and bowed courteously. 'Forgive this intrusion,' he said.

Wulfrun could see that even he was a little awed. It was hard not to stare, for Nelda's appearance seemed almost insubstantial. Wulfrun had never seen anyone so thin, and the question came unbidden to her mind: what does she live on out here in the woods?

Nelda stood barefoot on the damp, mossy rocks, her feet pale and dusty. She wore a gown of homespun wool, as did all the nuns at Whitby, but on Nelda the garment made Wulfrun think at once of a shorn fleece; it seemed to fit her body closely, matted in parts and dotted with fragments of leaf and twig. Wrapped twice around the hermit's tiny waist was a girdle of neatly plaited grass and from it swung a simple cross of polished jet. Her hair was long and white, floating a little in the breeze, so that Wulfrun was reminded of stories her mother used to tell of the spirits who lived in the woods.

'You look different,' Elfled said, staring at her with open interest. 'You don't look any older, but you are very thin. What do you eat out here?'

'Berries, nuts, the shoots of all the woodland plants – God provides quite enough for my needs.'

'You smell of the woods,' the young girl told her frankly.

'That does not surprise me,' Nelda answered, quite unoffended. 'I have become a woodland creature.'

Wulfrun looked about her in the cave, searching for small signs of homeliness and comfort, but there were none. It was indeed as if a woodland creature lived there.

'Where do you sleep?' she asked, curiosity getting the better of her.

'On this ledge.' Nelda's hand smoothed the mossy surface as though it were a coverlet.

'So cold.' Wulfrun could not help but shiver at the thought.

'No, no.' Nelda smiled. 'When the bitter weather comes I cover myself with leaves and dried grasses. Now sit down, for I think we have much to say. Tell me, who was it that tried to prevent you from speaking to me?'

They stared at her, aghast, for though they'd

been shocked to find the piece of ironstone, none of them had been able to put their fears so clearly into words.

'That must have been what happened,' Adfrith agreed. 'But we did not realize it until now.'

'Did someone try to kill us?' Elfled was outraged.

Wulfrun remembered that Nelda had been watching in the woods. 'Could you see who it was?' she asked.

Nelda shook her head. 'Someone from the abbey – dressed in a brown-dyed monastic robe.'

'Like the lay brothers and sisters?' Wulfrun was disturbed at the thought.

'Just such a dye,' the hermit agreed. 'They were up on the ledge above the ravine, fast and young and lithe, but making a terrible noise, such a crackling of twigs. They left their horse further down by the stream.'

'You could tell all that?' Elfled spoke almost accusingly. 'You made no noise at all, when you came up behind us.'

'No. I've learned from the deer to move silently . . . if I wish to. And though I am old my ears have become more sensitive. I know what each sound means. I heard you coming, chattering like magpies, plodding along the path like a train of mules. That other one tried to come and go secretly, but their feet did not know the paths.'

They all went quiet, wondering who might be trying to prevent them from seeing Nelda, but then the hermit spoke again and reminded them why they had come. 'What was it that you wanted to speak to me about?'

Adfrith nodded at Wulfrun, urging her to begin. Elfled fell silent for once, deferring to her Wolf Girl.

Wulfrun sighed. 'It is my mother, Cwen the webster . . . she is accused of a terrible theft and it is my fault.'

'Wait, child, you are hurt.' Nelda tore a handful of moss from her soft bed and pressed it gently where the rock had hit Wulfrun's head. 'Put your hand up to hold it while you speak,' she said.

It felt surprisingly soft and comforting so Wulfrun did as she was told. Nelda listened in silence as Wulfrun struggled to explain all that had happened. She nodded now and then to encourage the telling and show that she understood. Only once did she interrupt, holding up her hand to bid her stop.

'Do not describe this necklace!' Nelda ordered. 'Let me tell you.'

Wulfrun caught her breath.

'It is heavy gold, with a single cross and set with garnets. A beautiful sparrow in flight supports the cross; King Edwin's sparrow.'

'Yes,' Wulfrun breathed. 'You have seen it before!'

'I have indeed.'

Elfled pushed back her wide sleeve, and there beneath the edging braid of her gown was the matching gold and garnet bracelet.

'Ah.' Nelda smiled with pleasure and touched the tiny golden sparrow with one finger. 'This is its little sister – such blessed workmanship. Now carry on and tell me all.'

Though she felt that she was gabbling, fearful that she'd forget something important, at last Wulfrun came to the end of her story. 'And so you see – we wondered if you could remember anything about that terrible year that might help us prove that Cwen could have been given the necklace by right.'

Nelda sat there frowning, then drew breath and spoke. 'There are many possibilities. All I can tell you is what I remember and hope that it will lead you towards the truth.'

Wulfrun took courage from her own strong conviction that her mother was no thief, even though the evidence might seem to point the other way. 'My mother is innocent.' She felt she must say it yet again.

'Oh, that I do believe,' Nelda said at once.

Wulfrun looked at her gratefully and Nelda smiled back at her with such kindness that it made her feel as though the sun was bathing her in warmth and light, even though they sat in a gloomy cave.

'You came here searching for the truth,' Nelda told her. 'But somebody is trying to prevent you; this suggests to me that they are guilty in some way.'

'Yes indeed.' Wulfrun saw the wisdom in that.

Both Adfrith and Elfled sat as still as the rocks they perched on, impressed by the hermit's words.

'Now I will tell you what I remember of that terrible year: there are many things I would like to forget, but cannot. Hild and I were at Catterick, waiting on Queen Tata, when the dreadful news came of Edwin's death. It was the monk Paulinus who told her; he kept the warrior Bassus outside, though he'd ridden all night to warn the queen. Paulinus came into the queen's parlour; a tall, thin man with a beak of a nose that gave him the look of a hawk. That day he was all gentleness; his cheeks white as snow, his hands trembling. He spoke to the queen so softly that I don't think she really understood what he told her. Hild and I were stunned in disbelief, while Queen Tata sat there silent and unmoving. Young Ianfleda started to cry, and that seemed to break the spell – the little one had heard his words.'

'My mother,' Elfled murmured.

'Yes.' Nelda nodded. 'She was much the age that you are now. Your mother seemed to be the first to understand the terrible thing that had befallen us, and her crying shook us out of our frozen fear and made us act. Suddenly Hild began speaking fast and low to the monk. "So, Brother," she said, "it is time for our plan." He nodded and left the room at once, saying that he would fetch the horses. Hild pulled the queen to her feet. "We leave at once," she said. "Paulinus and I have planned for this. Your brother agreed to send a Kentish ship north to wait off the coast, just in case the battle news was bad. It will be anchored off the coast, just west of Whitby Beacon, and we must ride straight there. A signal will shoot up the coast, setting all the beacons blazing, and when the Kentishmen see it, they will come in on the next tide to pick you and the little ones up. We will go with you and see you safely to Kent."'

'The little ones,' Wulfrun murmured thoughtfully; those words were familiar to her.

'Why did they have to flee away so fast?' Elfled struggled to understand.

'King Penda and his ally, Cadwallon of Gwynedd, were wild with bloodlust after their victory on the battlefield. Cadwallon and Edwin had been bitter rivals, ever since Cadwallon's father, the King of Gwynedd, had taken the young boy Edwin as his foster child. Cadwallon looked on Edwin with envy and called him the Usurper, for the King of Gwynedd had showed more love to the orphaned Edwin than he ever did to his own son. Hatred slowly grew between the two of them.

After Cadwallon and Penda had finally slaughtered Edwin in battle they wanted rid of all his bloodline. None were to be left alive to seek vengeance or to claim to rule Northumbria again. All the family were in danger.'

'They would have murdered them?' Elfled's lip curled with bitterness. 'But . . . my mother was just a girl.' She shuddered and leaned close to her Wolf Girl for comfort.

Wulfrun took the pad of moss from her head and wrapped her arms tightly around Elfled. She was eager to hear what the hermit had to tell them, but knew that the princess was listening and understanding properly for the first time the terrible things that had happened to her mother as a child.

Nelda shrugged. 'Ianfleda was Edwin's daughter, a girl whose husband might well avenge his wife's father and claim the throne of both Bernicia and Deira. Indeed, Oswy has claimed both thrones.'

'You said . . . the little ones,' Wulfrun murmured. 'Cwen spoke of the mother and her two little ones. Could "the mother" have really been Queen Tata?'

'No.' Elfled shook her head. 'I know that I had an uncle killed in the battle and another foully murdered by Penda, both sons of my grandfather's first wife, but there was only one little one and that was my mother.'

Nelda spoke gently. 'Dear girl ... there was another child, a baby boy. Your mother had a young brother, Wuscfrea; he could have grown up to be heir to Edwin and a great threat to Penda and Cadwallon if he'd ever become a man. Alas ... they saved him from Penda and Cadwallon, only for him to die of a sickness, still a child.'

Adfrith spoke with awe. 'I knew of Wuscfrea, but it never occurred to me that "the two little ones" could be our Queen Ianfleda and the baby prince.'

'So ... my mother and her baby brother had to run for their lives?' said Elfled, her voice full of sadness.

'Yes.' Nelda nodded. 'And that was why I remember the necklace so very well. You see, Hild was always the strong and practical one; she'd faced the possibility of Edwin's defeat long before it happened. She and I had prepared clothing for their escape; we knew that if it came to fleeing they'd have to go on horseback to the coast, carrying nothing that might slow them down.'

'You prepared the clothing?' Elfled was puzzled and Wulfrun held her breath.

'I myself with these two hands stitched the garnet necklace inside the skirt of Ianfleda's robe.'

Wulfrun's heart beat fast. 'You stitched it with linen thread,' she murmured. She well remembered the strong twist of thread that had been wound so tightly between two of the gold beads that she could never pick it loose.

'I did.' Nelda raised her eyebrows, impressed. 'I stitched everything with linen thread. They had to carry only the most valuable things – things that they could sell.'

'Did you ride with them?' Wulfrun asked.

Nelda shook her head. 'I would have slowed them down. I went up into the hills to hide in the caves, as did all the poorer folk who had any connection with Edwin. Paulinus and the warrior Bassus went with Tata, and Hild went too, for she could ride like the wind and they needed someone young and strong at their side.'

'So she went with them to Kent?'

'No . . . I thought I'd never see my wild young fosterling again, but she returned to me within the month. Tata and her children got safely away, but it had been a close-run thing. They reached the coast, but knew that they were being closely pursued. The Kentish vessel was there, as promised, waiting for them out in the deep water. They could see it in the distance, but the tide was out and all the time they could hear behind them a murderous hullabaloo. Their pursuers followed them down the steep cliff-side.'

Wulfrun shuddered at the thought of such a situation: to be chased to the very edge of the country and then forced to wait, fearful that your enemies might appear at your back at any moment.

'But . . .' Nelda looked at Wulfrun and raised a faint silver eyebrow. 'They did not have to wait, for a young fishergirl was there on the beach, putting away her father's small boat. When she understood what danger they were in, she dragged her boat back into the water and rowed them out to the Kentish ship. Hild did not go, for there wasn't room in the boat. She helped to push them out as far as she could and then rode fast away up the beach towards Whitby, taking the horses with her.'

Wulfrun's eyes widened with hope. 'The fishergirl . . . could it have been . . . ?'

Nelda nodded. 'Yes – why shouldn't that fishergirl have been your Cwen?'

Wulfrun smiled bitterly and tears sprang to her eyes. 'Mother,' she whispered. 'She said she'd been given the necklace in payment for "the lives of the mother and her two little ones" and she said there was a warrior and a monk.'

'Paulinus,' Adfrith said with satisfaction, but then he frowned. 'But why would Paulinus go in the boat and not Hild?'

'Have you ever tried to argue with Hild?' Nelda asked him with an expression of wry amusement. Then she shrugged. 'Tata depended on Paulinus for everything and it would have meant certain death for him if he'd been captured. Bassus had sworn to Edwin that he'd protect the queen and the children with his life. Hild knew Deira like the back of her hand and the Deirans' loyalty to her was un-shakeable. That was why Oswy was so clever when he gave her Whitby to rule. No – Hild was the one who could be left behind and survive; she returned to Catterick and stayed there, quietly helping James, the deacon, comfort those in distress. Our help was greatly needed, for both Deira and Bernicia were raided and robbed. Penda and Cadwallon's war bands left a foul trail of slaughter wherever they went. Hild's healing skills grew fast and I taught her all I knew.'

They sat in silence for a moment, picturing in their minds the misery of those years.

'So . . .' Wulfrun turned to Adfrith, concerned that Cwen should not be forgotten. 'Do you think this might prove my mother's innocence?'

Adfrith pressed his lips together. 'I'm not sure,' he said reluctantly. 'It is not exactly proof, but it seems to agree in every point with what Cwen said. The time fits and so does the place; it makes a link between Queen Tata and Cwen that none of us could have dreamed possible, but . . . have we proof that the necklace was given? Why did Cwen hide it away if it was a reward that she might be proud of?'

'She would not dare to show her treasure in the

year of terror.' Nelda spoke with certainty. 'That would have meant certain death. But if your Cwen was that fishergirl, then Queen Ianfleda owes her life to her. If this is your mother, child, then she must be a woman of great resourcefulness and courage.'

Chapter 16

uneasy truth

Wulfrun lifted her chin with pride at the hermit's words. 'My mother is both resourceful and courageous,' she said.

'Well then, keep faith with her,' said Nelda. 'Listen well, for I have more to say about that garnet necklace.' She shot a warning glance in Wulfrun's direction. 'Remember this: the truth is not always easy. Years afterwards, when Ianfleda was a girl of about sixteen and still a landless refugee at the court of Kent, Hild was sent by Oswy to visit her with the priest Utta, and I went as waiting woman. Hild and Utta's purpose was to persuade our lost princess to come north as a peace-weaver bride and marry Oswy. Such a marriage would unite the two warring royal houses of Northumbria and at last bring us peace. Oswy could claim to rule Bernicia in his own right, but if he married the daughter of Edwin, then he could claim kingship of both Bernicia and Deira. It was a clever plan – your father is no fool, my little Elfled – and Hild was just the right person to speak for him.'

'But what did the garnet necklace have to do with that?' Wulfrun could not bear to lose the thread again.

Adfrith raised his hand to hush her. Nelda understood her need and chuckled. 'Patience,' she commanded. 'You must let me tell it my way. When we arrived at the Kentish court, there was a wild and joyful reunion between those who thought they'd never see each other again. After the hugs and kisses we began to speak of shared memories; some good, some that made us weep. It was then that the garnet necklace was remembered. Most of Queen Tata's jewels had been saved, so carefully had we stitched them into their clothing, but they'd had to be sold. Only a small gold and garnet bracelet had been kept as a special treasure, and I am so glad to see it there on your small wrist, Princess, where it should be.'

Elfled smiled. 'Mother Hild gave it to me.'

'No, child.' Nelda shook her head. 'That bracelet did not come from Hild. Your own mother, Queen Ianfleda, fastened it about your wrist, tiny though it was, the day she gave you into the abbess's care. I was witness to it. "Let my little Elf not forget that she's King Edwin's grandchild," she said.'

'She called me . . . Little Elf?' Elfled murmured.

'Oh yes,' Nelda said. 'That was her pet name for you.'

It was very hard for Wulfrun to hold back her own urgent questions, but the tense silence that followed and the thoughtful wonderment on Elfled's face told them that this piece of information was important to her. She opened her mouth and her lips trembled a little as though she'd ask more, but then suddenly her eyes widened as she stared at Wulfrun's head where the moss had been. 'The blood has all gone and your head is almost mended,' she said.

Wulfrun smiled, surprised, and gently touched the spot.

'What about the garnet necklace?' Elfled asked on behalf of her Wolf Girl.

Nelda pressed her lips together, almost as though she was reluctant to speak. 'Ianfleda told us that she'd accidentally dropped the garnet necklace into the sea – it had been lost.'

'Ah no!' Wulfrun groaned, remembering Nelda's warning. She understood now why the hermit had said that the truth was not always easy to hear. 'Do you think my mother found it and took it home with her?'

'No, I do not.' Nelda shook her head, surprising them. 'Remember what I said: *Keep faith with your Cwen*. I said nothing at the time, but I was troubled. Who was I to question the future Queen of Northumbria? But I stitched those jewels into her gown and I did not mean them to come loose. I worked with many lengths of thread and wound them carefully between the jewels so that even if one was lost the others would still stay in place.'

Elfled was shocked. 'You mean that my mother lied?'

'I cannot answer that,' Nelda insisted. 'All I can say is that the only way those jewels could have been lost was if someone had cut them away with a good sharp knife, and there is only one person who can really know what happened.'

Wulfrun looked at her uncertainly. 'You mean Queen Ianfleda herself!'

They sat there for a while, quietly wondering about what had been said, but Nelda suddenly rose to her feet, her woodland senses alert. 'The one who tries to walk in secret has returned.'

They all got up and edged cautiously towards the cave mouth, blinking as the bright noon sun struck their eyes.

Rooks rose screaming from the sides of the ravine, and above the waterfall's steady roar they heard a whinny, followed by the sound of galloping hooves and branches cracking. Elfled rushed to the edge, all caution discarded. 'Sea Mist!' she screamed. 'Come back – come back here!'

They pulled Elfled into the safety of the cave, though they'd all glimpsed a rider wearing a brown habit astride a grey. The intruder had loosed their horses and was leading them by their reins out of the forest, back towards the heather moors.

'How can we return to Whitby?' Adfrith was agitated. 'We must get back and fast.'

'Yes,' Nelda agreed. 'But you cannot rush after them on foot. There is no doubt that someone is working against you – you must be careful until it all becomes clear.'

'How dare they?' Elfled was furious. 'I will have them whipped.'

'You will have to identify them first,' Wulfrun pointed out.

'I will walk to the edge of the forest with you,' Nelda told them. 'You are safe within the woods with me. Come, follow.'

They hurriedly did as she said, more puzzled and shaken than ever at this latest turn of events. They scrambled down the steep pathway after the old woman, who moved at a surprising speed.

'We cannot walk like this all the way back to Whitby.' Elfled's voice was high and childlike.

Nelda stopped for a moment by the bridge and turned round. 'You are young and strong, my Princess,' she said reprovingly.

'I could go to fetch help,' said Adfrith, his brows

knit tight with worry. 'Princess ... perhaps you and Wulfrun would be safer staying here with Nelda for the night.'

'In that cold cave?' Elfled was horrified.

Wulfrun saw Adfrith's anxiety and understood it well. What was the Lady Irminburgh going to say if the horses came back without their riders? She'd surely have all the guards out combing the hills and moors to find them; she'd be furious. 'I could go for help, while you stay here to look after the princess,' she offered.

'No, you are not to leave me, Wolf Girl.' Elfled's fingers caught at her sleeve and twined tightly in the loose material at her wrist. Though her words were imperious, her voice sounded more than ever like that of a small, frightened child.

'Best to carry on walking then,' Nelda told them, with firm good sense. 'The light will not go for a while and you can easily reach the mill on the river bend and take shelter there. Eva and Borg are my friends and they will keep you safe and make you as comfortable as they can.'

Elfled said no more, and once again they followed Nelda in silence, walking fast along the woodland paths. At last they reached the edge of the forest, where Nelda stopped. 'I must turn back here,' she said solemnly. 'I have not gone beyond these bounds for five years. I call on a thousand angels to guard you against all foes, Woden to keep his ravens from your shoulders and Brig to defend you with her magic arrows.'

Though her prayer was a strange one, they all three bowed their heads in reverence, feeling suddenly safer for her words. They kissed Nelda in turn as she took her leave of them. There at the edge of the forest she appeared to be just a skinny and very old woman with tangled hair and dirty feet, but as she walked away, it seemed the trees closed protectively about her.

'Like a woodland creature she goes back to her lair,' Wulfrun murmured.

'We must hurry,' Adfrith urged them, setting off downhill towards the river, his hand gripped tightly on the handle of his seax.

Elfled marched behind him, uncomplaining at first, but as the sun moved over their heads, her steps slowed and she began to fret a little. Just as they came in sight of the mill, the sound of galloping hooves made Adfrith freeze. 'Friend or foe?' he murmured.

'Into the ditch,' Wulfrun hissed.

She grabbed Elfled's arm and dragged her quickly down into the damp undergrowth. Adfrith crouched beside them, a warning finger to his lips.

Elfled said nothing, though her wide eyes betrayed fear.

'Just one rider,' Adfrith whispered.

The speeding hooves slowed to a trot and then a

walk. A black and white riderless horse came into view as they all rose smiling to their feet. 'Magpie,' Wulfrun cried out with delight. 'You have come back for us.' She went at once to reach up and throw her arms around the thickset shoulders with their stubby black and white hairs. Magpie rolled her dark eyes and tossed her head for a moment, but then settled quickly at the familiar scent.

Adfrith's face was radiant with relief. 'Trust Cadmon to know which beast you can rely on; with Magpie's help we shall make it back to Whitby tonight.'

'She is so clever.' Wulfrun dropped a grateful kiss on Magpie's muzzle.

Elfled crossed her arms and looked about hopefully. 'I would have thought Sea Mist might have returned for me.'

Wulfrun's heart soared with love for her sturdy mare, but she tried to be fair. 'Sea Mist might have had no chance to turn back, but three horses is a lot for one person to control at once.'

'Yes,' Elfled acknowledged with a sigh. 'Magpie has done very well to escape, even though she's slow and fat.'

'Princess, will you ride her?' Adfrith bowed courteously, offering a leg-up.

'But she's Wulfrun's mount,' was Elfled's surprising reply. 'Perhaps I can walk.'

Adfrith and Wulfrun glanced at each other, both impressed by Elfled's sudden reticence.

'Princess,' Adfrith tried again, 'you should ride – you must be tired and Magpie is very strong – she could carry two.'

Elfled looked from him to Wulfrun. 'You mean that I should ride behind my Wolf Girl?'

'I think your safety is the most important thing at this moment.' Adfrith spoke with his usual quiet sense.

Elfled nodded. 'Climb up, Wolf Girl,' she ordered.

They set off, moving quickly beyond the spreading fingers of the purple heather moors, Adfrith striding along beside the horse. Wulfrun took the reins and Elfled rode behind, her arms clinging tight round the older girl's waist. They passed the mill and forded the river. A sensation of heavy warmth at her back and the sound of regular breathing told Wulfrun that Elfled had fallen asleep – just like Gode did when she carried her home piggy-back after a hard day's digging in Fridgyth's garden.

'The princess sleeps,' she whispered.

'That's good,' Adfrith said, but Wulfrun saw that his face was still white and worried in the gathering darkness. He had every right to be fearful: they must get back inside the safety of the monastery stockade as fast as they could. But even that thought must bring unease, for it seemed that there was one within the abbey bounds who wished them ill. Wulfrun did not want to point it out to Adfrith at the moment, but they should have heeded the warning rune. Who could have taken the trouble to put it there in Magpie's stall?

It was dark by the time they splashed through the second ford and rode up the hill to the main gate. 'Princess' – Wulfrun raised her voice a little and turned to Elfled – 'we are almost home. Shall I get down and let you ride in alone?'

'No,' Elfled murmured sleepily. 'I'm warm and comfortable – why should you get down?'

'At least the place is not alive with guards searching for us,' Adfrith whispered.

'No,' Wulfrun agreed, echoing his relief. 'It is almost as though nobody has missed us.'

'Indeed.'

But as they went in through the main gate they saw that both the stables and guesthouse were a blaze of torches and activity. 'Guests,' Adfrith said. 'Important guests have arrived, by the look of it.'

Wulfrun caught her breath. 'Could it be the abbess returning?'

'She went by sea and I'm sure she will return by sea,' said Adfrith. 'We'd have seen the *Royal Edwin* in the harbour. Come – lead Magpie into the stables. We will soon know who it is.'

He was right. The stables were filled with strange stamping mares and geldings and stable lads running frantically in all directions. They were glad to see that Cadmon was there, helping settle the beasts in their stalls.

Adfrith took Cadmon's arm and spoke low to him. 'Have Midnight and Sea Mist returned?'

The cowherd nodded quickly.

Adfrith closed his eyes, relieved. 'Has nobody noticed how late we are?'

'S-Sister B-Begu,' Cadmon stammered, taking charge of Magpie.

'Ah! Not Lady Irminburgh?'

'N-no; too busy with the prince. Sister Begu c-came in here and whispered to me, "Any sign of the princess?" I said no . . . and I d-didn't tell her Sea Mist and Midnight came back – no riders and spooked. I settled them.'

'Thank you.' Wulfrun spoke with feeling.

Now another concern came to Adfrith. 'The prince, you say . . . Which prince?'

'P-Prince Ecfrid.' Cadmon glanced quickly at the sleepy Elfled.

Wulfrun turned to help the young girl down from Magpie's back, her head spinning with new fears. What could this royal visit mean? Prince Ecfrid was one of the most powerful men in Northumbria, even though he had no kingdom of his own as yet. 'Princess' – she gently shook

Elfled's shoulder – 'wake up. Your brother Prince Ecfrid has come to Whitby.'

Elfled rubbed her eyes. 'Ecfrid?' she said, puzzled for a moment; then, when she opened her eyes properly, she smiled. 'That teasing fellow – where is he?'

Sister Begu appeared at their side, giving Adfrith a sharp, reproving look. 'At last,' she said. 'Elfled – your brother is asking for you, and I have told him that you were resting after a ride. Come, you must quickly wash yourself and put on a clean gown.'

'I'm so sorry, Sister,' Adfrith mumbled.

'Well, at least you are back and safe,' she said, giving him another sharp look as she steered Elfled away.

'You told a lie, Begu,' Elfled accused.

'Lucky for you I did!'

'I must go too,' Adfrith said. He nodded curtly at Wulfrun, turned on his heel and followed them.

Wulfrun felt suddenly bereft. She looked at Cadmon, but he turned his back on her in an unfriendly way and set about rubbing Magpie down. She knew that it was their seeming careless-ness with the horses that had upset him, but this was not the time to try to explain. She pushed her way out of the crowded stables, past the bustle and smells, feeling afraid and alone. The coming of Prince Ecfrid had served to remind her of the great gulf that lay between her and those she'd begun to think of as friends. While riding back she'd felt more like Elfled's big sister than her slave, and for a while she and Adfrith had seemed to have an understanding that needed no words.

Just as she was about to leave, she stopped, realizing that there was something she'd meant to do. She went back into the stables and saw at once what she should have been looking for all the time. A big pale grey had been hastily fastened by the bridle outside the nearest stall, steam rising from its flanks. She marched back to find Cadmon, whether he was angry with her or not.

'Who brought in that grey?' she demanded. 'It is really important to know.'

Cadmon looked where she pointed and shrugged. 'D-didn't see,' he said.

Wulfrun sighed in frustration. 'Well . . . it needs rubbing down,' she told him and marched outside again.

She crept round to the vegetable garden, where the contrast with the guesthouse and stables was stark. All was in darkness but she picked up the sound of voices – a man and a woman arguing. She moved on quietly and soon could hear what they said.

'She will be angry.' The woman's voice was familiar.

'Tell your mistress she should have sent army – not one alone,' the man replied.

'What – for two little lasses and a soft oblate?'

'I could not prevent them,' the man replied. 'You tell her – send army next time. I cannot work alone for her.'

'Huh! I think the army has arrived.'

The man seemed to shrink away into the shadows, and all at once the woman began hurrying back down the path towards the spot where Wulfrun was standing. Though she backed away from the oncoming shadow, Wulfrun's hand caught the woman as she pushed past her.

'Who is that sneaking about?' The voice was Bertha's.

Wulfrun said nothing, but for a moment they stood there in the darkness very close; so close that they could hear each other breathing.

'Is it the Wolf Girl?' Bertha hissed very low.

Still Wulfrun dared not speak and at last Bertha growled angrily, 'Very well then! Woden knows what will be! I tried to warn you!' and set off again towards the guesthouse and refectory.

Wulfrun stared after her, her mind whirling. She replayed the conversation that she'd overheard in her head. What did it all mean? Could it really have been Bertha who had scrawled the warning rune?

At last she moved on and stumbled towards the distant light that burned in Fridgyth's hut. She stopped again, resting her hand on the wooden lintel, realizing that she'd missed something else. What she'd touched as Bertha pushed past had been the rough woven wool of a monastic habit, with the sharp scent of thyme still clinging to it. She remembered the glimpse they'd had of the rider in the forest. 'It could have been anyone, dressed in that robe,' she murmured to herself. 'But I know that it was Childeric out there in the woods.'

She was too exhausted to work it all out, so she pushed opened Fridgyth's door and went inside.

Chapter 17

gold and garnets

Gode was fast asleep in the shadowy firelight that came from the herbwife's hearth, wrapped in a woven rug, a smear of milk at the corner of her mouth and a small bowl with the dregs beside her. Fridgyth sat by the fire, crumbling dried lavender into a bowl. The wonderful clean smell of the herb filled the hut, and the sight made Wulfrun's eyes water and her throat catch, reminding her of the way that it had been in the weaver's hut before she had betrayed her mother. What a true friend Fridgyth had proved to be.

'Prince Ecfrid has arrived,' Wulfrun announced. 'Did you know?'

Fridgyth chuckled. 'All of Whitby knows. Even the lower town is a-buzz with the news.'

'Was he expected?' Wulfrun frowned.

'Not that I knew of – and not that Ulfstan knew of either, judging by the panic he flew into. Riders came to warn him this morning.'

'Ah.' Wulfrun remembered the two riders who'd splashed through the ford. So they'd been Prince Ecfrid's men.

Fridgyth looked at her, frowning now. 'You are late,' she said. 'And you have a nasty lump on your forehead. Are you hurt?'

Wulfrun shook her head and sat down. 'It has been a very strange day,' she said with a great sigh. She told Fridgyth about the ironstone boulder and how their horses had been stolen, though she held back some of the information about the necklace that she'd gained from Nelda. 'And now,' she finished, 'we get back and find that Prince Ecfrid has arrived, and though Adfrith and I fretted over the princess's safety it seems nobody even noticed that we were in trouble. Only Cadmon was concerned when the princess's riderless horse came galloping back without its mistress, and I think he was more bothered about the horse.'

'Humph!' Fridgyth was unsurprised. 'Sister Begu was fluttering about in a worried way – I'm sure she missed you, but she had the good sense not to start a fuss. The one who should have been upset by your absence was otherwise engaged.'

'The one . . .' Wulfrun frowned. 'Ah yes, my Lady Irminburgh. What was she up to?'

'She went out to greet Prince Ecfrid dressed like a queen, and though none other seemed ready for his visit, I'd say she was well prepared. And there was something else . . .' Fridgyth paused and hesitated.

'What?' Wulfrun was puzzled.

'Well,' said Fridgyth, lowering her voice as though she feared to be overheard, 'around her neck my Lady Irminburgh wore a very beautiful garnet necklace: garnets set in heavy gleaming gold!'

Wulfrun's mouth dropped open in amazement. 'She was wearing it quite openly?'

'Yes. I was close enough to see Prince Ecfrid bending to admire it when Irminburgh presented the welcome cup of mead. I swear his lips touched her neck, just for a moment. It was a good job Princess Audrey was not there to see it.'

'He kissed her . . . on the neck?' Wulfrun was shocked. A kiss on the cheek would be polite and most acceptable, but a kiss on the neck from a married man was quite another thing.

Fridgyth nodded. 'Just brushed her skin with his lips, there where the jewels lay.'

Wulfrun sat by the herbwife's hearth, deep in thought. What did this mean? Why wear the garnet necklace so openly? Was that not drawing attention to the fact that Irminburgh had taken it herself? If what Nelda had told them was true, the necklace should be handed over to Elfled's mother, the Queen of Northumbria. The connection that Fridgyth hinted at between Irminburgh and Prince Ecfrid was shocking.

'Why has Princess Audrey not come with her husband?' she asked.

Fridgyth gave her a knowing look. 'Rumour has it that Audrey begs her husband to agree to a divorce so that she may become a nun. It seems she has gone to stay with Ecfrid's aunt, Abbess Ebbe of Coldingham – perhaps to beg her help.'

Wulfrun's eyes were wide. 'Does that mean the prince looks for another wife?'

'Huh.' Fridgyth shrugged. 'So it might seem.'

'But surely not Irminburgh . . . she is a dedicated nun.'

'It makes a strange kind of sense. Why not exchange a princess who wants to be a nun for a nun who wants to be a princess?'

Wulfrun smiled, but there was something in it all that troubled her.

'Now I come to think of it' – Fridgyth frowned in thought – 'Ecfrid and Irminburgh must be distantly related, for Irminburgh has always claimed to be some kind of cousin to Queen Ianfleda through her mother's side of the family.'

'But isn't Irminburgh a nun dedicated to live in chastity like Abbess Hild? Isn't she one who has vowed never to take a husband?'

'Huh! She hasn't made her vows yet and there are many who claim chastity but do not stick very rigidly to it. I've heard that in Princess Ebbe's abbey the nuns do as they wish, and Ebbe is King

Oswy's sister – Elfled's aunt. I'm not sure it will suit Princess Audrey's ideal of nunlike behaviour.'

'Hild herself would never—'

'Certainly not!' Fridgyth exclaimed. 'She sets a fine example of chastity, though she has never pressed her lay brothers and sisters to live in so dedicated a way.'

'What is Prince Ecfrid like?' Wulfrun could not suppress her curiosity.

'A handsome lad with golden curly hair and an imperious manner, though he's not yet twenty. He had poor Ulfstan running round in frantic circles, while to Irminburgh he was all charm.'

'So . . . Irminburgh must be older than him.'

'Yes, that's true, she is older, but you have to admit that Irminburgh is young enough and she is beautiful.'

Wulfrun agreed reluctantly. 'She is very beautiful.' She picked at the fine braid on the gown that Irminburgh had given with such seeming generosity. She could not judge the lady too harshly for wanting a handsome prince rather than a life of monastic service, but she could not forget the conversation she'd heard out there in the dark, and she touched her head where the heavy lump of ironstone had hit her. Could Irminburgh really have sent Childeric after them? Had she wanted to prevent them speaking to Nelda? Surely she could not wish to harm Elfled, although she might well want rid of the Wolf Girl, with her stubborn insistence on her mother's innocence and her knowledge of a gold and garnet necklace.

'Elfled rushed off in excitement to greet her brother,' she told Fridgyth.

'That child craves affection,' she replied, 'and an older brother might have much to offer. He should understand and sympathize after the childhood that he suffered.'

'How has he suffered?' Wulfrun was learning fast that the royal children of Northumbria did not have as perfect lives as she'd once thought.

Fridgyth dropped her voice again. 'Never repeat this to a soul – to speak so might be judged treason – but believe me, Oswy has ruthlessly used both his wives and his children to help him claw his way to power. Ecfrid was sent at the age of seven or eight as a hostage to King Penda's court.'

Wulfrun was horrified. Sebbi had been thirteen when he was sold as a slave and that had been terrible enough. 'A hostage?'

'Yes.' Fridgyth pressed her lips together. 'His father sent him to live with his worst enemy. Penda was demanding land and tribute from North-umbria and Oswy wasn't much of a battle leader then. His tactics were to slip away with his warriors into the hills every time Penda rode north with his war band, only to reappear when they'd finished ravaging the countryside.'

Wulfrun listened with interest. This was yet more of Northumbria's past that she had never heard before.

'The ordinary folk suffered bitterly.' Fridgyth's face crumpled with the pain of the memory. 'I was a young wife with little bairns when my husband was killed in one of Penda's raids. My babies starved – I couldn't feed them.'

'Oh, Fridgyth . . . I never knew,' Wulfrun whispered in sympathy. 'I never knew you'd been a wife and a mother.'

'All long ago,' she murmured. 'When peace returned I set myself up as a herbwife, swearing that I'd do my best to prevent such sorrow happening to others.'

'You live by that still.' Wulfrun leaned forward to press her hand. 'Nobody knows that better than I. You saved me when I wanted to throw myself over the cliff.'

'Thank you, honey.' Fridgyth smiled, then went on with her story: 'Well, Oswy tried to buy Penda off and make peace. He paid a huge tribute and offered his elder son Alchfrid as husband to Penda's daughter and his younger son Ecfrid as a hostage. That's why Penda's daughter is now Sub-queen of Deira.'

'But King Oswy fought Penda at the great battle and won.' Wulfrun found it hard to understand.

'Eventually he did,' Fridgyth agreed. 'This came

before . . . Penda accepted the bribes and the hostage. He sent his daughter to marry Alchfrid, but he still continued to raid our lands. He even attacked Oswy's great stronghold of Bamburgh and burned it to the ground while the king was away. When at last Oswy was forced to face his enemy, he won more by his wits than his courage. He knew that the river Winwood near Leeds flooded at that time of year and he lured Penda's fiercest warriors into the mire. They were drowned and smothered in mud, not killed by fighting. Oswy is sharp as a knife – I give him that.'

'So . . . what happened to Ecfrid? He must have been in great danger at that time.'

'Yes indeed. I understand that Penda's queen protected him; a pagan lady with a strong sense of honour. He was lucky to survive – but how did it make him feel to be used like that by his own father? Now his elder half-brother, Rhienmellth's son, is made king here in Deira, while he, the direct descendant of Edwin, gets nothing.'

'You are right in saying that Oswy has used his children,' said Wulfrun. 'He took Elfled from her mother's arms and sent her here to Whitby in order that he might win his battle.'

Fridgyth nodded.

'She was a baby and could not choose, but I wonder what kind of a mother would give up her child and allow him to do that?'

The herbwife shrugged and then Wulfrun thought of Sebbi. She hung her head in weariness and shame, remembering that her own mother had done something similar in desperation – perhaps Ianfleda had been desperate too.

'You need sleep,' said Fridgyth. 'No more talking now. I have another rug; settle down and sleep here.'

'But the geese – and the weaving . . . ?'

'Gode and I took the geese out to graze and locked them up safely for the night,' said Fridgyth. 'You are far too tired to set about weaving now. Lie down and sleep.'

Wulfrun nodded obediently and crawled onto the pile of straw beside her sister. As Fridgyth bent to tuck the rug about her, she suddenly stopped. 'I have just remembered something else,' she said. 'I think it was Begu who once told me that Irminburgh had been betrothed as a child to one of Penda's sons, who died.'

Wulfrun frowned. How did that help?

Fridgyth gave a knowing smile. 'That would be it. Do you see the link? Irminburgh would have been sent as a young girl to the court of Penda's queen.'

'And Ecfrid was a child hostage there.' Wulfrun picked up the significance now.

'Those two may know each other very well,' Fridgyth said thoughtfully. 'But let us not rack our brains about it now. Shut your eyes and sleep.' She dropped a gentle kiss on Wulfrun's forehead, remembering sadly the children that she'd lost.

'Have I told you what a good friend you are?' Wulfrun murmured.

Fridgyth smiled. 'Go to sleep,' she said.

The next morning was Saturday and Wulfrun spent the day working hard at her wall hanging, which was now growing steadily. On Sunday she was preparing to do the same, even though the abbess insisted that only essential work should be done on the Sabbath. She took the geese early to the pasture, and when she returned to her hut, leaving Gode once again in Fridgyth's care, she found Sister Begu standing by her doorway, looking anxiously inside.

'Did you want me, Sister?' she said.

Begu turned at the sound of her voice. 'You are wanted in the abbess's parlour.'

'Me?' Wulfrun asked, surprised.

'Yes, child. The princess wants her brother to see you.'

Wulfrun's heart thundered and her hands went up nervously to pluck at her hair.

Begu took her by the arm and pulled her along, hobbling fast beside her. 'You may comb your hair as we go, but we must not keep Prince Ecfrid waiting.'

Wulfrun combed her hair frantically as she went. 'Is there trouble?' she asked.

Begu looked at her with understanding. 'I don't think so, honey. We are all unprepared for this visit. Elfled says she wants her brother to see her Wolf Girl, and I think the prince is amused at the way she speaks of you. He has heard all about you and your mother and the necklace.'

Wulfrun's stomach turned over in fear and she stopped, afraid to go on.

Begu pulled her along again. 'The prince seems to be in a very cheerful mood,' she said. 'You cannot disobey: he outranks us all – even Elfled. He is the king's second son, and if Prince Alchfrid were to die . . .'

'Yes, I know,' Wulfrun acknowledged. 'He would become King of Deira and heir to the whole of Northumbria.'

The abbess's parlour was a warm, comfortable room, heated by four braziers, one in each corner. The prince lolled in a finely carved chair, two wolfhounds at his feet – one lying down, the other alert. Irminburgh sat demurely on the abbess's small chair, dressed in a gown of rich golden silk, plying her embroidery needle. Elfled stood at the prince's shoulder, laughing and reaching across him for a string of silver beads, from which dangled a small ornate silver cross. He held them just out of her reach, teasing her as he might a kitten. Irminburgh glanced up at them with tolerant amusement.

'Give it to me,' Elfled demanded. 'I know it is for me.'

'Why should you think that?' the prince asked, raising his eyebrows in mock severity.

'Because it has a cross,' Elfled said. 'I've been given to the Christian God, whose symbol is a cross, so it must be for me.'

Ecfrid shook his head and laughed, then let her snatch the beads. 'Do not forget that you are also descended from Woden.'

Begu's sharp ears picked up their bantering words. 'Descended from Woden or not, I do not think Mother Hild would like to hear you display such greed, Elfled!' she said.

'Well, she isn't here!' Elfled snapped back and laughed again. 'Come here, Wolf Girl!' She beckoned imperiously as she saw Wulfrun hesitating in the doorway.

One dog barked and the other pricked up its ears and leaped to its feet. They growled fiercely, sensing Wulfrun's fear. Both Ecfrid and Elfled threw back their heads and laughed, so that the cosy parlour was suddenly filled with uproar.

'Down!' the prince ordered, when he recovered. The dogs subsided obediently, as Ecfrid chuckled. 'I think you are right, little sister: my wolfhounds recognize your Wolf Girl as their enemy, though she does not look very fierce to me.'

'She's clever though.' Elfled was enthusiastic. 'And she can do much more than your wolfhounds – she can write words in Latin.'

'Can she indeed?' Ecfrid was smiling thoughtfully now and staring at Wulfrun in a way that made her feel uncomfortable. 'So, Wolf Girl,' he said, 'I hear that your mother is accused of theft.'

Wulfrun swallowed hard. 'I swear my mother is innocent,' she said.

'Poor girl.' Irminburgh spoke with sweet sympathy. 'She is so loyal to her mother.' But as she lifted her beautiful gaze up from her needlework, Wulfrun saw that the garnet necklace gleamed about her neck.

Chapter 18

day of slaughter

It seemed that Elfled suddenly noticed it too. 'That is the necklace,' she said, leaning forward and pointing across her brother. 'Irminburgh is wearing the necklace that Wulfrun's mother is supposed to have stolen.'

Irminburgh shook her head. 'My dear Elfled, you are quite mistaken.' She touched the necklace tenderly. 'This is the necklace that I inherited from my grandmother when she died. I have owned it since I was a child. Now this' – she searched in the pouch that swung from her girdle – 'this is the necklace that the weaver woman stole.'

Wulfrun could not stop herself from moving forward so that she could see. She gasped as Irminburgh drew from her pouch a necklace that looked almost identical to the one that she'd once played with, but there in place of the sparrow was a tiny pouncing cat.

'No.' Elfled flared up with frustration that she

couldn't contain. 'You've had that made – I swear you have. Look at the necklace that she wears, brother. It bears the standard of Edwin, our grandfather, and should belong to our mother the queen – that was the necklace that Wulfrun's mother had in her chest.'

'No, dear.' Irminburgh was all honey. 'Mother vowed this necklace to be my proof that I too am descended from Edwin, and have a claim to the throne of Deira – or my husband would, if I had a husband.' She flashed a coquettish glance at Ecfrid, who coloured a little and shuffled in his chair. Wulfrun and Sister Begu watched in silence, deeply disconcerted by this interchange.

'That is our mother's necklace.' Elfled pushed her brother's face round to make him look at it, but he shook her off, annoyed.

'Be quiet, sister,' he ordered.

'Dear little Elfled.' Irminburgh still spoke with patient sweetness. 'I would advise you to think carefully about what you are saying. If this necklace belonged to the queen and Cwen the webster stole it, then the crime would be treason and the punishment must be slow death by fire. The prince could pass judgement on the woman; he has every right and it supersedes yours, dear Elfled.'

'No!' Wulfrun could not help the cry that escaped from her lips. She struggled for breath, her heart beating like a drum. Suddenly she understood why Adfrith had warned them to keep quiet about their belief that the necklace was of royal origin. Why had she not realized that theft of royal jewels would be seen as treason and incur the harshest punishment?

Elfled shot a frightened glance at her Wolf Girl. She opened her mouth to say more, but then shut it, understanding that she'd already said too much.

'Prince Ecfrid?' Sister Begu intervened gently. 'There are those who would speak in defence of Cwen the webster and affirm her honesty. One is a respected carpenter who has travelled here from Fisherstead, having known her as a child; he works in the building of the new guesthouse and patiently awaits Mother Hild's return. Ulfstan the reeve will speak on Cwen's behalf and I myself would add my voice to her defence. We would all be willing to bear witness with our hand on the altar and swear her to be an honest woman.'

The prince looked very uncomfortable. Begu was the abbess's close friend and he knew that Hild would trust her word above all others. Swearing with a hand on the altar was a serious matter; those who lied risked eternal damnation. He bowed his head respectfully to the old nun and shot an apologetic glance towards Irminburgh. 'Be at ease, Sister Begu. I know that Ulfstan wishes the webster to be judged by the abbess and I would not wish to offend our cousin Hild.'

Irminburgh shrugged. 'Very well, dear Prince,' she said obediently, her ivory complexion flushing a delicate rose-pink as she spoke. Then she turned to Begu. 'The Wolf Girl may go, Sister.'

Begu steered Wulfrun out of the room with surprising speed, but as soon as they were outside she paused for breath, looking a little white and shaken herself.

'You'd think Irminburgh was the queen, the way she speaks.' Wulfrun was outraged.

'Indeed you would,' the old nun agreed. 'But I think we may have been lucky to get out of there without more trouble. Go back to your geese and weaving, Wulfrun, and wait patiently for the return of the abbess. That is the best advice I can give you.'

'Yes, Sister.' Wulfrun was still trembling at Irminburgh's suggestion of treason.

Then, as she crossed the courtyard, she saw Adfrith come out of the guesthouse, accompanied by Ulfstan. They walked quickly towards the abbess's parlour, passing close by her. Wulfrun stopped and hesitated, wanting to speak, troubled by the anxious glance that Adfrith sent her.

But Ulfstan urged the young man on, ignoring Wulfrun's pleading look. 'We must hurry. Don't keep the prince waiting.'

Adfrith bowed his head and followed the reeve.

Wulfrun turned and watched them go into the abbess's house, wondering what the prince would have to say to Adfrith.

She related the incident to Fridgyth and Cadmon that afternoon, as they sat in the wattle wind shelter on the upper pasture, watching Gode play among the calves. Now that the likelihood of the necklace being Queen Tata's had been spoken of openly, she felt no need to keep it from her friends. They listened with great concern, and sat there for a while in silence. Their quietness frightened Wulfrun more than anything. Eventually Fridgyth got up and touched Wulfrun's cheek. 'I must gather the last of my herbs,' she said quietly, and wandered away to the gardens, Gode following at her heels.

'You'd almost think Fridgyth was Gode's mother now,' Wulfrun murmured with what she knew to be unfair resentment. She sat on beside Cadmon, fretting about her mother and fearfully wondering if Irminburgh could really wish them both dead.

The cowherd could not stop his anxious gaze from wandering to the growing calves that frolicked together in the cool breeze. Then suddenly Wulfrun understood his distraction.

'The day of slaughter,' she murmured. 'The day of slaughter draws near.'

Cadmon turned to her and his face was full of pain. 'Tomorrow,' he whispered.

'So soon?' Wulfrun had been so fretful about her own problems that she had not noticed the speed with which the year was slipping away. 'Blood Month is here?'

'It is here,' Cadmon said quietly.

Wulfrun put out her hand to touch his arm. He glanced at her gratefully, though his eyes had filled with tears. Every year at this season Cadmon must bid farewell to the calves that he'd reared patiently through their early days. He'd watched them grow into strong, skittish young beasts that butted and jostled for food and sunshine.

Wulfrun tried to offer some comfort. 'They have a short life, but in your care they have a grand life.'

Cadmon nodded agreement. 'Th-that is why I do it,' he said.

'Leave the slaughtering to those who are paid for it,' she suggested. 'There's no need for you—'

But he shook his head. 'I . . . I must be with them to the end,' he said calmly.

Every time Blood Month came around Cadmon would put himself through the misery of taking each calf to the slaughtering shed. He would soothe and hold the young beast while the foul work was done by the men of the slaughtering gang; only then did he feel that his work was truly over till the spring. Wulfrun decided to neglect her

weaving and moved closer to the cowherd, pushing her arm companionably through his, so that
warmth grew where their bodies touched. They sat
there till the sun began to go down, sadly watching the calves tugging at the lush grass.

The following morning Wulfrun took her sister to
eat breakfast in the refectory as usual, and then,
leaving her in Fridgyth's care, went on to the
scriptorium. She wasn't surprised to find that Elfled
hadn't arrived yet and waited patiently, stirring the
ink carefully as Adfrith had shown her. But all
the ink was well mixed and three fine quills set out
and ready when she heard the soft sound of leather
boots. Adfrith came in, looking very solemn.

'What is it?' she asked.

'I'm not to give the princess any more lessons,'
Adfrith told her, his tone cold and formal. 'The
prince forbids it, and he has ordered his sister to
have no more to do with her Wolf Girl. Only the
Lady Irminburgh will attend her – your services
are not required.'

Wulfrun stared at him, aghast. 'Is it because my
mother is accused of treason? Oh, Adfrith . . . I
understand now why you told us to keep what we
suspected secret.'

He nodded, slipping back to his usual kind
concern. 'I was afraid for both you and your
mother,' he admitted.

Wulfrun was filled with rage. 'Does Elfled agree to this dismissal of her Wolf Girl?'

Adfrith looked away, a forlorn, defeated expression on his face. 'It is not our place to ask, I fear. Maybe we are getting off lightly; there was no more mention of treason. You are nobody's slave now, Wulfrun.'

'But Elfled was doing so well – even Sister Begu praised her work.'

The young oblate sighed and shook his head. 'This means that your lessons have to stop too: I am to help Brother Bran in the stables.'

'You . . . in the stables?'

'I don't mind.' He shrugged and looked at her with just a hint of a smile. 'I'll be happy tending the horses. You'd best go back to your weaving, Wolf Girl.'

Wulfrun turned to go, but then she stopped and grabbed his arm. 'Beware,' she warned. 'I think it was Childeric who stole our horses yesterday and hurled the lump of dogger down at us. I heard him and Bertha talking together in the dark. I know it is very surprising, but I think it was Bertha who drew that warning rune in Magpie's stall – though I have always believed that she has little love for me.'

Adfrith did not scorn her words. He bent down and gently kissed her cheek. 'I will beware,' he said. 'Goodbye, Wolf Girl – I have so much enjoyed teaching you.' With that he quietly turned and went.

Wulfrun's thoughts swung into chaos. She stood quite still in the scriptorium, staring down at the fragment of parchment that she'd been getting ready for Elfled. 'She cannot have agreed to this,' she murmured. 'Never!'

At last she bent to pick up a quill. She dipped it in the ink and with a fast flourish she wrote the word *NUMQUAM* in large letters; then she went outside to find Cadmon.

Faced with an empty pasture and an open gate she remembered again that it was the day of slaughter; Cadmon would have taken his flock down to the slaughtering sheds close to the stinking tannery in the deep folds of the valley. Even now he must be going through the torturous process of dispatching his beasts. She sat down in the empty wattle shelter and stared across the river into the distance. Seagulls swooped about her, mewing and crying; dark rainclouds rolled in from the sea. Never since the fearful day of her mother's imprisonment had she felt so terrible. 'Is it my fault again?' she murmured.

A horrible feeling of tightness had knotted itself in her throat and she wanted to cry, but her eyes remained dry. 'Sitting here will help nothing,' she growled. At last she made herself get up and go to the gardens, throwing herself vigorously into the smoky work of burning leaves.

Later she picked up her shuttle, but found a tangle in the weft two rows above. 'I'm not unpicking again,' she snarled, throwing the shuttle away. When she eventually lay down beside Gode to try to sleep, thunder started to rumble and lightning flashed. It rained heavily and water began to find its way through the worn-out thatch, making the earthen floor cold and damp, so that Wulfrun wondered whether to wake Gode and go to Fridgyth to beg shelter for them both. Then she remembered that the side gate could only be opened from the inside and she didn't think there was much chance of the watchmen letting her in through the main gate. As she searched in Cwen's chest for more rugs to keep them warm, she heard the creak of the side gate opening and the pounding of quick, light hooves. She wondered why the prince was sending men out in the middle of night – and why through the side gate? At last, in the early hours of the morning, her eyelids began to droop, but she was destined not to sleep.

'Wulfrun! Wulfrun!' Someone was calling her name, but the caller spoke so quietly that at first she thought she was dreaming and ignored it.

'Wulfrun, honey, are you there?'

Suddenly her eyes flew open in astonishment, for she knew that soft, creaky voice. Sister Begu was up in the night and calling her.

Chapter 19

woden's daughter

The feeling of being wide awake returned swiftly to Wulfrun as she opened the door. 'What is it, Sister?' she asked.

The frail nun crept in to crouch beside the fading embers in the hearth. 'Thank you for trusting me, honey,' she whispered. Wisps of grey hair strayed from her hood in disarray and she clutched her wet cloak about her, looking distraught and very fragile. 'It's Elfled – she has done a foolish thing. She has crept from her bed and taken Sea Mist and gone – I don't know where!'

'By Freya!' Wulfrun swore under her breath. 'Oh, I'm sorry, Sister, I meant no offence.'

'I might swear by that goddess myself,' Begu replied, 'if I thought it would do any good. Our princess is still Woden's daughter, it seems. I had a troubled dream that I was searching and searching for Elfled, but couldn't find her, though always I could hear her laughter. Then I heard a strange voice saying to me over and over again: "By her heritage she shall be saved." I couldn't think what it might mean, but I went to check on her and found she'd gone. I knew she was angry and distressed at her brother's orders. She did not rage or cry, but she wouldn't speak, and with Elfled that is more worrying. Her bed had not been slept in.'

'Does her brother know that she's gone?'

'No, not yet, but when he does all Woden's wild ravens will be loosed in Deira. The prince will be looking for someone to blame.'

'How could she have got out without the guards . . . ?' Wulfrun frowned, then remembered the creak of the gate and the fast horse galloping away. 'Ah . . . I think I heard her go. I should have known those fast light hooves to be Sea Mist's.'

The old nun nodded and a tear oozed from one of her rheumy eyes. 'I found Adfrith before he returned to his bed after Matins and begged for his help. He went to the stables, searching with a torch, and saw that Sea Mist's stall was empty. Fridgyth's garden is trampled with hoofprints and the side gate was hanging open. I crept through it and came to you. Can you think where she might have gone?'

Wulfrun thought hard, but shook her head. 'I can imagine her riding off in fury – but where to I cannot say.'

'Adfrith is in the stables, saddling his horse. I

should not ask you to go with him, Wulfrun – but if there is a chance of bringing her back before anyone knows, it might save a great deal of trouble, and you are the one person I think she might listen to.'

Wulfrun glanced down at Gode, who murmured and wriggled in her sleep. 'Will you see my sister safe into Fridgyth's care?' she asked.

'Of course,' Begu answered. 'Do not wake her now. I will sit by your fire and take her to Fridgyth as soon as she wakes; then I shall return to the abbess's house and pretend that Elfled is ill to give you as much time as I can.'

'Won't Irminburgh see that she is gone?'

Begu raised her wispy eyebrows. 'She never rises early. You have at least till midday before she discovers that her charge is missing. The problem is guessing which way you should go to look for her.'

Suddenly a very frightening idea of where Elfled might have gone crossed Wulfrun's mind. She remembered the princess's sudden interest in the mother who had given her away as a baby; but Queen Ianfleda resided in Bamburgh, far away to the north. That was where the abbess herself had gone in the royal galley. She said nothing to Sister Begu and pushed that thought quickly to the back of her mind. 'Uskdale?' she murmured. 'Or perhaps Fisherstead – she revelled in the kindness shown to her there.'

Begu nodded. 'Go in by the side gate and you'll find Adfrith in the stables.'

Wulfrun struggled into the riding breeches that Adfrith had given her and fastened her mother's girdle around her waist. She took the warm cloak that had been a gift from Irminburgh; though the very sight of it made her angry now, she knew she must be practical and wrapped it around her shoulders. She hesitated as she moved to the door, then bent to kiss the nun's cheek. 'We will do our best to find our unhappy princess,' she said.

Begu's mouth trembled. 'I know you will,' she said. 'That I can see clear.'

Wulfrun stumbled through the darkness that covered Fridgyth's trampled garden, heading for the faint light of a torch inside the stables. When she got there she saw that Adfrith had saddled Midnight and Cadmon was leading Magpie out of her stall all rigged and ready.

Adfrith looked up as Magpie caught Wulfrun's scent and tossed her head, neighing a gentle greeting. He had no time for formality now. 'You do not have to do this, Wulfrun.' He spoke quietly, though the stable lads lay heavily asleep in their cubicles after a night in the mead hall. 'Cadmon will come with me.'

'I must go with you,' Wulfrun insisted, and suddenly she knew that that was true. She could not sit here feeling desperate; she must take some kind of action. She also knew that it was not because Elfled was the King of Northumbria's daughter that she must go, nor because they'd all be in grave trouble if they couldn't find her. 'If it were Gode,' she said, 'I'd go at once to search for her, and it's just the same with Elfled.'

Cadmon gave her Magpie's reins. 'W-we knew you would,' he said. 'W-we'll all go together.'

He turned to lead Sea Coal out of the next stall, already saddled and bridled. Wulfrun smiled at his choice. 'Yes,' she said. 'If anyone can find Sea Mist it will be her brother. I'm glad you are coming too.' She always felt safe with Cadmon, and at least he would be forced to think of something other than the terrible day of slaughter that he'd endured.

'The question is where to head for?' Adfrith looked perplexed.

'Fisherstead – where else does she know? I do not think she'd go to Uskdale,' Wulfrun said.

'No indeed,' Adfrith agreed with a smile. 'A night in the forest was not to her taste. Fisherstead seems as good a place to start as any.' He stuck a sheathed seax into his belt and covered it with the dull brown monastic cloak that he wore. 'Come,' he said. 'We must go if we are to have a chance of catching our young runaway.'

They led their horses across the vegetable garden and out through the side gate. The first rays of morning light appeared in the east as they mounted and trotted down the steep path towards the ford. It was only as they neared the river that Wulfrun turned to Adfrith in panic.

'The tide is coming in, and fast! We are too late to cross!'

In the murky dawn light they could see the sea flooding in through the harbour and up the valley, drawn by the power of the autumn moon. Water was swirling across the ford.

Adfrith moved, grim-faced, into the lead, still heading towards the river crossing. 'Remember,' he called back to her. 'Cling on tight. Grip with your thighs – it's all in the legs.'

'Can we do it?' Terrified, Wulfrun turned to Cadmon.

He nodded. 'W-we must.'

As they reached the water, Cadmon held his mount back a little, indicating that Wulfrun should go ahead and he would bring up the rear. She moved gratefully in between the two men, understanding quickly why they must risk this. If they went the long way round they would waste so much time that they'd have little chance of catching up with Elfled. Wulfrun swallowed hard and ploughed on into the water; riding Magpie along a steady track was one thing, but urging her into a deep, fast-moving river was quite another.

'Forward,' she muttered, gritting her teeth.

Magpie needed little urging: the sturdy mare

followed Midnight into the ford as water washed about the gelding's haunches. Wulfrun gripped with her legs, trying not to mind the coldness of the water as it crept up to her knees, all the time keeping her eyes on the dark cloaked shape of Adfrith's back. Midnight seemed to skitter to the side, but then moved forward with a lurching roll, his rider adjusting his weight a little to keep his seat. Magpie went on, tossing her head and rolling her eyes, but never wavering from the watery path she took. Wulfrun dared not turn her head to see how Cadmon fared.

The water was up to her thighs, and suddenly she felt the same sideways motion, countered with a gentle lift and dip that told her Magpie was swimming. 'Grip tight!' she muttered as freezing water flooded all around her legs; but quickly the mare found her feet again. They were through the deepest part and into shallower water. Wulfrun sank forwards onto Magpie's neck, overwhelmed with relief. 'I love you,' she whispered in her ear. 'You are the best horse in the world.'

Adfrith clattered out of the water ahead of them, foam spraying from Midnight's haunches. At last Wulfrun felt brave enough to turn her head and see how Cadmon fared. He followed on Sea Coal's back, a smile of triumph on his face; his poor lost calves forgotten for the moment.

'This will work in our favour,' Adfrith said. He

brought Midnight to a standstill while he squeezed water out of his cloak. 'They will not be able to send anyone after us that way; the ford will be impassable now until noon.'

'I'm glad you can be so cheerful about such a soaking,' Wulfrun told him with a wry smile as she did her best to wring out her own wet skirt and cloak.

The sun rose behind the now distant watch-tower, bathing the pathway ahead of them in pink light. Their mounts shook themselves. A bubble of excitement warmed Wulfrun's stomach as the horses snorted and galloped on towards Fisherstead.

They made good speed and struggled down the steep cliff path into the village just as the inhabitants were stirring. Wulfrun went straight to Emma's hut, but the fisherwoman could only stare at her damp riding breeches and tunic, amazed that anyone would think the King of Northumbria's daughter might come to Fisherstead seeking shelter.

'I beg you keep this quiet,' Wulfrun asked.

Emma nodded but she clearly thought that Wulfrun had gone quite mad. They swiftly searched the village, but the people only seemed astonished that a young oblate and two abbey servants should be there at all so early in the morning. The three urged their horses back up the steep slope, dismayed that their hunch had proved so wrong, and stopped at the edge of the heather moors, uncertain where to go next.

'Should we try Uskdale?' Wulfrun asked.

Adfrith frowned. 'I would not have thought she'd go there, but where else?'

The troubling idea that Wulfrun had pushed to the back of her mind came creeping to the fore again. 'I wonder . . .' she murmured. Then she looked up and saw in the distance a rough-hewn stone cross. 'What is that?' she asked.

Adfrith and Cadmon both turned to look where she pointed.

'That is one of the old marker stones,' said Adfrith. 'They were set up by King Edwin to guide travellers across the heather moors.'

'Elfled's heritage,' she murmured. '*Her heritage will keep her safe.*' The words of Begu's dream had come at once into her mind. King Edwin's marker stones must be Elfled's heritage.

'She might well have seen that stone and headed towards it.' She pointed ahead.

'Do you think so?' Adfrith asked uncertainly.

'We have nothing better to help us,' Wulfrun said. There was no time to explain properly, and like everyone else Adfrith might think Begu's dreams very suspect.

But he bowed his head to acknowledge that they didn't have any better clues to follow and turned

Midnight towards the cross. They rode on, gaining speed, and as they drew close they saw that a copse of oak trees lay just beyond the marker stone. A horse neighed in the distance and Sea Coal lifted his head and answered it at once, rearing a little and pulling in the direction of the sound.

Cadmon turned to Adfrith. 'Beast to beast, brother calls to s-sister,' he said, soothingly stroking Sea Coal's rump.

Adfrith stared for a moment, then picked up his meaning. 'You think it is Sea Mist over there in the copse. Let's hope our princess may not be far away.'

They cantered towards the trees and were quickly rewarded by another horse greeting, but when Sea Mist appeared they saw that she was riderless and dragging her reins. She came willingly to them and Cadmon dismounted and caught the mare, fastening her reins to the pommel of his saddle. They looked at each other with dismay, but then a small bedraggled figure emerged from the bushes, wrapped in a long cloak.

'I did not tell you to follow me.' Elfled spoke as imperiously as ever.

Wulfrun swung down from Magpie's back and went straight to the princess, seeing that despite her brave words the young girl clutched her cloak tightly about her as though she were very cold. There were traces of tears on her cheeks.

'Are you wet?' Wulfrun asked, fearing that the princess had been soaked crossing the river just as they had.

'Wet? No – why should I be? I waited till the rain had stopped; I'm not stupid.'

'Are you cold?'

Elfled shook her head. 'I have my cloak and my long fur-lined boots.'

'Come back with us, Princess.' Wulfrun tried to make her voice as gentle and reassuring as she could.

'I cannot go back.' Elfled's voice wavered again now.

Wulfrun was prepared for this and had her argument ready. 'If we turn back now we can have you in Whitby by noon and none shall be the wiser.'

'No,' Elfled repeated seriously, her eyes wide with meaning. 'I cannot go back.' Slowly she released the grip on her cloak, and with a little self-conscious gesture she opened her arms to reveal that round her slim childlike shoulders she was wearing the heavy gold and garnet necklace decorated with the tiny golden sparrow.

'It is the true necklace,' she said. 'Not that copied thing that Irminburgh had made and pretended was the one Cwen stole.'

'You took it from her?'

'I did,' she said, her voice strong with a sense of right and justice. 'I took it from her chamber, where she was supposed to be sleeping, though her bed was empty. I have more right to it than she.'

'And what did you mean to do with it?'

But Wulfrun knew already what the answer would be; she had known ever since Sister Begu woke her in the night.

Elfled spoke with confidence and determination. 'I mean to take it to my mother, the Queen of Northumbria, who lives in the fortress of Bamburgh.'

Chapter 20

hunting

They stood looking at her, trying to take in what she'd said. A journey to Bamburgh seemed an impossible task. Elfled spoke again, but this time the mature tone had fled, though she struggled to keep her dignity. 'Though I was born at Bamburgh – it seems that now I cannot remember the way.' Her voice was suddenly child-like and shrill.

Wulfrun simply opened her arms and Elfled's face crumpled as she came to her. Adfrith and Cadmon watched quietly as their princess cried into Wulfrun's neck.

'Hush!' Wulfrun soothed. 'We are here to help.'

'I am so glad you've come,' Elfled howled.

When at last they pulled apart Adfrith moved to speak. 'Princess,' he said, 'there is still no great harm done. We can return to Whitby before noon and I'm sure you could slip the necklace back in place or even admit to Lady Irminburgh that you borrowed it – perhaps to admire it. She must forgive you for that.'

'No.' Elfled shook her head and wiped her eyes with the back of her hand. 'There is something else that I must show you. Come with me, Monkman – leave the horses here.' She snatched Adfrith's sleeve and pulled him along with her, dragging him back towards the copse. They left the horses tied together and followed. Elfled put a finger to her lips to warn them all to be silent.

They glanced at each other anxiously, but obediently bent down when she signalled to them. They crept through the copse of tall trees and out onto the other side, where thick gorse grew. As they emerged, Elfled had no more need to warn them, for at once they understood her concern. Just below the dip of the hill was a wide expanse of rough scrubland, bordered on the far side by the heather moors, and on it an encampment of warriors' tents.

They stared, open-mouthed, then moved quickly back behind the gorse. For a terrible moment Wulfrun thought of Nelda and Fridgyth's tales of the merciless raids of King Penda. Was it possible that one of his sons had returned to punish the Deirans again? But through the prickling gorse she could see battle standards set up before some of the tents. She recognized them only too well – gold-painted orbs topped by the shape of a sparrow in flight – while some of the men who wandered sleepily from the tents were dressed in the green livery of Prince Ecfrid's guards. Though it was still early in the morning, they were greeting newcomers who arrived on horseback armed with spears and seaxes and swords.

Wulfrun looked to Adfrith for help, but all he could do was frown and bite his lips. At last he gestured to them all to follow him back into the copse.

'What can this mean?' Wulfrun gasped. 'Are they Ecfrid's men? But there are so many of them.'

Adfrith shook his head. 'I do not like this at all. They seem to be Ecfrid's men, but this is a war band and growing fast. What does the prince need a war band for?'

'T-trouble,' Cadmon said.

'It's something to do with Irminburgh,' Elfled insisted. 'It must be. First she took the necklace and claimed it as her own; now this. She has cast a spell on Ecfrid; he would not dare to gather an army on his own. He was kind and funny until Irminburgh started ordering him about. We cannot just go back to Whitby and forget this, can we?'

'No, Princess,' Adfrith agreed. 'You are right. This is too serious. Can Ecfrid really plan to claim the throne of Deira and marry Irminburgh? Might they claim the throne of Deira together?'

Wulfrun remembered how Fridgyth had warned

that Irminburgh could cause a lot of trouble if she was not kept sweet. 'I think they might. Fridgyth says there are many who resent Alchfrid and call him the Stranger.'

Elfled grasped the heavy jewels that still gleamed about her thin neck. 'But Ecfrid would not fight his own half-brother,' she said. 'Surely he would not do that.'

Wulfrun spoke with terrible certainty. 'As you say, Princess, Irminburgh has him under her spell. I think she means to use the necklace to support her claim to Deira. Did she not say only last night that the necklace proved her bloodlink to Edwin?'

'Yes, she did,' Elfled confirmed. 'Though it is all lies – that necklace was never hers.'

Adfrith knitted his brows in thought. 'King Oswy would not sit by and allow them to do this. He has placed Alchfrid on the throne of Deira.'

'Th-they will set us all s-slaughtering each other again,' Cadmon broke in fearfully. 'It will be th-the end of peace.'

Adfrith put a soothing hand on the cowherd's shoulder. 'Perhaps we can prevent it. If we go with the princess and see her safe to Bamburgh, then both the abbess and the king will be warned of this gathering war band. They are not yet ready to strike, I think.'

Wulfrun's heart began beating very fast at this suggestion. Perhaps she shouldn't be thinking of her mother at this moment, when the whole country might erupt into violence – but if they could get to Bamburgh she might also beseech the abbess to set her mother free.

'I would like you to come with me,' Elfled begged, looking from one to the other. This was no high-handed command, but a heartfelt plea.

'Never been far from Whitby.' Cadmon looked worried.

'I will look after you.' Elfled turned a charming smile on him.

Adfrith and Wulfrun glanced at each other uncertainly. 'Either way there is danger,' he said. 'Either way we three are like to be blamed.'

'I will not let you be blamed,' Elfled insisted.

Wulfrun hesitated, thinking of Gode, who would not know why her sister had deserted her, but at the same time she knew she could trust both Fridgyth and Begu to see that the little one was safe. There seemed to be nothing she could do for her mother by going back – she must trust to Ulfstan's sense of justice in that, just as she had all along.

Adfrith saw her confusion and suddenly raised an amused eyebrow. 'What do you say, my fierce Wolf Girl?'

Wulfrun loved the way he said 'my' Wolf Girl and she answered him with a wry smile. 'You said the princess should see her father's kingdom – so let us show it to her. But one thing, Princess: you must put away that precious necklace. It will certainly bring us trouble if we are stopped.'

Elfled allowed them to pack the necklace into Adfrith's strong leather pouch.

'Very well.' Adfrith took a deep breath and closed his eyes for a moment in thought. 'The next question is: which is the best route to take? The main track lies straight ahead through that great gathering, but we must keep well away from them. If we stay close to the coast we can go from one small fishing village to the next, using the small tracks. If we keep in sight of the sea, then eventually I believe we'll reach the great strong-hold on the rock. I know that it stands high, facing across the sea towards the island of Bishop Aidan.'

Wulfrun looked at him suspiciously. 'You have never been to Bamburgh, have you?'

'No,' Adfrith admitted. 'But I have always wanted to go and I long to see Bishop Aidan's island too.'

'We set out on a journey and none of us know the way.' Wulfrun suddenly felt she wanted to laugh like a wild dog.

'There c-could be w-worse things,' Cadmon said sadly. 'Much worse.'

'We go to find my birthplace,' Elfled reminded them. 'I cannot remember it, but I was born at

Bamburgh and I believe I shall know it when I see it.'

'C-come, Princess.' Cadmon glanced anxiously in the direction of Ecfrid's men. 'If we are going w-we should go fast.' He helped Elfled to mount Sea Mist again, gentling the beast as she swung into the saddle.

Adfrith picked up his sense of urgency and leaped up onto Midnight's back. 'Cadmon's right: your brother may send men after us. Our warning must be delivered soon or it will come too late.'

They headed back towards Fisherstead, but instead of going down the bank, this time they set off northwest, over Boulby Head, the huge cliff that stood out like a great green whale into the sea. They rode fast all morning, for Adfrith was filled with an urgent desire to get away from Ecfrid's camp of warriors. By noon they were riding downhill again into a valley where a beck ran through a cleft and out to the sea. The fisher huts were poor, ramshackle things built clinging to the craggy cliff-side.

'I am hungry and thirsty,' Elfled cried, bringing Sea Mist to a halt beside a stone gathering trough that caught water from a small spring. 'We have to stop to eat and drink.' She flashed a determined look at Adfrith.

He reined in Midnight, his face tense with worry again, his hand griping the handle of his seax. 'The problem of food has been troubling me, Princess. We set off to look for you believing we'd be back at Whitby for breakfast: I brought a weapon, but no food or money or goods to exchange for food.'

Wulfrun gave him a sharp, exasperated glance.

'Will we have to pay for food?' Elfled was astonished. 'At Fisherstead they gave me crabmeat!'

Wulfrun reminded herself that both Adfrith and the princess had lived in the monastery almost all their lives. Meals had been provided and Elfled must never have known hunger before this moment.

'At Fisherstead they knew you were their princess,' Adfrith reminded her. 'You were their honoured guest. If we announce you here as the King of Northumbria's daughter, I fear your brother will get wind of what we do. At least we can drink at this trough. It must be one of those set up by your grandfather, King Edwin. See here – this little iron ring set in a pole once bore a cup on a chain. Edwin had them put up beside the tracks so that everyone could drink.'

'Where is the cup now?' Elfled dismounted, more interested in satisfying her needs.

'They did not survive Penda's raids,' said Adfrith. 'Now we must make our hands into a cup as people did before your grandfather's reign.'

Wulfrun smiled: was this not Elfled's heritage again keeping her safe? It boded well.

They all slaked their thirst, but Elfled wasn't satisfied. 'My stomach groans for food,' she moaned. 'I cannot part with the necklace but I have other jewels to sell.' She pulled a fine gold ring from one of her fingers.

Wulfrun shook her head. 'Princess . . . that ring would buy bread for a year for one of these fishing families; they'd know at once that royalty had passed this way.'

As she spoke the words, a sharp understanding came to her of why Cwen could never have sold the garnet necklace, even though it might have been the saving of Sebbi. They let their horses graze for a while, wondering what to do. Wulfrun fingered her mother's precious belt of tools; it was a great sacrifice but one she'd just have to make.

'I have a girdle full of work tools,' she said. 'One or two of them will buy us food – and selling tools will cause little stir.'

Adfrith watched her with a feeling of helpless shame as she unhooked the sharp wool shears and tweezers from her girdle. He fingered the gleaming jet cross around his neck that marked him as an oblate and then the seax that swung from his belt, but he knew that selling his seax might put them all in grave danger.

'Wolf Girl, you cannot,' Elfled cried. 'How will you slice and trim your wool?'

Wulfrun answered her in a calm, businesslike

manner. 'Princess . . . if we ever get to Bamburgh and manage to avoid punishment for kidnapping the King of Northumbria's daughter, then I shall expect a fair recompense from you.'

Elfled stared at her, trying to understand. 'Yes . . . of course,' she managed. 'Recompense – I promise it. That's if they will believe me,' she added with a small tremor in her voice.

'Princess, they will,' Adfrith said, his courage returning. 'We should have known the Wolf Girl would not let us down.'

Wulfrun left Magpie in their care and went marching down into the village, taking only Cadmon with her, each of them carrying an empty saddle-bag. They found the people there living in even more severe poverty than at Fisherstead, but the smell of freshly baked bread drifted over the fences and ditches and every dwelling reeked of fish. Wulfrun asked her the way to the webster's hut and offered the woman her sharp shears in return for smoked fish and bread.

'Bread? How many for?' the woman asked, eyeing them both with suspicion.

Wulfrun swallowed hard. 'Ten,' she said. 'And they're big hungry lads.'

'Aye . . . they are,' Cadmon backed her up. 'S-slaughtering lads,' he added with feeling. 'Travelling fast – got a lot of work on.'

The woman glanced nervously about as though they might be hiding around the corner. Such gangs might well be passing on the cliff paths at this time of year. She took the shears and tried them, slicing a tuft of straying wool from the work on her hanging loom.

'You'll never find better shears,' said Wulfrun.

The woman made no reply, but they could see that she was impressed with their strength and sharpness and she called from her doorstep to the bakewife across the way. 'Ten flat loaves and quick about it!'

Cadmon and Wulfrun exchanged a quick smile.

The saddlebags were soon filled with bread, six smoked herrings, a pot of boiled crabmeat and two smoked mackerel.

'Can we have some crab claws – for the lads like to suck claws?' Wulfrun asked, seeing that they'd been boiling crabs that day and remembering Elfled's pleasure at Fisherstead. 'And some of those oats,' she said, thinking of the horses.

The webster looked affronted for a moment and Wulfrun feared she'd gone too far. 'You'll never get the chance again of a better pair of shears,' she insisted. 'And here's tweezers too.'

The webster added the oats.

Wulfrun and Cadmon heaved the saddlebags, now heavy with goods, onto their shoulders. It would be a hard struggle back up the hill, but they were pleased with what they'd got; this haul should last them that day and the next.

Elfled greeted them with delight. 'My Wolf Girl's been a-hunting . . . a-hunting,' she sang with delight, as Wulfrun handed her a pair of good-sized crab claws.

Chapter 21

Riddles

Only Cadmon sighed as they sat down to eat and they looked at him with sympathy, understanding that despite their success at bartering, harsh memories of the day before had crept back into his mind.

'What scents the air and grows in a corner, covered with cloth?' Elfled asked him.

Cadmon managed to smile at her and pretended that he didn't know the answer. 'Sc-scents the air? It must be a flower, Princess.'

Elfled crowed with delight, waving a hunk of bread at him. 'Covered with a cloth . . . it is bread set in a corner to rise! Now you must eat it.'

Cadmon took the proffered bread obediently and they all ate well. When they'd finished they rode on, still following the small tracks that linked village to village, staying high up on the cliffs whenever possible and keeping away from the bigger settlements and farms. After noon they had to turn away from the sea and head inland as a great wide river mouth opened up before them.

'What river is this?' Elfled asked.

'I think it is called the Tees,' Adfrith told her. He pressed his lips together in worry again. 'I believe you have to travel a good way inland to find the crossing place. 'And the tide is going to be against us again, as it was when we left Whitby. We should ride fast to find the ford before the water makes it impassable.'

'Ride on, Monkman,' was all that Elfled said.

They found a river crossing that was deep but not yet fully flooded. Wulfrun approached it with much less fear than she had early that morning. She was ready for the lift and lurch as Magpie lost her footing and swam, for the river Tees was considerably wider than the Usk. Once on the further bank they rode fast to dry and warm themselves, but as the sun sank they felt the cold and dampness of their clothing. They came near to the coast again and saw in the distance, dark against a pink sunset, a large, rounded hammerhead of land curving out into the sea. It almost made an island, with only a stubby neck linking the headland to the coast. A fishing village had grown up around the inner edge of the natural harbour that was formed by the curve of the land. Above it on the blustery headland stood two high thatched halls, each one bearing a large wooden cross above the gable where a lord might set his own symbol.

Elfled slowed up. 'What is this place?' she asked. 'Those churches and the little huts that surround them put me in mind of Whitby.'

Adfrith's lips moved in wonder. 'We have travelled far,' he said. 'Much further than I ever thought possible in one day. This must be the monastery of Hartlepool.'

Elfled had another reason to stare when she heard that name. 'I have been here before,' she whispered. 'This is where they sent me as a baby when I was given away to God. Mother Hild was abbess of this place and this is where she brought me.'

'That's right,' Adfrith agreed.

'Mother Hild is still abbess in charge of this place.' Elfled's eyes lit up. 'The monks and nuns will give us warm beds and a good supper, when they know who we are.'

No answer came from any of her companions and she quickly understood their silence. 'Ah no,' she said. 'I see that we cannot do that. The nuns would keep me here; they'd think it their duty to see that I was safe.'

Still there was no reply; then Adfrith spoke. 'Perhaps we would be wise to take you to Hartlepool Abbey, Princess. We could leave you there in safety, while we travel on to Bamburgh to speak to the king.'

'No.' Her voice was firm at first, then rose in panic. 'You will not do that – they do not know me there. I want to give the necklace to Queen Ianfleda – I must give it to her myself.'

Adfrith sighed but said nothing, clearly uncertain where his duty lay.

'Well, where else can we sleep?' Elfled's voice was now plaintive with fatigue.

'A c-cowherd's shelter, just a way back,' Cadmon said. 'No one's there – calves all gone.'

'I saw it too,' Wulfrun added. 'We have plenty of food and our cloaks to keep us warm.' She herself was bone weary and hungry and she knew that Elfled must be too.

'Yes,' Adfrith agreed at last. 'The horses must rest and graze; they have carried us much further than I ever thought possible.'

They turned back towards the empty shelter and found dry straw inside. They ate until they were full and then Adfrith and Cadmon gave their cloaks to Wulfrun to make a bed for Elfled in the most sheltered corner.

Elfled yawned. 'Tell me a riddle,' she begged.

They racked their brains, but nothing would come, until at last Cadmon spoke in a soft, sad voice. 'Perfect, without s-stain, I danced in the sun beside my dam. I never knew the chill of winter frosts, for I saw no more than three seasons. They bled me till my life had gone; a stainless sacrifice.

They shaved off all my hair and scraped my skin; they stretched my p-pelt to dry.'

Cadmon's voice broke and he stopped. They'd listened intently, understanding only too well what the answer to the riddle was.

Elfled sighed. 'That is clever, but it is too sad,' she said. 'The answer is a vellum calf.'

They sat in solemn silence for a moment, but then Adfrith leaned forward and touched Cadmon's arm. 'But there should be a second part to your riddle,' he said. 'They cut my skin, straight as an arrow flies. Then a bird's feather moved over my surfaces, leaving marks that have meaning. A man bound me together with my brothers and sisters and adorned us with gold. Now they handle us with deep respect; they speak of us in soft tones and call us precious. In our golden binding we will live for ever.'

Cadmon looked up at Adfrith. 'Y-yes,' he agreed. 'A little part of my calves will live for ever in your gilded books. Thank you for that.'

'That was a good riddle,' Elfled said, sighing again, this time with satisfaction. 'With a happy ending. Now I will sleep.' She got up, swaying on her feet, and staggered towards the piled-up straw that Wulfrun had prepared for her. 'Sleep beside me,' she begged.

'If that's what you want,' Wulfrun agreed.

'Where are they going to sleep?' She turned her head wearily to the two men.

'We will sleep outside and keep guard,' Adfrith answered at once.

'No.' Wulfrun shook her head. 'Without your cloaks you will freeze. Sleep over there on the far side,' she insisted. 'And take my cloak to cover you both.'

Adfrith hesitated. 'It would not be right,' he said.

'I order you – do as my Wolf Girl says.' A small sleepy voice spoke up from the corner.

'Very well, Princess,' Adfrith agreed at last.

Wolves howled in the distance, but Elfled murmured sleepily, 'I'm not afraid of them – I have a Wolf Girl at my side.'

When they woke in the early morning, they found that Cadmon had quietly gone outside and was keeping watch, Adfrith's seax in his hand. They struggled up from their makeshift beds and walked stiffly about, easing their shoulders and backs until they found a water trough to wash in as best they could. As the first gleams of the sun lit Hartlepool and the headland in the distance, they ate again.

'Hard for y-you, Princess,' Cadmon murmured as Wulfrun tried to drag her comb through Elfled's wild, untidy hair.

But Elfled shook her head vigorously, making Wulfrun's work more difficult. 'I am enjoying myself,' she said, her mouth full of cold smoked mackerel. 'This food tastes better than any I've ever had and I feel alive – alive. What has no feet and still moves fast? What has no hands, but makes a meal? What gleams silver like the stars, but gives no light?'

'Has no feet and still moves fast?' Wulfrun frowned in thought.

Cadmon and Adfrith shook their heads.

'Ah!' Elfled groaned at their stupidity. 'It is hanged and burned only to be eaten. That must make it easy for you.'

Wulfrun shuddered at those words, but Cadmon had the answer. 'M-mackerel,' he said. 'No feet . . . but still moves fast and gleams silver like the stars. We eat it smoked.'

'Well done.' Elfled applauded him.

They smiled, relieved that she seemed to be finding some pleasure in what they knew to be a most dangerous undertaking. Adfrith said that they must set off again if they were to have any chance of achieving their aim. They avoided Hartlepool monastery, skirting the settlement and heading northwest once more beside the sea. They rode all through the morning along a flat, sandy shore edged with grassy dunes, though they saw higher hills inland. They didn't stop until they arrived at another wide river that Adfrith thought must be the Tyne, the edges populated with small farms and fishing hamlets. They feared they must waste more time heading inland, but discovered that the benevolent son of the local lord had set up a ferry to carry both people and horses across.

'Blessings on him,' Adfrith said as they were carried across on a flat punt.

'Aye, there's many round here as bless that young man,' the ferryman told them. 'He's of your religion,' he said, observing Adfrith's monkish robes and cross. 'We call him the bishop, though he's not even a monk. He will be a bishop one day; we have no doubt of it.'

Adfrith's face was alert at once. 'I think I've heard of him. He has travelled across the sea and journeyed through many countries. I would like to do that . . .' His voice trailed off.

Wulfrun felt a small crumb of resentment grow inside her against this bishop who was not a bishop: at the mention of him Adfrith's face had grown happy and eager; but she pushed such unjust thoughts away and tried to remind herself that if it hadn't been for him they'd be riding far inland to cross the river Tyne. Her gratitude was even greater when the ferryman warned them that a warrior band had been riding along the bigger tracks questioning travellers and dealing roughly with them if they did not give the replies they wanted.

'We must find more food tonight,' Adfrith said with a frown.

'B-best get on then.' Cadmon too was tense. 'Are we in Bernicia now?'

'Indeed we are,' Adfrith agreed.

They said no more but rode on fast, stopping only for a small meal, their supply of food almost gone.

They continued through the flat Bernician countryside, past beaches with wide sweeps of pale golden sand, always edged with dunes, until they came at last to a winding river that cut through more flat, marshy land and flowed out into the sea. A small town had grown up there on a low headland. A round, flat-topped green island could be seen in the distance.

'An island,' Elfled sang with glee, pointing ahead. 'We are here, I think. Bamburgh has an island near to it; I remember from what Mother Hild told me.'

Adfrith stared where she pointed, but shook his head. 'It cannot be,' he said. 'We could not have come that far. Bishop Aidan first built his small church and huts from wattle and mud, then Bishop Finan raised a bigger wooden church in its place. This island has nothing on it at all.'

'Perhaps we're not close enough to see,' Elfled insisted.

Wulfrun forced her to be practical. 'It cannot be, Princess. If your father's stronghold is close to the island, then where is this stronghold?'

Elfled scanned the horizon ahead of them. 'Not here,' she admitted, disappointed. 'But that is a lovely island, and if I were in charge of monks and nuns I'd build a fine monastery there.'

'Maybe one day you will get your wish, Princess.' Adfrith smiled tolerantly. 'But now we must find more food, then keep going towards Bamburgh – and fast.'

Wulfrun and Cadmon went into the small town to see if they could barter goods for food once more. This time Wulfrun had been forced to exchange her mother's girdle, with its remaining tools and precious comb, as none had the value of the shears. They came back with fresh bread, herrings, goats' cheese and some hard-boiled seabirds' eggs.

They fell on the feast and ate their fill. 'That island is named for the river,' Wulfrun told Elfled. 'Coquet Isle. There's nothing on it but grass and screaming gulls, and that's where these eggs came from. The children paddle there in their skiffs and steal gulls' eggs.'

'I love it,' Elfled said, gazing happily at the small shape in the distance.

'*An emerald jewel set in silver.*' Cadmon sang the words softly, making them all smile with pleasure. '*A centre of peace, this island floats in the ocean, while seabirds soar and swoop around it, screaming their wild music.*'

'Cadmon understands.' Elfled spoke with satisfaction. 'He should be a scop and sing in the mead hall.'

Cadmon shook his head shyly.

Wulfrun smiled: many a time she'd said the same thing to him, but she knew that Cadmon always crept away from the herdsmen's mead hall whenever he saw the lyre being passed around. He'd go early to his bed and settle to sleep alongside the beasts rather than risk the mocking laughter that might come should he stumble in his song. Cadmon could only find beautiful words for his friends and feared to lift his mellow voice to entertain a larger gathering.

Elfled was weary and begged them to let her sleep close to the river Coquet, but Adfrith insisted that they ride on until the sun had gone. 'We must sleep where we can,' he warned. 'You may not be comfortable, Princess, but the closer we get to Bamburgh, the safer we shall be.'

'My brother's men would never dare harm me,' she said.

Adfrith made no response.

His silence made Wulfrun wonder what would happen if they were to be caught by Ecfrid's men. Elfled might come out of it safely enough, restored to her brother and berated a little; but a young oblate, a goose girl and a cowherd could disappear without trace and none would demand justice in their name.

'Ride a little further, Princess,' she urged gently.

Elfled turned a white and weary face to her. 'Very well,' she agreed.

Cadmon helped her onto Sea Mist's back and they rode on northwards as the sun moved down towards the rolling hills. They came in sight of yet another river mouth, with a small settlement on the far bank, just as the last gleams of light were sinking into the sea. They saw with relief that though the tide was coming in, the estuary was shallow. It seemed they could cross without fear.

'What river is this?' Wulfrun asked. Adfrith seemed to carry a map of all the lands inside his head.

'I think it must be the Aln,' he told her, 'if my memory serves me right.'

'Your memory has served us well,' Wulfrun replied warmly. 'We should stop here and rest now. The princess cannot go further, and who knows what tomorrow may bring?'

Adfrith put his hand on her arm in gratitude for her support. 'Let us cross this river first, while the tide is out, then I think we may come to Bamburgh in the morning.'

So they rode fast onto the fine white sands, gleaming pink as the sun went down. Elfled urged Sea Mist out in front, full of confidence, but the lively little mare slowed down abruptly, tossing her head and neighing.

'Onwards! Onwards!' Elfled ordered, kicking her heels into her horse's sides and slapping her rump hard.

'No . . . n-no,' Cadmon cried. 'S-sinking sands!'

Chapter 22

begu's magic

Then Wulfrun saw that Cadmon was right. Sea Mist was sinking up to her delicate fetlocks with each step that she took.

'Come back!' Wulfrun howled.

'Dear Christ!' Adfrith muttered.

All three dropped down from their horses and let their beasts go free to follow their own instincts. Elfled turned to them with terror on her face, only now understanding the danger. She swung her leg over the pommel of her saddle and prepared to jump down.

'No!' Wulfrun bellowed. 'Stay there! Let Sea Mist carry you back to us.'

But it was too late; Elfled had leaped down onto the sand. Released from her load, the little mare managed to struggle back, but now her mistress was sinking fast. As they strode grimly on towards her, they too felt the powerful suction beneath their feet. Elfled took a step in their direction but fell full length, grasping wildly at the sand. 'Help me – help me!' she screamed.

'Stay still!' Wulfrun barked out her order, though her own feet were sinking now and her heart thundering. 'Be still and quiet,' she added more gently.

Adfrith and Cadmon tore the cloaks from their backs and threw them down onto the sand in front of them. They crawled forward on hands and knees, then on their bellies, as Wulfrun dropped full length beside them.

They could see Elfled's white face in the gathering dusk. 'Be brave.' Wulfrun spoke softly to her now, keeping her voice low and steady. 'Be brave and trust us – we will not leave you.'

Adfrith stretched and strained, but he too began to sink, his cloak vanishing beneath him. Elfled tried so hard to obey Wulfrun's order; she did not struggle or scream any more, but they could hear her small, pathetic groans and whimpers. Wulfrun saw that they needed something to stretch out to her and turned to the seax that Adfrith still had tucked through his belt. 'Keep still,' she ordered him, as she eased it from its sheath. She turned the handle towards Elfled, taking the sharp blade into her own hands.

'Now, Princess – you must reach out to us,' Wulfrun cried. 'Grab it!'

'No!' Adfrith was horror-struck when he saw

what she was doing. 'Your hands will be sliced!'

'Can't . . . can't,' Elfled wailed.

Adfrith quickly loosed his belt and threw it out towards the struggling child. The pouch that contained the garnet necklace fell onto the sand and was at once half buried. Wulfrun saw it happening, let go the seax blade with one hand and lunged at the gleaming jewelled tail. The pouch was lost, but Wulfrun managed to snatch the necklace with bloody fingers.

'By her heritage she shall be saved,' she gasped, her mind working like lightning. Begu's dreams were proving to be powerful magic; without hesitation Wulfrun flung the necklace towards the fast sinking princess, keeping tight hold of her end of it. 'Elfled – come get it!' she yelled. 'Your mother's jewels!'

As soon as her eyes lighted on the necklace, Elfled stopped wailing, gritted her teeth and reached out towards it. 'I will . . . take it to my mother,' she growled. 'I will.' She strained for the seax handle with one hand and Adfrith's belt with the other, but her eyes never left the sand-covered garnets set in gold.

'We've got you,' Wulfrun cried. 'Hold tight!'

Cadmon stretched forward, groaning with the effort, and managed to grasp the princess by a hank of her wild hair. 'Forgive me, Princess,' he murmured.

'Now!' Adfrith growled.

All three heaved at once and Elfled howled in pain as they dragged her free. The knife blade cut into Wulfrun's palm again, but they managed to haul Elfled closer, so that Cadmon could grasp her by her arms. Slowly they worked their way backwards and at last lay together in a gritty heap on firmer sand.

'You have c-cut yourself,' Elfled cried as they rolled over and struggled to their feet.

'But you are safe,' Wulfrun soothed. 'That's all that matters.'

'The necklace!'

'It is here.' Wulfrun dropped it into Elfled's hands. They stumbled back towards their horses, covered in fine damp sand, Wulfrun dripping with blood.

'We must make camp where we can.' Adfrith's teeth were chattering as he spoke. 'I cannot believe I was such a fool!'

'We all went willingly,' Wulfrun told him sharply.

They found a thicket above the river. The horses followed them and began to crop grass. The two girls huddled close together, shivering violently, desperate for warmth. Cadmon filled his waterskin from the river and insisted on washing Wulfrun's cut palms. Then he tore thin strips from the bottom of his tunic and bound up her wounds; she let him tend her like a child. Then he removed the saddles from the horses and set about rubbing them down, soothing them all the while with his soft singing.

'You had better take charge of the necklace again,' Elfled said, holding it out to Adfrith.

He took it and put it carefully into one of his saddlebags. 'I'm glad you still trust me, Princess,' he said.

'I trust you with my life,' she said sleepily.

They settled down close together for warmth, with only Wulfrun's and Elfled's wet sandy cloaks to cover them. Despite their discomfort and the frightening ordeal they fell asleep from shear weariness.

While it was still dark Wulfrun opened her eyes to realize that Cadmon was shaking her gently. 'Lady Moon sails in the sky' – he sang the words low in her ear – 'Lady Moon hails a miracle: a pathway for our brave princess.'

Wulfrun got up, rubbing her eyes and blinking in the moonlight. Cadmon turned her round and pointed inland so that she could see what he meant. Though frost had touched the edges of the bracken, a silver moon sailed in a cloudless sky. The tide had gone even further out and the river Aln had shrunk to a mere trickle, revealing a neat line of wide stepping stones. They could make a crossing now without trouble.

'It is a miracle,' Wulfrun agreed.

They woke Adfrith, who was full of wonder at the sight. Elfled took a little time to rouse, but once she was awake she smiled, her energy renewed. They mounted their horses and crossed the stepping stones without a splash.

Once safely across and leaving the small township behind them, Adfrith turned to his companions. 'We could rest again now,' he offered.

But Elfled shook her head. 'The sun is rising,' she said. 'I am wide awake and I want to ride for ever.'

'Let's hope Sea Mist feels the same way,' said Wulfrun.

It seemed that the horses were as willing as their riders, for they trotted and cantered steadily through the day. Their spirits rose at the lovely landscape around them. Oyster catchers chirruped in the grassy dunes and a bright sun warmed them as wide, rolling beaches spread out on the seaward side. The smooth white sands were broken only by a few rocky outcrops stretching out into the sea. Gleaming black snouts of seals poked out from the water and seabirds soared overhead. At last, as the sun began to sink, the horses slowed up and protested a little. Adfrith was elated with the distance they had covered. Though they were still uncomfortable from the previous night, he guessed that it could not be long now before they saw the great fortress on the rock.

'Will we be there by nightfall?' Elfled asked. 'I have sand down my neck and inside my breeches. Will I have a comfortable bed tonight?'

'I cannot be certain, Princess.' Adfrith would not build up false hopes.

The path they were following grew wide and busy with lumbering carts carrying wood, cloth merchants' wagons and slaughtering gangs. Small groups of wandering monks in their undyed robes travelled on foot. Wealthy nobles rode fine horses, their women carried in litters with curtains drawn to protect their modesty.

At first they found the company that joined them unnerving, for they'd kept so much away from fellow travellers. But gradually they found that if they remained calm and looked as though they knew where they were going, nobody took much notice of them. Their dirty state and bedraggled appearance made people look away from them, uninterested.

They found it hard not to stare, for none of them had ever before seen such a range of people. Cadmon glanced about him suspiciously and Adfrith was very quiet and thoughtful.

The first warning of trouble came when travellers from the north rushed past them, pushing to get by. Two young monks, their foreheads shaven in the Columban style, turned back looking fearful, though the nobles with their great escorts of warriors and slaves carried on unperturbed.

'What is it?' Wulfrun slid down from Magpie's back and caught the arm of a girl who had come rushing back, dragging her young brother with her.

'King Oswy's men.' She spoke breathlessly. 'Stopping people . . . looking for a thief . . . an oblate from Whitby who's stolen horses and a novice from the abbey. They question young ones in small groups and they are rough and frightening.'

Wulfrun climbed onto Magpie's back again and urged her mount forward so that she could see well ahead. There was indeed a group of armed men stopping people, and one of them she recognized. She looked back at Adfrith and saw by the way the colour drained from his cheeks that he'd heard what the young girl had said and seen the familiar figure ahead. Though her heart thundered with fear, Wulfrun calmly took hold of Sea Mist's bridle and turned Magpie's head to lead them back in the direction from which they'd come. 'Come quietly,' she murmured.

Elfled allowed it, sensing that something was very wrong. Adfrith and Cadmon followed.

'By Oswald's bones!' Adfrith swore, when at last they stopped at a crossroads, feeling safe enough to dismount. 'I am accused of theft and kidnapping!'

'Did you see who was with them?' Wulfrun asked.

Cadmon looked puzzled. 'It was Ch-Childeric, the Frankish jeweller.'

'They're not Oswy's men. They are Ecfrid's, and Childeric is Irminburgh's – I am quite sure of that.'

Adfrith nervously ran his fingers through his hair. 'He has travelled fast along the main routes and got ahead of us while we took the small coastal tracks. They don't seem to seek the princess or even mention her name.'

'No.' Wulfrun was not surprised at that. 'The king himself would be here if it were spread abroad that Elfled was missing and they don't want that. I think they've guessed we mean to give warning of what they are up to and they're trying to prevent us reaching Bamburgh. Where can we go now?'

'Woden take my brother!' Elfled muttered resentfully, but then she corrected herself. 'But perhaps it is not him that I should blame – it is Irminburgh. He takes more notice of her than of his own sister!'

The others understood well enough why that might be: Irminburgh's beauty and powers of persuasion were great.

'A rose-petalled fly catcher, a golden honey trap,' Cadmon said.

'A poisonous flower,' Elfled growled, spiritedly joining in.

Adfrith was fretting. 'If we turn inland we head away from Bamburgh and I don't know whether we can ever find our way back. If we try to slip past them, I fear . . .' His voice trailed away.

'Childeric would recognize us,' Wulfrun finished for him. She felt sure the jeweller was there to pick them out and capture them and who knows what else. He had already shown that he was willing to attack them.

An ancient carved stone stood tall beside a well and many people were stopping to drink at the cross-roads. Another caravan of horses and slaves on foot came to a standstill beside them; the quality of their clothes and goods proclaimed wealth.

'We'll stop here for the night,' the lord called. 'Set up tents.'

A group of slaves headed for the well with beakers and water jugs. Wulfrun was watching them without interest, her mind on the problem that beset them, when her eye fell on the swinging gait of one of the young men. Her heart began to race at the sight of him: he was a tall lad and broad, with dark hair that curled just as her own did.

'What is it?' Adfrith asked as he saw her start.

Wulfrun shook her head and for a moment she pretended that nothing had happened, but she could not stop herself from looking again at the young slave. The sight of him set her chin trembling. She felt sure that it was Sebbi, taller and older as he would be by now. How could she deny him? How could she pretend that she wasn't his sister and he the dearest sight she'd seen since her mother had been dragged away from her?

Adfrith saw that Wulfrun was troubled and touched her arm in concern. 'Wolf Girl, what is it?'

She shook him off and turned without a word of explanation, running fast down the slope towards the young man, who had set off again to carry water to his master. She followed him, never taking her eyes off his broad shoulders.

He went not to the great man astride his horse but to a litter, where a woman was hidden behind thick curtains. Wulfrun watched as he attended to his mistress, and when he stepped back she came up behind him. 'Sebbi,' she called. He turned round at once but his gaze passed over her as though she were a stranger.

Wulfrun's heart sank. How could he know her as his sister? She'd been nothing but a skinny lass when he'd left home; he looked just the same but bigger and stronger, and with a twist of pain she saw that he bore scars across the back of his neck.

'Sebbi.' She whispered his name again and this time he turned and looked at her curiously. Suddenly his eyes widened and he knew her.

'Wulfie? Is it you?'

Chapter 23

sebbi

Tears welled up and spilled down Wulfrun's cheeks as she went to her brother, arms outstretched. They clung together.

'Wulfie, you have grown so tall,' Sebbi whispered. 'And how are you here? You have good clothes – but you are very dirty.'

'There is so much to tell,' she said, her mind working wildly, not knowing where to start.

Some of Sebbi's fellow slaves were watching them, though not without sympathy. 'I must go back to my duties,' he told her, his eyes fast searching the horizon. 'But can you meet me after dark, over there, where three trees stand tall?'

'Yes,' she answered firmly. Nothing on earth would stop her from doing that.

Sebbi kissed her cheek and walked away, picking up his water jug and carrying it into a tent that some of the other slaves were setting up. Wulfrun turned round and saw that her three companions had followed where she went and now stood at a distance, staring at her in amazement. She walked back to them biting her lips: she knew she must give them some explanation and she promised herself that she would never deny Sebbi again.

'Who is that?' Elfled demanded. 'You were kissing him.'

Wulfrun swallowed hard. 'He is my brother,' she said.

They stared at her, shocked.

Elfled's eyes narrowed in thought as she struggled to remember. 'Is this the brother who had to go away?'

Wulfrun sighed, her hands still shaking a little with the emotion and shock of meeting Sebbi. 'Yes,' she said.

'He is very handsome,' Elfled allowed. 'But . . . is he not a slave?'

'Yes,' Wulfrun said, lifting her chin. 'And I am very proud of him. He offered to go as a slave to make sure my sister and I were fed.'

Adfrith and Cadmon walked ahead a little way in silence, concern showing clear on their faces. They found an oak tree with a patch of grass beside it and fastened the horses on loose reins so that they could crop the grass and rest. Then they sat down and turned to Wulfrun in sympathy. 'All here are your friends.' Adfrith spoke kindly, as was always his way. 'Tell us about your brother.'

'Y-yes . . . we are all your friends,' Cadmon agreed.

Wulfrun took a deep breath and began to tell them how Sebbi had been lost to them and how ashamed Cwen had been to allow such a thing.

Elfled listened, frowning. 'And all the time your mother had the necklace.'

'Yes,' Wulfrun admitted. 'But now I understand that she could never have sold it, just as we dared not sell your ring, when we needed to buy food. If you are poor you cannot just sell precious jewels and hope that nobody will question how you came by them. You will be accused of theft!'

Elfled nodded her understanding and her hand crept forward to take hold of Wulfrun's. 'I am sorry for your mother and I am very sorry that I ever called you slave. You are not my slave – you are my friend.'

Wulfrun looked at her with tears in her eyes and pressed her hand in gratitude.

'There are many like Wulfrun's Sebbi,' said Adfrith.

Cadmon agreed. 'M-many,' he said. 'M-my own mother. The m-master who owned us offered her freedom but she begged him to set me free instead.'

Wulfrun was shocked now. 'I never knew,' she said. 'I thought your mother must have died. And did this master set you free?'

Cadmon nodded. 'I believe m-my mother is still alive . . . and still a slave,' he said sadly.

Wulfrun reached out and pressed his arm; they all sat together in silence for a while.

Then at last Adfrith brought them back to the present. 'I say we should stay here so that Wulfrun can go to meet her brother tonight and we can think carefully what's best to do in the morning. It seems a waste of time to go inland, but I fear we may not get past Prince Ecfrid's men any other way – there will be no fine bed for you tonight, Princess.'

'I do not care.' Elfled shrugged, still sad at what she'd heard.

They made themselves as comfortable as they could and as soon as darkness fell Wulfrun set off towards the three tall trees that her brother had pointed out to her. Adfrith offered to go with her, but she firmly refused, fearing that Sebbi would be afraid to approach if he saw anyone else there. The penalty for a disobedient slave would certainly be whipping and could even be death.

Wulfrun did not have long to wait, but she was surprised when she saw that Sebbi did not come alone. It was hard to see clearly in the shadows, but it seemed he walked towards her with a young girl at his side. Brother and sister hugged each other again, but then Sebbi drew his companion forward. 'This is Cissa – we are fellow slaves and owned by Alfged, Lord of Linithdale. We are friends' – he hesitated for a moment – 'more than friends . . . we love each other and have sworn to stay together – or die together.'

He added the last words with a quiet passion that shook Wulfrun. She caught her breath, peering at the shadowy face of Cissa, but all she could see was a gleam of silver moonlight on the girl's fair hair. 'I am glad my brother found somebody to love,' she whispered.

Cissa leaned forward and kissed her cheek. 'Thank you,' she murmured. 'I love him dearly and we will not be parted.' Her gentle voice contrasted with the strength of her words.

'But . . . Alfged was not the lord who took you from us?' Wulfrun turned to her brother.

'No, indeed,' Sebbi said at once. 'I have been sold twice since then, and as for my second master – I cannot speak his name without a curse. I thought he'd done for me: he whipped me so that I thought I'd die – but then Freya must have looked down on me with pity, for his treatment made me so weak that I was of little use to him and he sold me on.'

'Oh, Sebbi.' Wulfrun's voice broke with pain at what he told her.

His hand went out to stroke her shoulder. 'No truly, sister . . . Freya smiled on me that day for I was bought by Lord Alfged to serve his mother the Lady Elgifu, and that is how Cissa and I met.'

'Is Elgifu the lady in the litter?' Though she could not see the expression on their faces she sensed that both Sebbi and Cissa smiled.

'Elgifu is full of kindness; she is a Christian lady who does not believe in slavery, though her son will not be persuaded to set us free. She treats us well and allows our love to flourish – our only fear is that she will die, for she is very old and frail.'

'Will she not free you?' Wulfrun was suddenly hopeful.

'She cannot make that choice – we belong by right to her son.'

Wulfrun blinked back tears. Though she was glad that Sebbi had found this love, their situation still seemed to be very sad.

'But tell me, sister: how is my mother and little Gode?' Sebbi asked, as she knew he must.

Wulfrun steeled herself to tell him the truth without hiding her own guilt. He listened quietly, asking a question now and then, but he betrayed no surprise at all when she told him about the garnet necklace, only shook his head in sorrow. Suddenly she understood why.

'You knew about the necklace!'

'Yes – I knew. Mother and I wondered if we could break it up and try to sell it bit by bit, after Father died . . . but it was such a beautiful necklace and we had no proof that we had any right to it.

We feared that even a small gem from it would bring suspicion and accusations. We should have told you, sister. If we had, then maybe this terrible thing would never have happened.'

'So . . .' Wulfrun saw here a chance to find out more. 'Were we right in thinking that Mother was given it by Edwin's queen?'

Sebbi frowned, puzzled. 'She helped a mother and her two little ones, rowing them out to a Kentish ship. The woman was travelling with a priest and they were fleeing for their lives from Penda's men – we assumed they were the family of one of Edwin's thanes.'

They stood in silence for a moment while Wulfrun thought hard.

'But why are you here in Bernicia?' Sebbi asked. 'Why are you here if our mother is awaiting judgement?' There was a hint of accusation in his voice.

Wulfrun dared not tell her brother that she was riding across Northumbria in the company of King Oswy's daughter, so she told him a much simpler version of the truth. 'We – me and my companions – feel sure that Prince Ecfrid is planning to overthrow his brother Alchfrid the Stranger and take his place as King of Deira,' she said.

'Sister . . . you risk much for the quarrels of our rulers.' Sebbi was still surprised.

'Abbess Hild is at Bamburgh and if we can warn her of this, she will speak to the king and make him take action to prevent war breaking out between his two sons. At the same time I shall plead with her to come back to Whitby and hear our mother's case. I trust that her judgement will be fair.'

'Ah.' Sebbi understood her actions better. 'They say the king does listen to Abbess Hild, but I understand that he has gone north with his army to punish bands of Picts who invade his borders.'

Wulfrun was shocked to hear that. If the king was not in Bamburgh with his army then how could he come to Whitby to berate his rebellious son? 'I must still see Abbess Hild,' she insisted. 'She will know what to do.'

'Hild is both strong and merciful,' Cissa agreed. 'I heard it from the Lady Elgifu.'

Sebbi shook his head. 'Not all Christians are merciful. Cadwallon and Edwin were both Christians, but they battled and slaughtered all their lives.'

Irminburgh's fair face swam before Wulfrun's eyes. 'No,' she agreed. 'And it seems that we cannot get into Bamburgh to speak to the abbess. Just a little way up the road Prince Ecfrid's men are camped and they stop most of the travellers to search for us. They say they are looking for a young oblate in the company of a young novice. They accuse him of having stolen her away and I cannot tell you how far that is from the truth;

Adfrith has risked everything to protect us. I fear the prince has guessed that we mean to warn the king.'

Sebbi was quiet for a moment; then he spoke. 'I wonder if we might help,' he murmured.

'Yes . . . yes.' Cissa encouraged him, as though she guessed his thoughts.

Wulfrun looked from one to the other. The moon had come out from behind the clouds and she saw now that Cissa's round, gentle face would make any young man love her. Something about the girl's eagerness to help made her heart skip with hope.

'How?' she asked.

'Tomorrow we travel on to Bamburgh. Lady Elgifu goes to the fortress to pay her respects to the queen. If I explain this difficulty to her I think she might take you along, but your oblate would have to discard his monk-like robe and your young companion would have to dress as a slave – that fur-trimmed cloak of hers would have to go.'

Wulfrun's mouth dropped open a little as she began to understand what her brother was suggesting. Disguised as the Lady Elgifu's slaves they might certainly pass Prince Ecfrid's men, and even Childeric might not notice or recognize them. But what would Elfled think of this plan? Could she possibly pass as a slave girl? Would it be treason to even suggest such a thing?

'Who is this young girl who travels with you?' Sebbi asked, almost as though he picked up her thoughts.

Wulfrun bit her lip, glad that shadows hid the flush that rose to her cheeks. 'She's Elfled, a young ward of the Abbess Hild.' After all, that was not untrue.

Sebbi nodded.

'I have heard the name somewhere before,' Cissa said thoughtfully.

'Would your Lady Elgifu really take such a risk for us?' Wulfrun asked quickly.

The two smiled at each other. 'The lady has her own ideas of right and wrong,' Cissa said. 'And she is a good friend of your abbess.'

'We will speak to her,' Sebbi said. 'You must go back to your friends and prepare them. Come back here at first light and be ready to go – if that is what you all wish.'

Wulfrun launched herself at him and hugged him tightly again. 'You are always saving us, brother,' she whispered.

She ran lightly back across the shadowy grass to where her companions were trying to sleep. Elfled had curled up close to Sea Mist for warmth. Adfrith and Cadmon had positioned themselves on guard, one on either side of her. Neither man slept; they just rested against their own steeds. Wulfrun stopped and looked at them for a moment. King

Oswy's daughter slept on rough grass out in the cold air, but she could not have two more stalwart guards.

'They'd give their lives to protect her,' she murmured. Then she also recognized with a sense of warm emotion that they would do the same for her. The two men stirred as she approached and rose catlike to their feet without a sound.

'I have so much to tell,' Wulfrun whispered, breathless with excitement, when she got back to her friends.

Even though it was dark Adfrith and Cadmon detected a new sense of purpose about her.

'Should we wake the princess?' Adfrith wondered.

'No. Let her sleep, for she will need her strength if we decide to do what my brother suggests.'

They listened carefully as Wulfrun described Sebbi and Cissa's situation and the offer they'd made.

'Won't Lord Alfged see us and question what we do in his train?' Adfrith asked at once.

Wulfrun frowned: why had she not thought of that? Surely Sebbi must have. 'I don't know,' she had to admit. 'We will all be dressed in his colours and there are many servants and slaves.'

'Perhaps . . . if we left the horses behind.' Adfrith seemed to feel that the risk was worth taking. 'Cadmon, would you stay here to look after the horses? It's not necessary for us all to get into Bamburgh, and I would return to you as soon as I could.'

'I will do wh-whatever is needed,' Cadmon said.

'The other slaves must see us and wonder,' Wulfrun acknowledged. 'But my brother seems to have faith that the lady will make it work. If Elgifu agrees to help us, then we shall be under her protection, and they tell me she is an old friend of Abbess Hild.'

'There is danger for us all,' Adfrith said, still worried. Wulfrun could see the dark shape of him hunched against the first gleams of light in the east. The warm rush of excitement faded, and instead an uncomfortable tightness began to grow in her throat.

Then suddenly Adfrith made a decision. 'Wolf Girl . . . I can think of no better plan.'

She heard the warmth in his voice and sensed that he too smiled in the darkness. The tightness in her throat vanished.

'We will do it?'

'Yes,' he answered firmly.

She spoke with wry humour. 'Then all we need now . . . is to persuade our princess to dress and act like a slave.'

Chapter 24

elgifu

All three turned their gaze to where the sleeping Elfled lay. For a moment or two they listened to the steady sounds of her breathing. 'Well, in that case you had best wake her now,' Adfrith said.

Wulfrun sighed. 'Always me . . . ?' she said. 'If I'm to wake her, fetch me water first and give me the last of the bread.'

Cadmon went off at once to the well and Adfrith obediently searched their bags for the last few scraps of food. Elfled woke hungry and thirsty, as Wulfrun had guessed she would. They offered her food and drink and began to explain the plan. She went very quiet, but listened to what she was told while she ate.

'And what must I wear if I am to pass as a slave and what must I do?' Elfled asked at last in a small voice that trembled just a little.

Her frightened acquiescence touched Wulfrun deeply. She stretched out to take Elfled's small hand in hers and stroked it. 'Cissa will bring us both simple gowns to wear, marked with the emblem of Lord Alfged. Then we will go to Lady Elgifu, and whatever she tells us to do, we must obey at once and never question anything she says.'

'And this will get us safely into Bamburgh and I will see Mother Hild and . . . and perhaps that other one?'

'We trust it will.' Wulfrun was determined to be positive. 'Can you do it?'

'Yes,' Elfled agreed. 'But I must take my mother's jewels with me.'

'We must hide them carefully,' said Adfrith, reaching up for his saddlebag. 'But where?'

'I shall wear them under my slave clothes,' said Elfled firmly, taking charge again. 'Will you help?' she asked Wulfrun.

The men turned away to the horses, while Wulfrun fastened the jewels securely around Elfled's tiny waist, where they would be covered by her shift.

'There . . . let us go and find this Cissa,' Elfled said. She went to drop a kiss on Sea Mist's nose. 'I will be back for you as soon as I can,' she whispered. The mare ignored her, cropping vigorously at the grass. 'Are we ready?' she asked, her dignity back in place.

'Yes, Princess,' said Adfrith.

As the first streaks of rosy light coloured the sky on the eastern horizon, they reached the three tall trees and found Sebbi and Cissa waiting there for them.

'What does the lady say?' Wulfrun asked urgently, but she could see from the bundles of clothes they were bearing that she must have agreed.

Cissa smiled. 'She says she hasn't had an adventure for a long, long time and she can't think of anything she'd like better.'

'But what of her son?' Adfrith asked, still anxious. 'He seems a man not easily fooled.'

'That's true,' Sebbi agreed, turning to him. 'But he's impatient with his mother's heavy litter and what he calls "her doting slaves"; he usually rides well ahead. But . . . we wondered . . . would it be ungracious to ask an oblate to take the place of one of the litter slaves? It is a hard job of work, but your face would be half hidden against the draperies and you'd be the last to be suspected.'

'I'd be most willing,' Adfrith answered without hesitation, and it was Wulfrun who looked up sharply, remembering how his long, slim fingers guided the quill pen and effortlessly produced such beautiful script.

'Be careful of your hands,' she warned. 'They are so important in your work.'

'I will, Wolf Girl.' He smiled. 'But what of the

other slaves? They must see that we are strangers joining them and question what we do.'

Sebbi smiled. 'If Lady Elgifu offers you her protection, then so do her slaves.'

Cissa held a cloak up for modesty while Wulfrun helped Elfled pull a rough high-necked gown over her shift of itchy undyed hemp. She struggled into a similar gown herself, while Adfrith discarded his monk-like robe in favour of a tunic marked with the rose emblem of the Lord of Linithdale. Cadmon packed the unwanted clothes into the saddlebags.

Elfled hesitated as they left Cadmon, but then she reached up and kissed him on the cheek. 'Thank you for looking after me so well,' she said. 'You are my friend – and I will not forget it.'

They left him smiling thoughtfully as he gathered together all the horses' bridles.

'Come.' Sebbi turned and led the way.

Adfrith followed him to where the other litter bearers were breaking their fast, while Cissa took Wulfrun and Elfled to Lady Elgifu's tent.

Elgifu was the oldest woman Wulfrun had ever set eyes on; she seemed even older than Nelda, though she recognized at once something similar in the eyes. Elgifu was tiny; her skin deeply wrinkled. She could not use her legs, but her eyes had the knowing brightness of a sparrow.

Two slave girls were tending her carefully, one

washing her hands, while the other gently combed her sprinkling of soft white hair. Wulfrun led the way and curtsied, giving Elfled a small nudge to do the same. 'We cannot thank you enough for your kindness,' she said quietly.

The old woman's birdlike glance flashed from the young girl to the older one, then back at once to the young girl. She waved the two maids away with a quick smile, then turned again to Elfled.

'Such hair! Come here, child,' she said, her voice soft and throaty.

Elfled stepped forward at once, determined to play her part well. Wulfrun bit her lip a little as Elgifu put out a trembling hand to touch the young girl's cheek, and she thought she saw the thin lips part for just a moment in surprise.

Elgifu looked sharply back at Wulfrun. 'A young girl promised to God, you say?'

'Yes, lady,' she replied.

'Yes indeed,' Elgifu said, turning again to Elfled. 'Let me see – what would Hild do? Child, you will travel inside the litter with me and carry my sweetmeat bowl. Can you do that, do you think?'

'Yes, lady,' Elfled answered obediently.

'And you' – she looked at Wulfrun – 'you will walk alongside us in place of Cissa, who usually carries my rugs.'

'Thank you, lady.' Wulfrun sensed that Elgifu

understood more than she let on, but her words brought relief; Elfled must be safer inside the litter than anywhere else. If the lady was a friend of Hild, it was quite possible that she'd seen Elfled as a young child and knew only too well who she was. This impression was heightened even further when Elgifu spoke again.

'We must disguise that hair,' she said, looking around her tent. 'Ah yes – that kerchief, bring it here.'

Wulfrun picked up a fine linen kerchief, dyed the dark blue purple that came from bilberries. Elgifu took it and reached forward to tie it tightly round Elfled's head, covering her wild golden curls completely. Elfled kept still, trusting the old woman instinctively.

'There now, what do you think?'

Wulfrun smiled and nodded. The young princess had been changed into a pale-faced, elflike servant girl, and Wulfrun could not help but smile at the aptness of the name she'd been given. But there was no more time to worry, for Lord Alfged's grooms came to enquire if the Lady Elgifu was ready to move off.

'Yes, quite ready,' Elgifu answered, her voice surprisingly strong.

Cissa and the other two slaves came back into the tent and between them they picked up the old lady and carried her out to the litter. Wulfrun and

Elfled stood back, but Elgifu turned to wave them forwards. 'Stay close.'

Elfled moved forward confidently, and as soon as the old woman was settled in her litter, she scrambled in after her. Wulfrun saw with a quick, grateful smile that Adfrith was there in place at the back of the litter, with Sebbi at his side acting as the other bearer. Cissa piled two rugs into her arms. 'You can hide your face in them,' she whispered.

Wulfrun saw with alarm that Lord Alfged was trotting back alongside the caravan towards them. 'Is all well with my lady mother?' he asked.

Elgifu moved with alacrity, sticking her head out of the gap in the curtains. 'I'm in a hurry to get to Bamburgh,' she snapped.

'As ever . . . Lady Mother.' He turned his horse's head with a touch of impatience and headed back to the front.

Wulfrun lifted the rugs to cover the lower half of her face as the caravan moved forwards.

Lord Alfged set a fast pace on his stallion, and the slaves and foot-servants had to struggle to keep up with him. Wulfrun soon longed for Magpie's rolling gait beneath her. She kept glancing back at Adfrith, for though the lady and Elfled were both light, the solid oak litter was heavy.

At the crossroads they turned and began to travel back along the path where they knew Prince

Ecfrid's men were camping. Again she saw that some of the travellers were turning back looking distressed, but she pressed on, praying quietly to Freya for protection – and to the Christian God.

At last they slowed and came to a stop; they could hear Lord Alfged shouting impatiently ahead of them. Prince Ecfrid's men had indeed had the temerity to stop the Lord of Linithdale, and Childeric came marching down the queue of servants, looking carefully at them all. Wulfrun lifted her pile of rugs even higher, hoping desperately that her disguise would work.

Two of Ecfrid's men made a young monk in the Linithdale train climb down from his pony. They pulled him about roughly, but could accuse him of nothing. 'If it's him, where's the lasses?' asked a man who'd been riding beside him. He was allowed to mount again and the men moved on to Lady Elgifu's litter.

Childeric reached right across Wulfrun and pulled the curtains open. 'Pardon us, lady,' he began in a much more polite tone of voice, when he saw the aged occupant.

'What is this all about?' Elgifu spoke angrily.

Wulfrun glanced up and saw that Elfled was leaning forward, directly in front of Elgifu, holding up a polished wooden bowl that contained sweet-meats. She ignored the man completely, her gaze never leaving Elgifu's face. Wulfrun looked hard but could see no sign at all of the precious jewels that lay beneath her rough gown.

'Prince Ecfrid searches for wicked oblate . . . he steals both horse and women – a very bad man.'

'How shocking.' Elgifu changed her voice to show concern. Elfled did not blink or move.

Then suddenly the man looked closely at Elfled and Wulfrun saw what had caught his eye. The little gold ring that they'd thought too fine to sell was still there on her middle finger.

Childeric stared for what seemed like an age, while Wulfrun's heart beat fast. Had Childeric even made that ring himself? It was quite possible. 'Lady . . . your slave is dressed very fine – good jewellery!' he said, indicating the small ornament.

'Oh, silly man.' Elgifu quickly saw what he was looking at. 'That's my ring of course – I was teasing the child by dressing her up.'

In a flash the old woman snatched the ring from Elfled and slipped it into place on her own little finger.

Lord Alfged rode back to the litter, an angry scowl on his face. 'How dare you question my mother?' he growled.

Childeric let the curtain fall, and with a sigh of annoyance went on past Adfrith without giving him a second glance.

'Move on!' Elgifu ordered.

Lord Alfged turned his horse and trotted back into the lead again.

Wulfrun and Adfrith glanced at each other to communicate their relief but dared not smile. It was only when they had put a mile or two behind them that Wulfrun felt confident enough to turn and give him a wide grin.

The caravan progressed quickly and it wasn't long before they caught their first glimpse of the great fortress that Oswy's father, King Aethelfrith, had built in honour of his first wife, Queen Bebba. It rose on its rock high above the sea. Three sturdy wooden stockades surrounded it, and the king's hall that rose in the centre could be seen for miles in every direction; it was hard to believe that Penda had once burned it down. Oswy had rebuilt it stronger and higher than ever. Wulfrun's spirits soared at the sight of it.

Elgifu pulled open the curtains. 'Can you see the fortress yet?' she asked.

'Yes, lady,' Wulfrun replied, her voice soft with wonder.

'You can get out now, child,' the old lady told Elfled. 'But stay close, ready to hop back in should trouble arise.'

Elfled leaped down from the litter and walked quietly at Wulfrun's side, her eyes wide with pleasure at the sight of the great fortress where she'd been born. 'Not one island but many islands,' she whispered, looking out to sea, where outcrops of rock rose from the dark slate-blue of the sea.

'Yes, but that one must be Aidan's Isle,' Wulfrun said, looking straight ahead and beyond the bulk of the fortress town.

Adfrith looked up at her words, straining to see. A great stretch of smooth white sand was revealed in the far distance, with a rocky island rising at the end of it. As the tide ebbed away it left a wide sandy pathway linking Aidan's Isle to the mainland.

'A magical island.' Wulfrun spoke warmly, understanding Adfrith's fascination with the place.

The fortress and the monastery faced each other across the wide expanse of sand and sea; as they got closer to Bamburgh their view of Aidan's Isle was lost as the fortress loomed above them and blotted out the sight of it.

They passed through the outer gate that protected the busy town. Lord Alfged came riding back once more to see his mother. 'Did those curs bother you?' he asked, not even glancing at the servants who surrounded her.

'It would take more than them to bother me,' Elgifu said with spirit.

Lord Alfged chuckled at her brave words and Wulfrun saw that there was affection between them, though there was much irritation too.

'Do you wish to stop and eat?' he asked.

'No,' Elgifu insisted. 'I want to see my friend Hild.'

'I hear from the gatekeeper that the abbess has her boat ready to return to Whitby.' He shrugged. 'I fear we may have come too late for you to see her.'

Elgifu looked dismayed for a moment and Wulfrun worked hard to hide her distress, squeezing Elfled's hand hard to warn her to keep silent. Who knew what kind of a reception they'd get if Abbess Hild had gone. Who would recognize and believe them? Would Queen Ianfleda even know Elfled as the tiny baby girl she'd given away to God?

Chapter 25

bamburgh

Though Wulfrun's heart sank at the thought that Hild might have left Bamburgh, Lady Elgifu was not going to give up easily. 'Tell them to move fast,' she ordered in a determined voice. 'Send a rider ahead to beg her wait for me!'

Annoyance showed again in Lord Alfged's face as he turned his horse to head back to the front. 'I'll do my best, Mother,' he said in a soothing tone that did little to convince Wulfrun that he meant what he said.

'Climb back in here with me, child.' Elgifu beckoned, and Elfled quietly obeyed.

The whole procession did speed up a little and they passed quickly through the outer gates in a wooden palisade surrounding the huge rock that the fortress was built upon. The wide uphill track went on and took them past well-built halls with carved wood lintels and high thatched roofs. There were market stalls, roaming cattle and goats and smoking cook fires that would have made their mouths water if the need for haste had not been so urgent.

At last, as they neared the main gateway of the inner palisade, Elgifu leaned out from her litter to speak to Wulfrun. 'Down that way are the quays,' she said, pointing to a series of sturdily built wooden ramps. 'Run down and through the outer seaward gate to where they moor the boats! See if the abbess is still here! I will keep this one safe. We'll be in the guesthouse waiting for you.'

Wulfrun looked at her in doubt. 'The abbess may be angry with us.'

Elgifu shrugged. 'Do not fear her; they do not call her Battlemaid for nothing. Tell her everything – now run!'

Wulfrun did not need telling again: she rushed towards the ramps, ignoring the shouts of annoyance that came from the Lord of Linithdale's men as she pushed past them.

'Who is that?' she heard Alfged himself demand at the sight of a wild young woman dressed in his colours running down towards the quays.

Wulfrun tore ahead and down the ramps, leaving them staring after her. It wasn't difficult to work out where she should go, for once through the outer seaward gate she could see that a long wooden quay had been built right over the white sand dunes stretching northwards and out into the sea. Boats of all shapes and sizes were moored along it. She stopped for a moment and shaded her eyes to see.

'The red sail, the red sail,' she murmured. She had seen the *Royal Edwin* moored in Whitby harbour every day for the last four years; surely she would know it and pick it out. But as her eye skimmed along the harbour side, she realized that there were many red sails on many such vessels, the larger ones moored further out to get the deeper water. How in Freya's name could she find the abbess's ship?

She stared at the line of furled sails, panic rising in her – were all their efforts to come to nothing?

Then she heard a woman's voice that was some-how familiar among the throng of people moving along the quayside where merchants sold their goods: 'Ten sacks of grain and another two of barley. Take them down to the *Royal Edwin*, please – as fast as you can!'

It was a voice that commanded obedience and Wulfrun gasped as she recognized it. She pushed her way into the crowd, as certain as could be that somewhere in there was Abbess Hild.

How could she find such a tiny woman among so many? Wulfrun moved in the direction of the voice, but then she had to turn sharply aside again, for it seemed the abbess had moved on down the row of stalls that supplied those venturing out on the sea. 'Ten measures of cinnamon spice and six boxes of dates' were being ordered next.

Although they were almost self-sufficient at Whitby, the abbess, practical as ever, was taking the opportunity to purchase a few rare commodities that the Bamburgh merchants kept in stock. Wulfrun pushed mercilessly in what seemed to be the right direction, making people grumble at her. All at once she realized that the small woman she'd reached out to shove next was the abbess herself, her head bent low as she examined a handful of beans.

'Courtesy, girl!' the abbess demanded, stumbling a little to the side.

'Oh, lady,' Wulfrun began.

'How dare you push me, girl?' Hild righted herself, regarding Wulfrun with annoyance.

'Mother Hild . . . it is me, Wulfrun, daughter to Cwen the webster.'

'What in the name of our . . . ?' Hild stared at her, amazed.

'Please, Mother, we need your help. Elfled needs you.'

'Elfled? But she is safe at Whitby.'

Wulfrun bit her lip and shook her head, her bandaged hands clasped together now, pleading. 'There is so much to tell . . . but please, lady, come back to the fortress – do not take to the sea at once. Only you can help us!'

Hild dropped the handful of beans and looked round at the three attendant nuns who stood behind her, bags of provisions in their arms, staring at Wulfrun with shocked disapproval. The abbess closed her eyes for a moment as she took in one deep breath; then, as she exhaled, Wulfrun saw with relief that the angry look vanished.

'Well, Sisters – it seems that this morning was not auspicious for travel after all. We will return to the fortress, but I warn you, child, this had better be of great importance – the winter snows will be on us soon and I must get back to Whitby. Come now.'

The abbess took Wulfrun firmly by the arm and set off back towards the ramps. 'The king has ordered me to host a great synod after the harvest next year: bishops and princes will be coming to Whitby from far and wide. I have much to do to prepare for it.'

'Mother, this is important – Northumbria's peace is at stake.'

Again Hild stopped for a moment to stare at her, then moved swiftly on. 'You had better start by telling me how a Whitby lass with bandaged hands comes to be wearing the colours of the Lord of Linithdale? Where is Elfled now?'

'She's safe in the guesthouse, in the care of Lady Elgifu.'

'Ah.' The abbess suddenly brightened and a wry smile touched her lips. 'Elgifu can never keep out of trouble. Now, start at the beginning and tell me as we go.'

For such a small woman and one no longer young, the abbess strode very fast, and as Wulfrun was already out of breath from running it was hard to tell her story in a sensible way. She gasped and puffed and struggled to speak as they marched along, but by the time they'd arrived back at the gates she'd managed to communicate a rather garbled version of events to the abbess. When she told what had happened to Cwen, the abbess came to a standstill again.

'Cwen a thief?' Hild looked amazed. 'That I cannot believe.'

Wulfrun felt as though her heart might burst with relief. Tears welled up and suddenly she felt she could not take another step. Hild saw the flood of emotion and took Wulfrun into her arms. 'Hush, child,' she said, her voice firm and low. 'There will be justice for your mother – I promise you that.'

Silently thanking both Freya and Hild's Christian God, Wulfrun dashed the tears away.

'Go to the guesthouse,' Hild told the guard at the gate. 'Find Lady Elgifu and the child that's with her and bring them to me in the queen's parlour. Bring the young oblate as well – she'll know who I mean – and Elgifu's slaves . . . bring them all to me.'

The guard called a companion over to take his place and hurried away at once with his message; it seemed that the abbess was obeyed here in Bamburgh, just as she was in Whitby.

'Oh, lady' – Wulfrun slowed her steps uncertainly – 'will the queen be there – in her parlour?'

Hild shook her head. 'No, no. The queen will be in the chapel praying; she is always in there praying – and just as well, until we have got this whole muddle cleared up a little.' Then she frowned, as though a worrying thought had come to her. 'And of course she has always said . . . But it cannot be helped.' It seemed she'd decided to dismiss whatever it was that had concerned her.

The queen's parlour was the most splendid room that Wulfrun had ever seen: the walls were hung with bright woven patterns, but it was still small enough to be cosy. Four braziers bore burning coals and the abbess made Wulfrun sit on a beautifully carved stool while she sent a young nun to fetch spiced mead.

'Now,' she said. 'You must tell me again slowly how you came to be riding wild across Bernicia with my young Elfled. You have made me look a somewhat careless guardian, I might add.'

Wulfrun tried again and managed to explain a little more clearly some of what had happened. The abbess made her take a few sips of warming mead, listening intently all the while, interrupting only to make sure that she'd understood. Before Wulfrun had quite reached the end of the telling, Elgifu and Elfled arrived. Adfrith and Sebbi carried the old lady between them in a small chair-like litter, while Cissa walked nervously at their side. Wulfrun realized from their shocked looks that they'd just discovered they'd brought the king's daughter with them in their mistress's train. Elfled, still dressed as a slave girl, began to run towards Hild. She looked as though she wanted to throw herself into the abbess's arms, but the stern look on her guardian's face made her manage a little more decorum. 'Mother Hild,' she murmured shyly, 'I . . . I am so sorry, but . . .'

Hild's flinty gaze roved over the small figure; then she cast a glance in Adfrith's direction.

'I told you to tutor my young ward, Adfrith, not go charging around the countryside with her. What do you think you were doing?'

'I am so very sorry, lady,' Adfrith said, his face downcast, but willing, it seemed, to single-handedly take the blame.

'None of this is Adfrith's fault.' Elfled spoke up for him at once. 'I went without his or anyone's permission. He and Wulfrun rode after me to try to keep me safe – and Cadmon the cowherd came as well.'

'The cowherd as well?' Hild spoke with shocked anger, but then she pressed her lips tightly together as though she was struggling to hold something back. Her face softened and she suddenly smiled wearily, holding out her arms. Elfled ran to her and hugged her.

'All that matters is that you are safe,' Hild acknowledged. 'Adfrith was right to make that his priority and it seems that you have found yourself a strange but loyal escort. We will sort it all out . . . somehow.' Then she turned to the old lady. 'We are good at sorting things, are we not, Elgifu?'

She bent to kiss her, and Elgifu answered with a chuckle.

'But . . . but Irminburgh swears that the treasure I have hidden beneath my clothes is *her* necklace.' Elfled touched her stomach, while a note of anger crept into her voice. She reached down inside the loose neck of her tunic. 'Help me, Wolf Girl,' she begged.

Wulfrun went willingly to her aid and quickly unfastened the familiar catch; then from beneath the slave tunic they carefully pulled the gleaming gold and garnet necklace.

'Ah,' Hild gasped and her eyes widened. 'So long since I saw those jewels.'

Elgifu's eyes gleamed at the sight of them. 'Tata

always had the most exquisite taste,' she said, smiling with satisfaction.

'So they *did* belong to my grandmother?' Elfled asked.

'They did indeed.' Hild spoke quietly, taking them into her own hands. 'And – Cwen's daughter – you say that they were in your mother's care?'

Wulfrun was touched at the generous way the question had been put. 'Yes,' she answered bravely. 'My mother had the necklace locked away in a secret compartment in her wool chest – my brother Sebbi knew of it.'

Hild turned at once to Sebbi. 'And this is Sebbi? What did you know, young man?'

Sebbi blushed at being addressed directly by the abbess, but he too struggled to speak out frankly. 'My mother said they were a reward for saving the lives of a mother and her two little ones. I swear she didn't know who the lady was – just a mother who needed help.'

At his words Hild's face became thoughtful and distant. 'Ah . . . the fishergirl – could she have been . . . ? It all happened so long ago and I must cast my mind far back to remember. It was such a wild and terrible time, but Nelda and I stitched the jewels in place so securely.'

'Yes, you did.' A deep, sweet-toned voice spoke and made them all turn in surprise to see that a woman, younger than Hild, in a richly embroidered over-dress, had entered the parlour quietly. She'd come from a curtained entrance behind the braziers and none of them knew how long she'd been listening. Wulfrun could see at once from her golden curls and the shape of her face that she must be Elfled's mother, Ianfleda, Queen of Northumbria.

'You stitched the necklace in place, but I could not bear the way it battered my legs, so I got rid of it,' she said.

With quiet dignity Ianfleda moved forwards and took the necklace from Hild. 'We had to ride and ride – you must remember . . . Then we had to run down the steep cliff-side to the beach, leading the horses, and all the way down it battered and bruised my shins.'

'But' – Hild frowned – 'I thought somehow it'd been lost.'

The queen was silent for a moment and Wulfrun saw that even she was a little in awe of Hild, and quailed before the abbess's keen glance. 'I . . . lied,' she said quietly.

'No.' Hild stared at her, amazed.

'Yes,' the queen insisted and colour flushed her cheeks. 'I tried to rip it loose, but you had stitched is so carefully into my skirt that it would not come free. I took out my small dagger and I cut it away from my dripping skirt.'

'And what did you do with it?'

Wulfrun's heart beat so that she thought it might burst; their whole lives depended on what came next.

'I gave it to the young girl who rowed us out to the Kentish ship. I said: "Here – take this, for you have saved our lives." '

Chapter 26

the peace weaver

Wulfrun gasped when she heard the queen's words. 'My mother,' she gulped. 'It was my mother and the necklace was truly given to her.'

'Yes,' Hild said with satisfaction. She put a firm, comforting hand on Wulfrun's shoulder, and the kindness in the gesture made tears run down her cheeks. Elfled quietly took hold of her hand.

'Why did I not see it?' Hild shook her head. 'I always felt that Cwen was somehow familiar to me.' She turned to the queen. 'This young girl's mother, Cwen, has been accused of stealing the necklace and is held in captivity at Whitby awaiting judgement. I am quite sure that Cwen was the young girl who rowed you to safety in her father's little boat. Surely she will now have the most trusted witness in the land to speak for her – is that not right, Ianfleda?'

Despite her relief and emotion, Wulfrun was a little shocked that the abbess should speak to the queen almost as though she were one of her novices.

'I . . . I was afraid,' the queen admitted, and it was dreadful to see her so shamefaced. 'I knew the necklace was of great value and that we needed it to buy ourselves a comfortable refuge in Kent – so I dared not tell what I'd done. I thought my mother would never forgive me.'

Hild went to the queen and reached up to hug her. 'You were a child,' she said, her voice warm with love. 'You were a very frightened child, trying so hard to be brave. I do remember that.'

'But it was a sin to lie.' Ianfleda hung her head. 'And it seems that it has brought much misery.'

'Well, now you have the chance to put things right, but we must go to Whitby at once.'

Suddenly Wulfrun saw Elfled's wide, wondering gaze and trembling chin. In the excitement of discovering the truth about the necklace, she'd almost forgotten the significance of this meeting for Elfled. The young girl could not take her eyes off the woman who'd given her birth.

The queen pulled away from Hild, regaining her dignity. 'I will bear witness to what I did,' she said, 'and speak for this girl's mother, but now I must go back to the chapel to beg forgiveness for my wicked sin.'

Wulfrun's jaw dropped in amazement, for the queen had turned away from them and started back towards the curtained side entrance.

She could not stop herself from stepping forward. 'But . . . but madam,' she cried out. 'Madam . . . you cannot go without speaking to your daughter.' Despite her fear and respect she simply could not let this happen.

Ianfleda stopped with her back to them for what seemed an age. Wulfrun looked to the abbess and saw that even Hild was troubled and uncertain.

At last the queen turned back, not to Elfled but to Hild. 'You promised me,' she spoke accusingly. 'You promised me!'

Hild seemed to regain her strength and composure. '*You* made me promise! It was not what I wanted and I couldn't stop this happening. The necklace is not the only problem that we have. There is more trouble afoot in Deira and Elfled has travelled across Bernicia with her companions to warn us of it.'

They watched as the two powerful women faced each other in tense silence; then the queen very slowly turned her head. For the first time in ten years she looked at her child. Deep, deep misery was written there on her face.

Hild went to stand by Elfled, her arm protectively round the child's shoulders, but she spoke to the queen quite sharply. 'This is the babe that you put into my care when Oswy made you pay his debt to God – I say you should be proud of her. Elfled is now the age that you were when you were forced to flee for your life. Remember how frightened you were and how brave. This young one that you carried in your womb is just as brave.'

Suddenly a low, beastlike moan of pain came from the queen. She stumbled towards her daughter, all dignity lost, putting out a trembling hand to touch the young girl's cheek. 'My little Elf,' she whispered huskily. Her words were heavy with sorrow and longing.

Elfled could still do nothing but stare into her mother's face.

Ianfleda dropped to her knees in front of the child. 'Forgive me,' she whispered, her voice husky with sorrow. She took her daughter's small hands in hers and covered them wildly with kisses. 'I was a peace-weaver bride – making peace was all my life. But nothing – nothing that I was ever asked to do to bring that peace was as terrible as giving up my tiny Elf.'

Elfled's eyes brimmed with tears too, but she smiled bravely. 'I understand,' she said. 'A peace-weaver bride must not think of herself. Mother Hild has taught me that and I am happy with my life at Whitby, but . . . I would so much like to see my mother the queen as well.'

Hild smiled with fierce pride at the astonishing generosity and maturity of her words, and

Wulfrun and Adfrith exchanged a look of deep satisfaction.

Ianfleda shook her head in torment. 'Little one' – her voice was full of pain – 'I thought only of myself. I made Hild promise to keep you away from me, because I could not bear the misery of seeing the precious thing that I'd given up. That was unworthy – deeply unworthy – and you have grown to be so very beautiful and strong.'

They hugged each other tightly, the two golden, curly heads close together. Hild turned to Wulfrun and took her arm. 'Come, Cwen's daughter,' she said. 'We will leave them for a while. We have much to do; it is vital that we get back to Whitby as quickly as we can.'

The abbess led the way from the queen's parlour and the others followed quietly, leaving mother and daughter alone; deeply touched by the scene they'd witnessed.

Elgifu was quick to recover. 'What now?' she asked her friend the abbess. 'What of Irminburgh and that silly lad Ecfrid? What will you do about them?'

'Go back to Whitby at once.' Hild was suddenly full of energy. 'The barge is ready and we can catch the evening tide. Ianfleda must come with us. The queen's presence will carry the weight we need, and Ecfrid is another of her poor neglected children – peace weaving is not all sacrifice.'

'But will she do it?' Elgifu asked. 'Oswy will expect to find her here when he returns. And I am surprised to hear you speak so lightly of peace weaving, my friend.'

Hild's eyes flashed dangerously. 'Peace is everything to me – you know that – but sometimes swift action is better than gentle submissiveness. The Battlemaid may bring peace too, if she strikes fast and times it well.'

'I do agree, dear Battlemaid.' Elgifu gave a wide smile of approval.

'We'll make sure that Ianfleda understands how much we need her with us.' Hild was full of determination. 'She must come for Cwen's sake and also for Northumbria.'

'Am I to come too and travel by sea?' Wulfrun asked.

'Certainly you shall,' both women replied at once.

Adfrith was ordered to return overland with a small but heavily armed escort of Bamburgh guards. He was to meet up with Cadmon and travel back through Bernicia in charge of the horses.

'We will meet again at Whitby,' Hild told him. 'And Elfled's education shall then be discussed.'

Wulfrun saw disappointment there on his face, and she understood it well, but he obeyed the abbess with courtesy and came to take his leave of them dressed once again in a monk-like habit borrowed from Brother Bosa, Hild's chaplain.

He left with the touch of a soft kiss on his cheek from Wulfrun, who'd suddenly turned shy. 'Take good care of Magpie,' she begged. Then she recovered her usual confidence with him. 'Race you back to Whitby, Monkman.' Her voice shook a little with excitement at the thought of the sea journey that lay ahead.

After he'd gone Hild caught Wulfrun by the arm. 'What troubled Adfrith?' she asked.

Wulfrun did not hesitate to tell what she knew to be the truth. 'He longed to travel on to the sacred isle of Aidan,' she said. 'He has seen it in the distance but . . .'

'Ah.' Hild smiled regretfully. 'Bless the lad! I shall bear it in mind next time I need to send a messenger there.'

The abbess flew about making arrangements and giving orders. She asked the royal servants to carry the queen's rugs and clothes chest aboard the *Royal Edwin*. Wulfrun was happy to fetch and carry, her spirits rising all the time at the small whirlwind of purpose and energy that seemed to surround the abbess.

'Does the queen sail with you?' a puzzled waiting woman queried.

'Yes,' Hild told her. 'Though she may not know it yet. We leave with the evening tide.'

Many sharp glances were exchanged among the queen's women, but none dare disobey Whitby's abbess. At last Hild turned to Wulfrun. 'I think mother and daughter have had long enough together for the time being,' she said. 'We need to rally our forces. Come with me – Wolf Girl. Was that what Elfled called you?'

Wulfrun smiled. 'That is the princess's name for me.'

Hild frowned, but her mouth twitched with amusement. 'I don't know whether I approve or not. Come with me, Cwen's daughter, and help me carry food to them.'

Wulfrun and the abbess went back to the queen's parlour with laden trays of bread, roasted swan and mead. They found them sitting close together; Ianfleda had dressed her daughter in a red silken gown. In Elfled's arms wriggled a baby boy, who crowed at her with delight and reached his tiny hand towards her curls.

'Wolf Girl, I have another brother,' she cried, her face alight with love for the little one. 'He is called Wini and I may come again to visit him.'

On a table in front of them lay a sheet of parchment, a silver-tipped goose quill and a pot of ink. Elfled had carefully written her name as Adfrith had taught her.

Ianfleda looked up at Hild. 'Such a clever one!' she said. 'You have taught my child so very well.'

Hild raised her eyebrows in surprise at the slightly shaky but clearly recognizable script. 'Not me.' She refused to take praise for it. 'That must be my young oblate Adfrith's work.'

'Yes,' Elfled agreed fairly. 'He has taught us both and my Wolf Girl can make her letters even better than I can.'

'He has been teaching you too?' Hild asked sharply and Wulfrun feared there was anger in the glance. 'I don't recall telling him to do anything of the sort.'

Elfled glanced down for a moment, then tossed back her hair and looked up at her guardian boldly. 'Mother Hild . . . you left Irminburgh to look after me and she did not care what I did or what happened to me. Wulfrun has become my friend and she has helped me very much.'

Hild looked truly angry now – her face was pale – yet her words were humble. 'I was foolish,' she said, bringing a tightly curled fist up to her chest. 'I thought Irminburgh would benefit from being given responsibility.'

Ianfleda looked at her with compassion. 'We are all to blame,' she said. 'They must be punished, but what is Audrey doing leaving her young husband alone with Irminburgh?'

Hild shrugged. 'Perhaps it was a mistake to marry him to one who clearly wants to be a nun rather than a wife. But yes, you are right, Ecfrid and Irminburgh must be punished, and I have already sent messengers off to Coldingham, begging Princess Audrey to travel to Whitby and meet us there.'

The abbess was stern with herself, but stern with others too, and now she looked straight at the queen. 'You must also come with us to Whitby, my dear Fleda, if we are to prevent more trouble brewing.'

Ianfleda frowned at that and shook her head as though the suggestion were ridiculous. 'I await my husband's return here in Bamburgh – as an obedient wife should.'

Hild sighed with barely concealed irritation. 'As a peace weaver you must come with us,' she insisted. She spoke with such boldness that both Elfled and Wulfrun gasped. 'As a mother you must come! Your son is in the clutches of Irminburgh and planning to attack his half-brother.'

'No.' Ianfleda stared at her in disbelief.

'Oh yes: Irminburgh has tried to claim Queen Tata's necklace as her own and use it as proof of her claim to the throne of Deira. Ecfrid is Edwin's grandson and the two of them together will find plenty of support from those who resent Rhienmellth's son sitting on that throne. You know that they call him the Stranger.'

'But Alchfrid is a dear good Christian man.'

Ianfleda spoke lovingly of her stepson. 'I cannot believe Ecfrid would challenge him!'

Hild shrugged. 'We suspect Irminburgh to be the driving force. Dear girl, you came to Northumbria to bring us peace: do not let it slip through your fingers now!'

Ianfleda got up. 'I will come,' she said. 'You are right, as ever. It is time I acted as a mother to poor Ecfrid.' She took the baby from Elfled and handed him to a waiting woman. 'Pack my boxes!'

The woman bobbed a curtsy as she took the child. 'Madam, they are already packed and on the boat.'

Once the queen was persuaded to go with them to Whitby, they moved quickly down to the *Royal Edwin*, waiting on the quay at Hild's command. Forty oarsmen were in place and the captain was there to receive them.

Wulfrun could not stop her tears flowing as she said goodbye to Sebbi. He stood at the quayside with Cissa and Elgifu. The old woman had insisted on being carried down to the harbour to see them safely away.

'Tell our mother . . . tell our mother that— I do not know what to say.' Sebbi's face crumpled in pain.

'Tell her that her son loves her and speaks of her every day,' Cissa intervened.

'I will,' Wulfrun agreed, still clinging to the brother she'd found but must leave again so soon.

'Tell your mother that I plan to visit Whitby in the spring,' said Elgifu. 'All my helpers shall be coming with me,' she added with a wicked smile.

Wulfrun let go of her brother and clasped Elgifu's frail, wrinkled hand instead, kissing it. 'I cannot thank you enough for all that you've done,' she said warmly.

'Oh yes you can.' Elgifu looked at her with mock severity. 'You get your mother free and we will all be together in the spring. I have much to say to that brave woman, and meeting her is all the thanks I need.'

Chapter 27

battlemaids

Many slaves waded into the sea to push the boat out into deeper water. At last the oarsmen had enough depth to haul away from the shore, while the captain set a sail to catch a steady northerly wind. Wulfrun stood in the prow, watching until even the great fortress on the rock had vanished from sight and the islands had become small dots in the distance. It was only then that she felt she could look properly about her. She'd often gazed with admiration at the *Royal Edwin*, moored in Whitby harbour just below the upper pasture. She'd never dreamed she'd be aboard it.

The hull was built of strong oak planks and the sides curved gracefully upwards to a prow at either end. The oarsmen moved together in perfect time, while the helmsman steered using a huge oar that was lashed to the starboard side.

Wulfrun sighed with pleasure at the sound of the gentle creak and swish that came as the oarsmen hauled and the boat moved forwards. Set in the middle was a stout felt tent fastened with ropes to provide shelter for important passengers. At the moment Ianfleda and Elfled sat beneath it on a bed of cushions, talking quietly together; young Wini had been left safely behind in Bamburgh with his nursemaids. The queen's arm rested comfortably about her daughter's waist; she was giving the girl her full attention. Wulfrun looked back at them and smiled. Since meeting her mother, Elfled had barely spoken to her Wolf Girl, but Wulfrun understood well enough why that must be. Abbess Hild hovered outside a second awning, giving advice to the waiting women, who were unpacking provisions stowed for the journey.

Wulfrun turned back to look at the distant coastline, wondering how Adfrith and Cadmon fared. 'Race you . . . race you, Monkman!' she murmured.

Suddenly Elfled was there at her side. 'Wolf Girl,' she cried, shouting wildly and pointing, 'it's my island. We are going to go past my island.'

Wulfrun turned and saw that Elfled was right: in the fading light a dark flat-topped shape rose out of the sea, surrounded by seabirds; they could see the faint white flashes of their wings.

'There!' Elfled cried. 'There's my lovely island, with all the birds.' And before Wulfrun could stop her she threw her leg over the sloping side of the ship and began hauling herself up.

The soles of her soft leather riding boots skidded on the smooth edge of the boat. Without stopping to think, Wulfrun reached up, grabbed Elfled round the waist and hauled her backwards with some force, sending her sprawling down inside the boat.

The queen leaped to her feet with a terrified scream and all the waiting women ran towards them shrieking, 'The princess! The princess!' They gathered about Elfled, fussing and fretting, lifting her up and carrying her back between them to the shelter of the felt awning. Unguents and a restorative drink were called for.

Wulfrun followed them slowly, trembling a little after what had happened. Abbess Hild stood back from the milling women, watching her with a stern and searching look. Once before in a moment of anger Wulfrun had unthinkingly raised her hand to the princess, and that had been the start of this terrible tangle. This time it had been an instinctive reaction – she'd hauled the young girl backwards just as she would have done if it had been Gode doing something wild and dangerous. But Elfled was not Gode; she was King Oswy's daughter, and Wulfrun feared that she had once again acted too quickly and brought trouble to those she loved. She had certainly handled the Princess of

Northumbria in a very rough and ready manner, and she'd done it right there, in front of the queen and her waiting women.

'Well, well, Wolf Girl,' Hild said quietly.

Wulfrun's stomach churned with worry at the words. 'You promised my mother justice,' she reminded the abbess, an anxious catch in her voice. At least she might make sure that Cwen should not suffer again for her daughter's lack of respect.

Hild frowned. 'I promised your mother justice and she shall have it,' she said sharply. 'Sit down now and eat.'

Wulfrun was both hungry and weary. She could not tell whether the abbess was angry with her or not. Exhaustion flowed through her and she simply obeyed, dropping down to the wooden deck.

Hild sent one of the waiting women to her with a beaker of mead and some soft bread and cheese. The food was excellent and comforting, while the mead was warm and spicy. Soon Wulfrun's head was nodding and she settled down to sleep wrapped in a borrowed cloak over the slave dress that she still wore, aware that the waiting women kept turning to look in her direction, whispering behind their hands. She was so worn out that she did not care.

*　　*　　*

Wulfrun woke with a fresh breeze on her face and a bright sun rising in the east. She knuckled the sleep from her eyes and looked about, trying to remember where she was. The boat was drifting while the oarsmen were replaced by fresh rowers. The new oarsmen quickly set up a steady rhythm again, while the others stumbled stiff-legged towards food and drink.

'Cwen's daughter, come here!' It was the abbess calling.

Wulfrun turned to see the small cloaked and hooded figure standing in the prow. She went at once to join her.

'Do you see that great river?' Hild pointed out a great divide in the land masses. 'What river do you think that is?'

Wulfrun frowned and narrowed her eyes. 'I'd say it was the river Tees, if it were not that I doubt we could have come so far.'

'Hah!' Hild laughed. 'Do not doubt yourself – you are quite right. The men have rowed steadily all night and with a following wind behind us. This is the river Tees.'

'Then . . . then it is not so very far to Whitby, and we will certainly have beaten Adfrith and Cadmon back home.'

'We will indeed,' Hild agreed, sharing in her pleasure. 'But as we move down the coast towards Whitby, it occurs to me that Irminburgh and that silly boy will receive good warning of our approach.'

'Yes.' Wulfrun saw at once the way that the abbess was thinking.

'I should like to arrive quietly and catch them unawares; that way we shall discover exactly what they have been up to. Now tell me, Wolf Girl, if we came in with the tide to that little fishing place where you once lived, would we be able to hire ourselves horses?'

Wulfrun frowned, trying to remember. 'Not fine horses, Mother,' she said. 'But higher up the valley Master Olwyn keeps horses that draw fish carts and heavy wagons. He would give them to you, Mother – there'd be no charge.'

Hild looked uncertain for a moment, but then she smiled with glee. 'To arrive back at Whitby in a fish cart would disguise us well.'

Wulfrun was shocked. 'Not the queen. Of course the queen could follow in the *Royal Edwin* . . .'

Hild shrugged. 'I shall take Brother Bosa of course, but I also need the queen at my side. We have the small landing boat that we can lower into the water. Do not look so fearful, Wulfrun: this queen is tougher than she seems. Remember how she fled this land – in your mother's small fishing boat? It seems to me highly suitable that she revisit the shores of Deira in the same way. Get yourself some breakfast, Wolf Girl!'

Hild turned on her heel and left Wulfrun staring after her. 'Yes, Mother,' she murmured. The abbess had such extraordinary control over her emotions that Wulfrun was never certain what she felt, but she was confident now that she could trust her with regard to Cwen.

The oarsmen worked on at a steady pace while the important passengers ate another meal, and as the sun climbed high in the sky, the dramatic cliffs of the Deiran coast rose on the landward side. Wulfrun watched Elfled and her mother from a distance: the girl looked pale and solemn since her near accident and her mother never left her side. At last the steep valley sides of Fisherstead came into view and the oarsmen slackened their pace. They dropped a heavy anchor-stone, while the captain lowered the small landing boat that was always kept aboard. He climbed down into it himself, and Brother Bosa followed once it was safely settled in the water. The abbess tucked her long skirts up into her belt and descended the rope ladder with alacrity, while the waiting women watched open-mouthed.

Not the first time she's done that, Wulfrun guessed.

'Now the queen,' Hild ordered as soon as she'd stepped into the unsteady boat.

The waiting women gasped and fussed about her, but Elfled's mother managed the undignified descent without incident. Elfled went next, though she stopped twice on her way down complaining that she was going to be sick. Once she was down, Hild called out for Wulfrun.

Again the waiting women turned to stare at her, with much whispering behind their hands. Wulfrun did not relish the wobbly descent, but she wasn't going to disgrace herself. She kilted up her skirt like the abbess and swung her legs over the side. There were many ropes to grasp, and though the drop seemed greater than ever, she managed to climb steadily down.

Elfled reached out to grab at Wulfrun's arm as she stepped into the boat, but the abbess made space for her at her side. 'Sit here by me, Cwen's daughter,' she insisted. Wulfrun could not help but wonder if the abbess were keeping her away from the princess.

Two oarsmen followed them down and they were soon moving steadily towards Fisherstead, where a small group of curious villagers was gathering at the waterfront.

'Now,' Hild demanded. 'Show me where the fish carts are kept!'

Wulfrun pointed to the field halfway up the steep hillside. 'Look towards those huts, Mother.'

'Ah yes, I see the beasts. Good sturdy nags – just what we need.'

By the time they reached the shore most of the

village was there to greet them, and as the queen and abbess waded through the shallow water, holding their skirts high, there was much curtsying and bowing and astonishment.

The abbess held up her hands to them, giving a brief blessing, but did not stop for more than a moment. 'Lead the way, Wulfrun!' she said. 'Waste no time!'

Wulfrun caught a glimpse of Emma's worried face but dared not stop to speak as she strode ahead of the Queen of Northumbria towards Olwyn's fish sheds. The man was astonished, but he recognized the abbess at once and set his sons to catch the horses and prepare the covered wagons. 'They must be cleaned.' He shook his head in concern.

'Certainly not!' Hild came back at him like a whip.

'But lady—'

'I've lived half my life with the wholesome smell of fish in my nostrils.' The abbess frowned at him. 'Speed and surprise is what we need.'

Olwyn nodded then, understanding that the surprise would be for Prince Ecfrid, whose men had recently become both a threat and a burden to all who lived close to Whitby. Two carts were set up and the abbess climbed aboard the first, telling the queen and Elfled to follow in the second.

'Bosa, you must skulk in the back and pull your

hood up, but be ready if I should need you. Wulfrun, you come with me.' Hild patted the wooden seat beside her as Olwyn himself took up the reins. Brother Bosa scrambled up behind them, while Wulfrun nervously took her place next to the abbess. The fisher folk thronged about the carts and Emma managed to reach out her hand to squeeze Wulfrun's for a moment.

The abbess bent down from the wagon to address the fisherwoman. 'Would you let me have the use of your good warm shawl?'

Emma's jaw dropped, but without hesitation she tore the shawl from her head and held it out to the abbess. Hild wrapped it about her head, covering the light undyed linen coif that she always wore. 'There – a battlemaid must have her headdress,' she said, giving Wulfrun a fierce smile. The shawl made her look the very image of an ageing, sharp-tongued fishwife.

Suddenly Wulfrun's anxiety fled and a warm ball of excitement began to grow inside her belly. 'Elgifu told us you were not named Battlemaid for nothing, Mother.'

Hild gave a low, delighted chuckle. 'Dear Elgifu,' she said.

Wulfrun did not notice the bumping of the cart as they rumbled over the rough track towards Whitby on the strangest journey of her life. They passed the place where Ecfrid's men had camped.

They'd vanished, leaving behind burned patches of earth and a good deal of human filth.

Hild held Emma's shawl closely about her face, and as they passed through small hamlets and villages nobody gave them a second glance. Few even bothered to look at the two royal women who sat well back in the following cart. The tide was swelling up the Usk as they reached the ford, but the abbess smiled again as Olwyn turned to her uncertainly.

'Forward, my man,' she said with gusto.

Wulfrun wanted to laugh out loud as they charged ahead, water splashing all about them, spraying their clothes. She glanced back to see Brother Bosa grimly holding onto the edge of the wagon, but saying nothing. The abbess seemed to be enjoying herself, and Wulfrun sensed that behind the usual dignity and calm demeanour was a woman who was capable of anything.

As they approached the main gate, it became clear from the tents and groups of cheerful fellows lounging in the pastures that Ecfrid's war band had settled itself closer to their master and the abbey's mead supplies. Two of the abbey guards came forward to greet them. 'The webster's daughter,' they said. 'You dare to return?' They recognized Wulfrun rather than the abbess.

Hild let the shawl slip down from her head and they both stepped back, shocked. 'Lady! Mother!' they whispered.

'Yes – I'm back,' said Hild.

Their mouths broke into broad grins. 'We're glad,' they said with feeling.

'I wish to arrive unannounced,' she said. 'Come with me and bring your weapons. Are you ready, Bosa?'

Olwyn brought the wagon to a halt outside the stables and they all got down. 'I must not lose the element of surprise,' Hild told Wulfrun. 'Ecfrid and Irminburgh first; then we will find your mother. Where will they be – the guesthouse?'

Wulfrun swallowed hard. 'The abbess's parlour,' she said with certainty.

'Will they indeed?' Hild's eyebrows shot up.

There was a rather uncomfortable shifting among some of Ecfrid's men, who hung about in the courtyard, huddled around glowing braziers, drinking and playing knucklebones. A weary travel-stained man came out of the stables, but as he saw the new arrivals he slipped back into the shadows.

'Childeric.' Wulfrun pointed after him. He hadn't been fast enough for her.

Hild nodded to Bosa. 'That's your man.'

The two guards and the monk ran at once into the stables.

'We will leave them to see to him,' Hild said grimly, then marched straight into the abbess's parlour, Wulfrun at her heels.

Ecfrid and Irminburgh were lolling together in the abbess's carved wooden chair. Irminburgh's legs were thrown across Ecfrid's knees, while her fancy laced gown lay open to the waist. They were both flushed and full of mead. Bertha stood beside them with a jug and a plate of honey cakes.

Wulfrun caught her breath, waiting for an angry tirade from Hild, but the small woman simply stood before them in silence, her arms folded across her chest. Bertha looked at the abbess and then at Wulfrun.

Remembering the warning rune, Wulfrun mouthed her own silent warning: 'Get out!'

Bertha shrank back and slipped away.

Chapter 28

judgement

Irminburgh and Ecfrid both stared up at the abbess as though they were seeing a vision. Still no sound came from Hild, and Wulfrun crept forward in concern. She saw that the abbess's face was white with rage; at this moment the woman who could control her feelings with such power did not dare let herself speak.

Slowly the reality of the abbess's presence dawned upon the two lovers, and even though their minds were blurred with mead, the colour seeped from their cheeks. Hild's silent anger was more powerful than any words could ever be. Then, with a rustle of silk and a tinkle of jewellery, Ianfleda, with Elfled at her side, followed the abbess into her parlour.

'Ecfrid!' the queen cried out, clearly appalled. 'What are you doing?'

It broke the spell, and at last Irminburgh moved to cover her bare legs and clutch her unlaced gown together; Ecfrid burst into a string of wild curses.

'Ecfrid – I will leave you to your mother.' Hild's words came slowly and her voice was low. 'Irminburgh – you come with me!'

Irminburgh got up and looked for just one moment as though she might flee the abbess's wrath, but then she seemed to understand that there was little hope of escape. She struggled to fasten her gown, head lowered, biting her lips.

'Follow me!' Hild ordered. 'You too, Cwen's daughter.'

The abbess strode ahead of them and Wulfrun glanced sideways at Irminburgh. The young woman refused to look at her, a sullen, defeated expression on her beautiful face.

She will always blame me, Wulfrun thought. She will hate me for ever and I will always have to look over my shoulder.

But the abbess was heading for the guesthouse now, and Ulfstan's quarters. Wulfrun quickened her pace to catch up with Hild and they found the reeve sitting at the table, his head in his hands.

'Lady,' he cried, when he looked up. He leaped to his feet at once, a mixture of relief and shame on his face.

Hild held up her hand to stop further explanation. 'I know, Ulfstan, I know,' she said.

Ulfstan looked past her to where Wulfrun stood,

with Irminburgh behind her; some light of under-standing dawned on him.

'Lady . . . I don't know where to start.' He shook his head.

Hild had no such uncertainty. 'Take me at once to Cwen the webster. Where have you kept her?'

Ulfstan turned to lift the door hanging that separated his work chamber from his living quarters. 'I will get my wife,' he said.

Both Hild and Wulfrun looked puzzled for a moment, but then the abbess smiled with under-standing. 'You have kept her prisoner in your own home?'

'It seemed the best thing – to be sure that she'd be safe,' he said.

Hild reached up to kiss him on one cheek and then the other. 'I chose well when I made you my reeve,' she told him warmly. 'I never knew how well until this day.'

'I hope you will still think well of me when you learn that I have now taken two prisoners,' he said, still looking a little worried. 'Please come this way.' He courteously held aside the curtain for all three women to walk through.

Alta came nervously forward, taking a key from the girdle hangers at her waist. She curtsied to the abbess. 'We hope we have done right, Mother,' she said.

'Show me,' Hild replied.

The guest-mistress led the way past the smoking hearth and through the family hall that thronged with children and servants, who stopped in both work and play to stare open-mouthed at the visitors. Alta moved on to an inner room, fitted with a strongly made door, and used her key to open the heavy lock. As the door swung wide they heard the sound of two women's voices quarrelling gently in a familiar and friendly manner.

'But if we use madder for the flowers, then what should we use for the birds?'

'Woad of course; we haven't enough madder to do both!'

The first voice belonged to Sister Begu, and Wulfrun recognized the second voice with joy: it was her mother's. The two women sat beside a stone-weighted wall loom, a basket of dyed wool at their feet and a fine patterned wall hanging almost completed. Wulfrun blinked at it – it was her own wall hanging, the one she'd struggled so hard to make. The room was warmed by a brazier and well lit from two high windows with wooden shutters. It was clean and comfortable.

'Begu!' Hild cried out in shock. 'What on earth . . . ?'

'Ha! At last!' Begu rose and threw her arms around her old friend. 'I swore that you would come and rescue us, did I not, Cwen?'

Hild looked up at Ulfstan with a frown. 'Why

have you imprisoned my dearest friend?'

Ulfstan glanced quickly at Irminburgh, who stood pale and silent in the doorway.

'I was ordered to whip her,' he said, shifting uncomfortably. 'But . . . I could not do that, so . . . as with Cwen, I took her into my charge to await your judgement.'

Hild's face was white again with barely contained fury as she turned to Irminburgh. 'And what had Begu done to deserve a whipping?'

Irminburgh looked away and would not answer, so the abbess turned to Ulfstan for an explanation. 'What had she done?'

'Sister Begu was accused of leaving her hut at night, ignoring her religious duties and spreading false rumours that the Princess Elfled had vanished.'

'As indeed she had,' Hild added, looking angrily back at Irminburgh.

At the abbess's words both Ulfstan and his wife looked at each other with horror. Then they turned to Begu, their faces full of apology.

'Is she safe?' Begu asked, ignoring them.

'Quite safe,' Hild reassured her. 'You did not know she had gone, Ulfstan?'

The reeve looked unhappy and shook his head, but his wife had none of his reticence.

'My Lady Irminburgh swore that the princess was confined to her room with sickness and far too ill to be disturbed. My husband could not break into the princess's room, Mother, and as Fridgyth had been called in to attend her, we believed it. My husband has tried so hard to be fair and just in his dealings.'

'And he has succeeded,' Hild said, but then she frowned. 'Fridgyth – has she been involved in this too?'

'You can be sure that Fridgyth had little choice in the matter,' Begu commented dryly.

Hild shook her head. 'I did not realize how far this trouble had spread, or how many people had suffered.' She turned then to Cwen, who had backed away into the corner of the room. 'And you, dear Cwen, have suffered above all, but now you are free.'

'But I . . .' she began uncertainly.

'You have suffered great injustice.' Hild spoke gently now, seeing that Cwen was still afraid. She took both the weaver woman's trembling hands and reached up to kiss her warmly on each cheek. 'You have suffered when you really deserve the highest praise and rich reward.'

'But . . .' Cwen still doubted that she was really free and vindicated. 'The necklace . . . ?'

Hild turned to Wulfrun. 'This sharp-witted daughter of yours has discovered where the necklace came from and proved your claim to be true – it was yours by right.'

Both Ulfstan and his wife gasped at these words. Wulfrun's eyes filled up with tears but she hung shyly back from her mother.

Cwen could still not understand. 'It was given . . .' she struggled.

'Yes.' Hild smiled at her. 'It was given just as you said, by a young girl whose life you saved. That young girl is now the Queen of Northumbria, and she herself has sworn that your story is true.'

Now it was Cwen's turn to gasp. 'The . . . the mother and her little ones?'

'The mother was Queen Tata, wife to the slaughtered Edwin; the tall monk was Paulinus, her chaplain. Dear Cwen – that wild young woman who helped you push the boat out, then rode away with the horses – that was me!'

'You, Mother? I cannot believe it . . . except that when we first came to Whitby I felt that I knew you somehow.'

'It was exactly the same for me, and I should have worked out why it was – but this girl of yours has picked her way through a web of confusion and at last discovered the truth.'

Then Cwen turned to Wulfrun with joy and pride in her eyes. 'Come here, my honey,' she whispered, and at last Wulfrun went to her.

'Mother, I have sold your girdle and all your fine tools,' she admitted.

Cwen laughed. 'My tools I can replace, but I

cannot get myself another brave daughter like you.'

They hugged each other tightly and wept.

Hild watched for a moment, a satisfied smile on her face, but then she glanced at Irminburgh, who sulked in the corner, her face distorted by an angry scowl. 'Begu – take Wulfrun and her mother to my parlour. You will find the queen there with Elfled and Ecfrid.' Her lips curled a little with distaste. 'I wish to be left alone here with Irminburgh.'

But Begu shook her head and boldly spoke up. 'I think there is another that they need to see first, my friend. For Cwen has another daughter, and she's been just as brave in her own way.'

Hild stared at her for a moment, but quickly understood. 'The little one – where is she?'

'In Fridgyth's tender care, I trust.'

'Then of course they must go to find her. Have no more fear, Cwen, you have nothing but our gratitude – we owe you much more, and payment shall be made.'

Begu took mother and daughter each by the arm and steered them past the shrinking shape of Irminburgh, though Wulfrun caught a venomous glance that came her way.

They found Gode safe in Fridgyth's hut, sitting beside the herbwife, shelling roasted chestnuts and blowing on her fingers. Cwen went in un-announced, quietly pushing aside the bunches of drying herbs that hung from every beam. For a moment the child stared up at her almost without recognition; then a slow wide smile spread across her face. 'Mam,' she said. 'Mam – you've come back!' Gode leaped up into her mother's arms.

'I've come back, my honey,' Cwen agreed.

Fridgyth hovered about them, smiling and excited. She made them all sit down while she brewed a comforting drink of honey and thyme. She bathed Wulfrun's hands and put marigold balm on the now healing cuts. Cwen sat with her youngest cuddled on her lap, but still would not let go of her older daughter's arm.

'Tell me where you've been,' she begged. 'I know from Begu that the princess took you as her slave – though Begu thoroughly disapproved of such a thing. I heard how you made the princess work at her studies and how you learned to read and write. I know nothing of what you discovered about the necklace.'

Wulfrun gave a great sigh of happiness. 'There is so much to say that I don't know where to start, but one thing I must tell at once.'

'What is that?'

'Sebbi,' she said with a smile. 'I have seen him at Bamburgh, and he is well and happy and I am to say that' – she frowned, trying hard to remember the exact words that Cissa had spoken – ' "he loves his mother and speaks of her every day".'

When she looked back at her mother, she was

distressed to see that Cwen's eyes had filled with tears. She tried to give reassurance. 'You will see him soon. His mistress, Lady Elgifu, is coming to Whitby in the spring. Mother, please do not weep; Elgifu treats him with great kindness and he has a young girl called Cissa whom he loves. They wish to be married.'

Cwen smiled through her tears. 'I am blessed with the finest children in the world,' she said.

They sat late by Fridgyth's hearth, talking over what had happened, until darkness settled about them and the candles were lit.

'Stay here with me tonight,' Fridgyth insisted. 'Gode and I have fastened the geese up safely in your close.'

Gode and Wulfrun settled down on the fresh straw that Fridgyth put out for them, while the two women talked on.

Cwen smiled at the herb woman. 'I thought the whole world had turned against me, until the reeve put Begu in with me; then I knew that I was blessed with loyal friends. I can never thank you enough for your care of my daughters.'

Fridgyth shook her head and looked down at Gode, now fast asleep by the hearth, a peaceful smile on her face. She looked sad for a moment. 'Irminburgh forced me to support her lie,' she whispered. 'She threatened to take this little one from my care if I did not obey her. I could not let that happen. I didn't think the princess would be harmed by me keeping her flight a secret. I knew that her friends had gone to find her, and if anyone could help the little lass, I trusted that they would.'

'We got back before Adfrith and Cadmon.' Wulfrun yawned, exhausted, but still trying to join in the conversation.

Fridgyth smiled again. 'Truth is, I've enjoyed having Gode here with me. Since my own little ones were lost to me, I have so much missed the company of bairns. Gode has become a fine gardener: already she knows the weeds to get rid of and the healing plants to cherish.'

Cwen smiled. 'It seems that both my daughters have learned new skills. Perhaps Gode could continue to come to work here in your garden. You should be training up an assistant, Fridgyth. Why should it not be Gode?'

Fridgyth smiled. 'I would like that.'

When they woke next morning the herbwife gave them bowls of porridge, then they gathered themselves together to walk round to their hut.

'You may have something of a surprise when you get there,' Fridgyth told them.

They looked at her uncertainly.

She laughed. 'Do not be fearful: the surprise will be good.'

Before they got to the hut they heard the sound

of an axe, and they found Leofrid working hard to make their tiny dwelling sound and waterproofed; smoke trickled out through small holes in a newly thatched roof.

'I hope I do not presume too much,' he said shyly.

Cwen smiled at him. 'I could do with a bit more presuming of this kind,' she said. 'And I have heard how you promised to swear on my behalf.'

Leofrid frowned. 'I have found something, Cwen. I dug out some mud from the back of the close and found a small pot with three sceattas.'

Cwen's face fell. 'For Sebbi,' she said. 'Though I know he is safe, I must still keep those coins and try to put aside some more.'

Chapter 29

wolf girl

Leofrid and Cwen were a little awkward with each other at first, but there was so much to say that the shyness soon faded. Leofrid passed on the rumours of what had happened. It seemed Prince Ecfrid's men had been turned out in the middle of the night and sent on their way. Though there were many more of them than the monastery guards, they'd put up no resistance. The sight of the Queen of Northumbria at the side of the angry abbess had soon persuaded them to obey. Brother Bosa and the guards had caught Childeric and taken him to the lock-up, but he'd fought his way free and then bolted.

'He is dead,' Leofrid told them, shaking his head. 'He made a run for it towards the cliffs. How could he think to get away by running in that direction?'

Wulfrun touched her fingertips to the rough scar on her head that the ironstone dogger had made. 'He fell over the cliffs?'

Leofrid nodded. 'He either fell or jumped and was smashed on the scars below.'

Wulfrun could feel neither sorrow nor anger for the man. Gossip had it that Hild had locked Irminburgh up in Ulfstan's prison room with nothing but dry bread to eat and water to drink.

Wulfrun left Leofrid and her mother together and took the geese out to the pasture. After her wild adventure it was good to be doing something simple and safe again. Sister Mildred came out from the kitchens to tip the peelings onto the grass. When she saw Wulfrun there, she took a piece of honeyed angelica from the bag that swung at her waist and offered it with an apologetic smile. 'I'm sorry for doubting you,' she said. 'I know from what Fridgyth has told me that you have been much misjudged. I've given Bertha refuge in my kitchens for the moment – I hope I have done right.'

Wulfrun took the sweetmeat graciously and glanced back to see the sorry figure of Bertha peeping out from the side gate. 'Yes – I think you've done right,' she agreed.

As the sun moved overhead, she chewed the sweetmeat and looked down with satisfaction on the scene below. The *Royal Edwin* had arrived back safely and was moored once again in the harbour; travellers splashed through the ford.

Suddenly a broad smile lit her face as she

watched two riders, leading two extra ponies behind their own mounts, approaching the shallow river crossing. 'Adfrith and Cadmon,' she murmured. 'Magpie and Sea Mist.'

She began at once to gather the geese together and herd them back to the close. When she got back, there was no sign of either her mother, Leofrid or Gode. She shut up the geese, feeling a little puzzled by the absence of the others, but set off to meet Adfrith and Cadmon as they struggled up the steep path to the monastery.

'All's well, all's well,' she shouted as she ran towards them. 'The abbess has taken charge and Childeric is dead.'

'I'm sorry for the fellow.' Adfrith shook his head. 'He was a fine craftsman and ignorant of our ways. It would have been hard for him to disobey Lady Irminburgh.'

Wulfrun shrugged. 'I cannot feel much for him,' she said.

'Well, it seems you won the race,' Adfrith said, smiling at last. 'Ecfrid's war band has melted into the mists.'

'The battlemaids have driven them out,' she told him. 'But I think Prince Ecfrid is still here: when I last saw him he was weeping and cursing, while his mother berated him.'

Wulfrun took Magpie's reins from Cadmon's hand, stretching out to pat her flanks. 'My poor

Magpie must be exhausted,' she said as she walked on beside them.

Cadmon nodded. 'No harm . . . n-no harm!'

'But . . . she's not mine. I must remember that,' Wulfrun told herself with a sigh.

'A m-mare gives herself to the rider she trusts,' Cadmon said. 'This m-mare has given herself to you.'

Wulfrun smiled, comforted by the thought, seeing that there was some truth in what he said. Whatever happened, nobody could stop her creeping into the stables with an apple for the mare. 'But now that the abbess is back,' she said softly, 'I think there will be no more lessons, no more Elfled, no more lovely Friday rides.'

Adfrith smiled sadly. 'I shall miss those things too.'

'Will the abbess stop you teaching the princess?'

'After all that has happened I'd be very surprised if she did not,' he said fairly.

As they reached the main gate, a great flurry of activity made them stop. A small cavalcade rode out from the abbey led by four mounted guards. A curtained wagon trundled past and four more riders brought up the rear. Childeric's parents followed behind, white-faced and weeping, with all their household goods piled into an open wagon.

Wulfrun watched with curiosity and saw a white

bejewelled hand catch the fluttering curtain of the wagon, drawing it closed so that the occupant could not be seen.

Adfrith, Cadmon and Wulfrun glanced at each other. 'Irminburgh,' Wulfrun whispered with relief. 'She has been sent away.'

'Yes,' said Adfrith. 'But will that be the last we see of her?'

'Ecfrid was not with her.'

Wulfrun went with them to settle the horses in the stables, but as soon as the stable boy saw her he became quite excited. 'Sister Begu is looking for you,' he said. 'She's been looking everywhere and she's quite annoyed. She says the abbess wants to see you.'

'You'd best go straight to the abbess's house,' said Adfrith.

Wulfrun twisted her fingers together in a painful knot. 'Are you sure it's me?' she asked.

'Yes. The webster's daughter – that's you!'

She turned, leaving them reluctantly to head across the courtyard, her heart pounding uncomfortably. Begu pounced on her in the entrance. 'I've been looking everywhere,' she snapped. 'Come straight in to see the abbess; your mother's with her now.'

In the abbess's parlour Cwen was sitting nervously between Hild and the Queen of Northumbria.

'There you are.' Hild looked up as Wulfrun came in. 'What did you think you were doing just vanishing like that?'

'I was pasturing the geese,' Wulfrun said simply.

'Come here.' The abbess beckoned impatiently, and as she moved close to them Wulfrun saw that the gold and garnet necklace gleamed on Ianfleda's breast. 'Yes,' Hild said. 'The necklace is back where it belongs.'

Wulfrun looked at her mother and saw that she was overwhelmed with emotion.

'The queen has agreed to pay the price that we believe the necklace to be worth,' said Hild. 'As long as the money is to be spent as we think best.'

Wulfrun frowned, unsure as to the fairness of this decision, but her mother laughed at the puzzled look on her daughter's face. 'The money is to be spent buying freedom for slaves,' she said. 'Sebbi and his Cissa are the first of many to be released.'

Wulfrun smiled at once, appreciating the cleverness and justice in such a judgement, but another captive slave came at once to her mind. 'Cadmon the cowherd's mother is still a slave,' she said.

'I will see to it that she is released too,' Hild promised. 'And as soon as I have had a chance to speak to him, I'm going to send Adfrith back to Bamburgh on the *Royal Edwin* to arrange the release of Sebbi and Cissa. Then I will send him on to Aidan's Isle with messages for Bishop Colman about the synod.'

'I'm sure he will prove to be an excellent messenger.' Wulfrun was happy for him.

'I am to take charge of the abbey's new weaving sheds,' Cwen went on, snatching up her daughter's hand, her face full of joy. 'We are to move within the abbey bounds and have our own little house built of wood. What do you think of that? We will live in warmth and comfort and have nothing more to fear. Leofrid is to build it to my own requirements and he will be well paid for doing it.'

'I think we are blessed,' Wulfrun agreed.

'But now,' said Hild with a sharp look, 'I wish to speak to Wulfrun alone, if you will allow me, dear Cwen. I have something to say to your daughter.'

'Of course,' said Cwen.

Ianfleda got up from her chair and took Cwen by the hand. 'You have given me back Queen Tata's jewels,' she said. 'Your neck must not go unadorned. Come with me, dear friend. I have some amber beads that I think will suit you well.'

Wulfrun curtsied as the queen led her mother from the room. She was happy to see Cwen so honoured, but the abbess's words had brought a touch of apprehension. Hild wandered over to the window and opened one of the wooden shutters so that a stream of cold air flooded into the room.

Wulfrun watched her, her heart beating fast. Once again she was unsure whether the abbess was angry with her or not.

'I've been meaning to speak to you, girl, ever since I saw you throw the Princess of Northumbria down onto the deck,' Hild said, still looking out across the river to the moors. 'But there have been so many other things to deal with first.'

Wulfrun's heart sank; so she *was* in trouble after all. There was nothing else to do but face it. Her mother was safe and rewarded – nothing else really mattered. 'I am truly sorry for that, Mother Hild,' she said. 'What must my punishment be?'

Hild looked back at her, frowning, and then she suddenly laughed. 'Punishment? I am not sorry at all: you saved the silly child's life! It seems to run in your family – saving King Edwin's descendants.'

Wulfrun gasped with relief. 'Then . . . you are not angry with me?'

The abbess gave a fierce smile that reminded Wulfrun of Elgifu. 'I'm far from angry with you. Do not disappoint me, Wulfrun; I thought you more quick-witted than that. I want to offer you a job.'

Wulfrun's mouth dropped open in surprise.

'Elfled told me how you saved her from being stoned in Uskdale Forest by covering her with your own body and how you pulled her from the sinking sands. I have been in the scriptorium with

Begu and seen some of the work that Elfled produced while working at your side. I saw your work too – it was good.'

The ghost of a smile touched the corners of Wulfrun's mouth. 'Then you will allow Adfrith to go on teaching the princess?'

'Of course I will.' Hild gave a swift nod and returned to her seat, patting the chair that Cwen had been sitting in. 'Elfled is lucky to have so clever and talented a teacher. As soon as he is back from Bamburgh he will be there in the scriptorium as her teacher again. Now, come here and sit down beside me.'

Wulfrun went obediently.

'I think I told you that the king has ordered a great synod to be held: we are to discuss the many disagreements between Christians in this land and try to find a peaceful solution. The king has asked me to host this important gathering, here at Whitby.'

Wulfrun stared at the abbess. What could she have to do with these great decisions?

'Oh, it is an honour to be asked to do it,' Hild acknowledged. 'But believe me, it is a huge task. Kings, queens, bishops, princes, abbesses – they are all coming here to Whitby: they will need accommodation, food, stabling for their horses and the outcome of it will bring either peace or strife to this land. Do you understand?'

'Yes, Mother.' Wulfrun was awed that the abbess should confide in her.

Hild shook her head. 'One thing that this whole sorry affair has taught me is that Elfled has needs that I have been ignoring— Oh yes I have. I love her dearly, as though she were my own child, but . . . I cannot give her the time that I should, and over the next year it will become even more difficult. I did not realize that she had been missing her mother so – and I should have seen it. She is a child and should be raised with other children – but what I think she needs most of all is someone to act towards her as . . . as a big sister might.'

Wulfrun's mouth parted in surprise. Was she being asked to act as Elfled's big sister?

'But it is more than that.' Hild looked intently at her and a chill ran down her back. 'Yes, it is much more than that. Elfled is the king's daughter and vulnerable to any who might wish to threaten his kingdom. She needs a bodyguard: one who will be fierce in her defence and unswervingly loyal to her.'

Wulfrun was doubtful now that she'd understood. 'Armed guards, do you mean?'

Hild shrugged. 'Armed guards? Yes indeed – there may be times when such a thing becomes necessary, but true loyalty is much more valuable than brute strength. What my Elfled needs is a fierce Wolf Girl at her side, and it seems to me that she has been very clever in finding just the right one all by herself. She needs someone who will not hesitate to pull her back if she behaves stupidly or knock her out of the way if she steps into trouble.'

'You are offering this job to me?'

'I am.' Hild's smile was wide. 'But as I have at last made clear to Irminburgh, here within the abbey of Whitby all possessions are held in common. There would be no money paid for this job. However, you would share all the benefits that Elfled has. You would share her education, her food, her living quarters; you would sleep at her side and you would have the right to ride the dappled mare whenever you wished. Indeed, I would expect you to ride always at Elfled's side. How does this sound to you?'

The joy on Wulfrun's face was answer enough. 'It sounds like heaven to me,' she said.

epilogue

It was early in Harvest Month and Wulfrun led Magpie out through the main gate, followed by Elfled with Sea Mist. Adfrith walked behind them leading Midnight. Cadmon had been left behind to tend his calves. His aged mother had been released from slavery and come to live with him in the new hut that had been built for them behind the cowsheds.

'Where are we going today?' Wulfrun asked.

Elfled gave a wicked glance towards Adfrith. 'Through the ford and northwards on the main track,' she said.

Wulfrun frowned, disappointed. 'We have been that way so many times before.'

Adfrith smiled and swung himself up into the saddle. 'All the synod visitors who come by land will be crossing the ford,' he said,

Wulfrun began to understand. 'You have seen so many of them before – and I never have.'

Elfled pulled a face. 'Some you'll wish you'd never seen,' she said. 'Fat bishops who almost kill the horses they ride and abbesses who fuss and fret over nothing. But some of them are wonderful. Cuthbert will come on foot, for he refuses to go anywhere on horseback, and you will never have seen a scruffier young man.'

'He's scruffy?' Wulfrun was surprised to hear that.

'Ah yes – but as soon as he opens his mouth you will understand that he is also the sweetest person alive. Wilfrid is quite the opposite – you will see him coming from afar with a great train of servants, and he will ride the finest horse that money can buy.' She sighed. 'He is the handsomest man in the world and the most dashing. My mother adores him, and so does Audrey; all women do.'

'But he's a monk?' Wulfrun was shocked.

Both Elfled and Adfrith laughed at her expression. 'Wilfrid is a law unto himself,' Adfrith admitted. 'And even I have to admit that he probably is the most handsome man alive.'

Wulfrun swung herself up onto Magpie's back. 'Let's head for the ford then,' she said with new interest. 'I must see this handsome fellow.'

Adfrith and Elfled exchanged a secret look of satisfaction and followed her.

The ford was indeed busy and they dismounted

and sat down on the warm grassy hillside to watch three dust-stained, bare-legged monks paddle through, their heads shaved at the front and their habits kilted up. They were splashed and soaked as a large party of mounted guards wearing the colours of Alchfrid of Deira caught up and overtook them. Behind the soldiers followed a broad-shouldered, well-dressed young man, mounted on a sturdy horse, a round-faced young woman riding at his side. Wulfrun glanced at them and something about the serenity and sense of completeness about them made her smile. Then suddenly her eyes opened wide as she looked at them more carefully. She rose to her feet and saw that both her companions were grinning up at her.

'You knew . . . you knew,' she howled at them.

Then Adfrith's smile faded and his lips pressed together for a moment in sadness. 'You know what this means, don't you?' he said gently.

Wulfrun's face fell too. 'Elgifu has died,' she whispered.

She knew that this must be so, for when Adfrith had gone to release Sebbi and Cissa from slavery they'd cried with joy, but Elgifu had been taken ill and they refused to leave her side, insisting that they should stay on as her servants as long as she needed them.

Seeing Wulfrun's sorrow, Elfled got to her feet and reached up to kiss her Wolf Girl on the cheek.

'Elgifu would want you to be happy,' she said. 'Your brother is a freeman.'

Wulfrun's eyes brimmed with both sadness and gratitude for this reminder. 'I know she would,' she acknowledged.

'I think they have seen you,' Adfrith pointed out. 'They have stopped and they're looking this way.'

Wulfrun smiled and ran down the hill to meet them.

αuτhoR's noτε

I have long been fascinated by the Anglo-Saxon history of Whitby and wanted to find a way of writing about it that might be interesting to young adults. Inspired by Ellis Peters's *Cadfael* and Peter Tremayne's *Sister Fidelma*, I decided to try some mystery/adventure stories using Hild's abbey for the setting.

I set about researching the period and found the work engrossing and exciting, but I also became aware that there is still much that is unknown about the period and that acknowledged historians interpret the evidence in different ways. Because of this I decided to create a picture of Abbess Hild and her monastery that is really Anglo-Saxon Whitby as I would like it to have been, rather than an attempt at accuracy. Where historical sources seemed clear and interesting I have used them, but I've also freely used my imagination.

The discovery of a gold and garnet necklace and

the planned rebellion of Ecfrid and Irminburgh are imaginary; though according to Bede, Ecfrid's second wife *was* called Irminburgh or Iurminburgh.

Elfled was dedicated to God as a baby by her father King Oswy and raised by Hild in her monastery to be a nun. Whether Elfled saw much of her mother or not during her childhood is not recorded, but on Oswy's death, his queen retired to Hild's monastery. On Hild's death Elfled and Ianfleda shared the role of abbess and ruled together for a few years. On her mother's death Elfled became abbess and ruled a double monastery of monks and nuns. She was a friend to both Cuthbert and Wilfrid and on many occasions acted as a peacemaker.

When studying this period I have found myself struggling with Anglo-Saxon names, so for ease of reading I have used the simplest forms – e.g. Elfled, rather than Aelfleda or Aellffled, Cadmon rather than Caedmon.

I have mainly used modern place names – e.g. Whitby rather than Streoneshalh, Bamburgh rather than Bebbanburgh.

Where there was an accepted nickname for a historical character I have used it – e.g. Queen Tata rather than Ethelburgh, Audrey rather than Etheldreda.

I changed Queen Eanfleda's name to Ianfleda

to help distinguish her from similar family names.

King Oswy's Northumbria covered a huge stretch of land from south of the Humber to beyond the present-day Scottish borders. His lands were divided into two sub-kingdoms: Bernicia, which roughly corresponded to present-day Northumberland, and Deira, which roughly corresponded to present-day Yorkshire and Cleveland.

The following works have provided much information and inspiration: Bede's *History of the English Church and People* (Penguin Classic); Horn and Borne's study of the Plan of the Monastery of St Gall; Peter Hunter Blair's *Northumbria in the Days of Bede*; John Marsden's *Northanhymbre Saga*; *The Anglo-Saxon World* – an anthology translated and introduced by Kevin Crossley-Holland (Oxford World's Classics); and Kathleen Herbert's *Peace-Weavers and Shield Maidens: Women in Early English Society*.

Visits to Whitby Abbey Visitor Centre, Whitby Museum, Bede's World, Bamburgh Castle and the island of Lindisfarne have provided further inspiration. The author would like to thank Flora Nelson for providing the Latin words.

Theresa Tomlinson, 2005
www.theresatomlinson.com

list of main characters

Hild: Abbess of Whitby, Elfled's guardian and her second cousin. Her father, Hereric, was poisoned, leaving his uncle, Edwin, as chief claimant to the throne of Northumbria.

Princess Elfled (Aelfleda): daughter of King Oswy and Queen Ianfleda.

Cadmon (Caedmon): cowherd at Hild's monastery – his story was told by Bede. He is often regarded as the father of English poetry.

Begu and Fridgyth: two of Abbess Hild's nuns mentioned by name. Begu dreamed of Hild going up to heaven on her death. I have invented the character of Fridgyth but given her the real name of one of Hild's nuns.

Ianfleda (Eanfleda): Queen of Northumbria, daughter to King Edwin – strong supporter of the Roman style of Christianity.

Oswy: High King of Northumbria. Edwin killed his father, Aethelfrith, and claimed the throne of Northumbria. Four-year-old Oswy fled with his elder brother Oswald to Iona, where they were raised by Columban monks. They returned to claim the kingdom of Northumbria soon after the death of Edwin.

Alchfrid (Alchfrith): Sub-king of Deira; Elfled's half-brother. His mother was Rhienmellth of Rheged, Oswy's first wife.

Ecfrid (Egfrith): Elfled's brother – sent to the court of the pagan King Penda as a child hostage.

Irminburgh (Ermenburg, or Iurminburg): a princess or noblewoman – she eventually married Ecfrid and became Queen of Northumbria.

Adfrith (Eadfrith): this character is based very loosely on Eadfrith, who eventually became Bishop of Lindisfarne and is believed to be the scribe and illuminator of the Lindisfarne Gospels.

Bosa: educated as a young man at Hild's monastery, he eventually became a bishop.

Audrey (St Etheldreda): She eventually divorced Ecfrid and became a nun.

INVENTED MAIN CHARACTERS

Wulfrun: daughter of Cwen the webster

Cwen: originally from Fisherstead; she works as a weaver for Abbess Hild

Gode: Wulfrun's young sister

Sebbi: Wulfrun's older brother – sold voluntarily as a slave to save the family

Ulfstan: Hild's monastery reeve

Nelda: hermit of Uskdale, once a nun at the monastery and Hild's old nurse

Elgifu: old friend of Abbess Hild

Childeric: Frankish jeweller at Whitby